The Kid From Custer

Dick Clāson

Lost Coast Press
〰
Fort Bragg, California

The Kid From Custer
Copyright © 1996 by Richard Lewis Clāson

All rights reserved. No portion of this book may be reproduced by any means, electronic, digital or mechanical, except for brief excerpts for the purposes of review, with the written permission of the publisher. For information, or to purchase additional copies, phone (707) 964-9520 or write:

Lost Coast Press
155 Cypress Street
Fort Bragg, CA 95437

LCCN 96-076091
ISBN 1-882897-05-6

Cover map courtesy of State Historical Society of North Dakota.

Cover photograph © 1994 Corel corporation. All rights reserved. Made in Canada. Corel is a trademark of Corel Corporation.

Manufactured in the United States of America

First Edition

*Dedicated to
my sons,
Ken and Chris*

Acknowledgments

Thanks to the following:

Antique weapons expert Ray Howser of Pony Express Sport Shop, North Hills, California, for valuable information about the kinds and operation of rifles used in the early west;

The ladies of the City Library at Custer, South Dakota, for information about the birth of that dynamic, historical little city;

John Fremont, Senior Editor at Cypress House in Fort Bragg, Califomia. His excellent critique of the manuscript made all the difference;

Louise Cabral, my writing teacher in Agoura, California, for valuable suggestions regarding writing techniques, especially composition and dialogue;

And my cousin, Montana Rancher Lester Morgan, for helping me with the horses in my story.

Introduction

On October 6, 1874, six covered wagons, each drawn by four oxen, left Sioux City, Iowa, and traveled westward along northern Nebraska to O'Neill, crossed the Niobrara River, and lumbered northwestward into Dakota Territory. Twenty-nine adventurous souls, twenty-seven of them men, one a woman and one a boy, made the long, treacherous journey as inconspicuously as they could to avoid contact with US Army personnel. They felt like criminals, and indeed they were, for they were bound for the Black Hills in violation of direct orders from the United States Government to stay off Sioux land. However, they had heard tales of fabulous gold finds there, and the prospect of becoming rich overnight stifled all reason, even the likelihood of being massacred by hostile Indians, upon whose ceded lands they were trespassing.

They found the Black Hills a formidable place. Its highest point was in the center, where Harney's Peak thrust its granite summit 7,424 feet into the Dakota sky. At the outer margins of the Hills lay stretches of limestone and red sandstone. From north to south the Hills provided some one hundred miles of the roughest country the Gordon pioneers had ever encountered. Deep, brush-entangled canyons and high, steep ridges sometimes made wagon travel impossible, and painstakingly slow at best. Thickets of aspen, willow, and birch proliferated and impeded passage, and beavers stopped up the creeks with dams which flooded the canyons. In many places deep valleys were walled in by limestone or sandstone cliffs, and travelers entering often had great difficulty finding their way out. On the slopes and ridges, even in the higher elevations, the jackpines grew so close together that covered wagons could not squeeze through, and pioneers had to seek other routes. Many beautiful lakes lay in the valleys, some in granite-walled ravines high in the mountains.

There were, however, occasional open meadows throughout the Hills where the pioneers found good grazing lands for their animals and which could be tilled for crops if one grew tired of gold seeking and wished to try his hand at farming.

Wild berry bushes flourished along some landscapes in the summer, and many a hungry pioneer sustained on berries or wild fruit. At almost any time one could find game like deer, antelope, or rabbits if he took the precaution of treading silently and alertly. He could even eat grizzly meat if he were careful the grizzly did not eat him first.

He did well to keep a wary eye on the weather, too. The winter brought snow and ice, but so did the spring sometimes, so heavy and relentless that livestock could not penetrate through to the grass. In the summer came the sudden, violent thunderstorms with accompanying lightning and flooding.

But the weather was good more times than not, and some winters saw virtually no snow at all in the lower plains and valleys. The Gordon party reported that among the majestic beauty of the tree-covered canyons and ridges they found an unusual silence they had experienced nowhere else. As they drove their oxen among the tall, straight pines, the crack of their whips echoed and re-echoed through the hills and valleys in a "romantic manner." Their own voices sounded strange and unnatural to them. Indeed, whether they found gold or disappointment, the Black Hills was a splendor to behold.

On December 23, 1874, after a journey of seventy-eight days without encountering any government agents other than surveyors, and sighting no Indians save a few friendly Cheyenne, the Gordon party arrived at French Creek in the Black Hills. To guard against Indian attack they built a fine stockade and erected several cabins within its walls. The site was a little over two miles south of where Custer City now stands.

They found enough gold to excite them, but the euphoria was short-lived. The U.S. Army arrived, placed them under arrest, and transported them to Fort Laramie in southeastern Wyoming. It was the end of their escapade, but it was also the beginning of the end for the Sioux Indians' legal habitation of the Black Hills of Dakota. Word got out, of course, that they had found gold, and others formed wagon trains and journeyed to the promised land. Before long more whites were scrambling into the Hills than the Army could catch and extricate.

The real rush began late in 1875 and the spring of 1876, when men of every conceivable profession and heritage traveled by any mode of transportation available — horseback, wagon trains long and short, lone wagons, mule back, and some even afoot. Their conveyances bristled with shovels, picks, pans, rifles, knives, ammunition, cook pots, bedding, and food supplies.

Soon miners' tents and makeshift shelters dotted the once peaceful and serene landscapes of the Black Hills. The awesome quiet gave way to the ring of the steel pick and scruff of the shovel. Unshaved, unbathed men of all descriptions crowded creeks and streams, swaying their pans to and fro to wash away the dirt as the yellow flakes settled to the bottom. In one short year the Hills changed from silence to bedlam.

The coveted area, called by the Dakotah Sioux, *Paha Sapa*, "The Hills that are Black," was part of the great reservation ceded them during the treaty of 1868. They took exception to the white man trespassing upon their land, and they attacked, killed, scalped and mutilated many of the miners. It proved to be a time of great anxiety for the travelers' kinfolk back home, and many never heard from their loved ones again.

The Army tried in vain to intercept and turn back these travelers. For every one intercepted, dozens got through. They grouped together, formed communities, built common buildings, and created towns in the Black Hills. Custer City, the first pioneer town, was the destination of a great many gold seekers. In July, 1875, a township company was organized and the site laid out. The sound of the chopper's axe, the saw, and the hammer joined that of the miners' picks and shovels, and early in 1876 they built 1,400 structures. Among these were hotels, restaurants, food stores, sawmills, dry goods stores, and, of course— the ubiquitous saloons.

At first they called their town Stonewall after Confederate General Jackson, but about a month later, in August of 1875, they took a vote and renamed it after their beloved General George Armstrong Custer who, a year earlier, had commanded the first military reconnaissance into the Black Hills and verified the presence of gold.

The quest for the yellow metal continued along French Creek and the area of Custer City for a few months until reports came in of rich deposits located in the area of Deadwood, another new town far to the north. Overnight Custer City became almost deserted, with dry goods and food stores standing vacant while their proprietors followed the stream of prospectors to Deadwood.

But they returned disappointed 'ere long to again work French Creek and other streams in the Custer area, for it was learned that while rich deposits were indeed found around Deadwood, they were concentrated in only a few locations.

In summer of 1876 the Sioux Indians, encouraged by the annihilation of General Custer's command at the Little Big Horn in Montana, began mounting attacks upon the miners, especially about the towns of Deadwood and Rapid City. The citizens of the Hills received reports of murders and mutilations, and they formed militias and built blockhouses for their protection. Eventually the Army found itself in a position where it had to defend the white encroachers from those who had a right to be there, and cavalry and infantry units marched in and established camps and forts.

Finally the United States Government informed the Sioux Indians they must give up the Black Hills and a new treaty would be drawn. Under the threat of having food and clothing rations withheld from the reservations, the Indians were compelled to yield, and in September of 1876 a new treaty was signed. The "trespasser" stigma was lifted from the heads of the pioneers to the Hills.

Shortly after the signing, a farmer, who was also a horse breeder, brought his wife and fifteen-year-old son to the Black Hills and settled on a farm a few miles from Custer City. He raised, bought, and sold horses and cattle, grew corn, alfalfa and hay. He supplied the miners and the citizens about him with these needs until the spring of 1880.

This is a story about his son, then nineteen.

This is about The Kid from Custer.

Chapter One

Custer County, Dakota Territory, Spring, 1880

Nineteen-year-old Casey Parkin had just caught what he was sure must be a nineteen-inch trout in the fishing hole on Earth Creek when he heard the shots. He was thinking how surprised Dad was going to be when he showed him the fish. They had seen several big ones gliding about in there, he and Dad, and tried many times to coax them into taking the big night crawlers. The fish had refused the tempting morsels time and again as if they were wise to the hidden hook.

"That's how they got so big," Dad had told him, grinning and touching his temple. "They're too smart for humans."

Dad had decided not to join Casey this Sunday at the fishing hole. It was less than a quarter mile hike, but he wasn't right up to snuff, he allowed, and besides, he was beginning to feel sorry for all the big fish he caught, and they had a good laugh over that because Dad seldom caught any but pan sized.

When he heard the shots, Casey guessed Dad was practicing on a bottle put up on the front fence, although if he didn't feel good, plinking wasn't apt to make him feel any better. Kind of strange, he thought, and then he heard hoofbeats and commotion. Something was going on at the Parkin farm.

He unhooked the trout and hung it on his string. As he wrapped the line around his willow pole, he heard men's voices, "Heyyyy-yuh! heyyyy-yuh!" The thudding sound of many hooves now came from the corral where Dad had shut in the horses this morning. He tried to see through the trees, but couldn't, so he stuffed his black hat on his head, snatched his home made fishing box, and headed up the slope at a jog. When he got about half way he could see a corner of the high corral jutting just above the rise. The horses looked to be circling inside, and for a moment he caught sight of a rider waving his hat and whooping. In that quick glimpse he saw that the man wore his bandanna over his face. There were only two reasons Casey could think of for wearing a bandanna that way, to keep out trail dust and to hide your face. And it sure as hell wasn't to keep out dust, because Dad hadn't sold any horses nor hired anyone to take any away.

He quickened his steps, and when he reached the top, he dropped his possessions on the ground. Across the plowed field to the west a dust cloud swirled high, and beyond the cloud galloped the Parkin horses, driven to stampede by three horsemen. Casey watched them ramble into the far canyon and out of sight. He stood with mouth agape and a sinking feeling in his stomach.

His mother stood in the pathway that led from the front porch to the wooden gate in the picket fence. She was a pale statue, motionless, not even breathing. Then, with the back of her hand to her lips, she screamed again and again and again.

"What, Ma?" he shouted. "What is it?"

He saw the terror on her face as she pointed. He shifted his gaze to the front gate where his father lay sprawled against the pickets, his head thrown back, his eyes open, blood pouring from an ugly hole in his breast. Casey ran to him and saw the death in his eyes. There was no mistaking the tiny pinpoints of light that twinkled deep in the pupils. Dad's handsome face was twisted grotesquely now, and the sight burned horribly into Casey's soul. It was a scene he would not shake in his lifetime. In that moment, though, before the overwhelming shock engulfed him, the thought came that he, Casey Parkin, would somehow have to fill Dad's boots. He decided to start at once, and he stooped and picked up the .45 caliber revolver Dad had dropped, and tucked it in his belt.

Sheriff Johnson came out from Custer City, fifteen miles to the east, to investigate the crime. Egor Baklanov, who owned the mortuary, came to take Dad in his one-horse, shiny-black hearse to prepare him for his "final journey." Before setting off for town, he assured Mrs. Parkin that Mr. Parkin had, indeed, stepped into a world much more beautiful and peaceful than this one, and we should not grieve for our dear departed loved ones. Then he sold her a nice casket and church service, set the funeral for Thursday at 2 p.m., and departed.

Casey tried to console Mom, tried to cheer her, when he, himself, was in near shock. The Sheriff rode into the wild hills in the direction the bandits had ridden, but returned after two hours. He came into the house and sat at the table with them. He was a big man, and his black shirt tugged at the white buttons that held it to his chest. His six-gun raked against wood as he squeezed into the chair Ma pointed to.

"I'm right sorrowful about what happened, Mrs. Parkin," he said. "I want yuh to know I'll do everything I can to find the fellers that done this." He pulled off his cowboy hat and held it in his lap. "I'll get a posse together and try to track the horses. But I can't make no promises, because trackin's mighty tough up in that high country."

Ma looked up with red-streaked eyes. "Thank you. I know you will do your best."

"To add to the problem, Ma'am, I ain't gonna be sheriff but a week or so longer. I'm turnin' the office over to a feller by the name of Brand. But I'll turn over all the reports and information to him. I just hope I can hand him the outlaws by then. Did you recognize any of 'em?"

"No."

"How about you, Casey?"

"I only saw one of 'em, and only for a second," Casey said. "He had a bandanna tied over his face. I couldn't see him good at all."

"All right. I'll be gettin' back now." He stood and put on his hat. "Again, I'm dreadful sorry, Ma'am. Mr. Parkin was a fine man. I knew him well. I wish fer you the best of everything. Good-bye."

"Good-bye," she said through her handkerchief.

Casey hurried to the door and out with the Sheriff. "Thank

you, Sir," he said. "If you catch the murderers would you ride by and tell us?"

The Sheriff swung up into the saddle. "You can bet yer britches I will, Son. Meantime, be tough. Your mama needs yuh now, more'n she's ever needed anyone before. You'll have to be a man."

"Yes, Sir. I'll try."

Chapter Two

The light from the campfire flickered off the rock face of the cliff high in the mountains north and west of Custer City. After Seth Dalby checked the stolen horses, he leaned down and felt in the darkness until he located his saddlebags on the ground. He slipped out his bottle, twisted off the cork, and glanced at his two comrades and the big red hound dog over at the campfire. Hermund Grim hadn't put him up very high on the smarts scale when he told him to tie up his bloodhound and not take him along on the caper at the Parkins'. Seth already knew that if he took old Slobbers along, the law would be looking for a feller with a hound dog from then on. Hell, Grim didn't have to tell him that! But Seth hadn't gave old Herm any guff when he told him; he just said "You betcha, Herm. I'll tie my dog up and leave him right here." That's why Seth was still alive. He never gave Herm any guff.

He tipped up the bottle and took a good snort.

"Ahhhhhh!"

Nothing like a shot of rotgut after a good meal, and Barty Hardwise had sure put together a dandy one on this night. He wasn't in no hurry to get back to the fire to share the whiskey so he stood in the dark where they couldn't see him and tipped the bottle a couple times more. He liked Barty, even though he was a damn wimp sometimes. Barty was almost as much a wimp as Hermund Grim was the other way. He guessed he liked Herm too, but now and then some little voice or other inside told him that it wasn't a *liking* he felt for Grim, but an out and out fear of the son-of-a-bitch. He'd been riding with Grim for three, four years now, and they'd been through lots of shenanigans together, enough to make Seth realize he would never be able to predict what Grim was going to do next. He knew he better do what Grim said to, because if you was to get the man irked up, you might wind up dead on the spot. Yet, most of the time Grim was like them saints Mama used to read about in the bible, just a passel of fun to be with, as nice and polite and entertaining as anybody you ever met in your life. And besides, he was downright generous when it came to dividing up the spoils of their capers.

And did he have a way with the ladies! My, Oh, My! Seth remembered a couple years ago in Saint Louie Grim saw in the Saint Louis Dispatch where some rich old coot had died and left his widow a basketful of money. Right away Grim started nosing around until he learned where she lived, where she went to church, and the fact that she lived alone. He also found out her relatives' names in New York, what they did for a living, and a bunch of other personal stuff. Grim began attending church then, the same one as the widow. He was most handsome, and he managed to make her acquaintance by pretending to have worked for her husband's brother in New York.

Seth and Barty hung around the pool hall and stayed low while Grim pulled off this incredible stunt. Although she was old enough to be his mama and was "already starin' the Grim Reaper in the eye," as Grim joked later, he swept her off her feet and of course she married him and gave him all her money.

The poor old lady died right away after the honeymoon of some sort of natural causes like a crushed spleen or something, and Grim and the boys went on the road again. With all that money they lived high up on the porker for the next few months until gambling and foolishness left them broke. They then took to collecting horses, mostly somebody else's. Hermund Grim had some contacts back east who would take all the horseflesh he could get as long as he could fix the brands right. It was working out good, and they were beginning to build up a little capital again. Their quest had brought them to the Black Hills of Dakota Territory, where remote farms and scant law enforcement made the fruit ripe for plucking.

Seth took another good jolt from the bottle before carrying it to the fire. The yellow glow lit up Barty's pale, pinched face. He and Grim were both laughing at something Grim had said. Seth was glad they had scored big at the Parkin Farm, not only because the horses would bring good money, but it put Grim in a jovial mood. He could be a downright mean hombre if things weren't going just right. Seth was pretty careful not to say or do anything that might rile the big man.

Grim looked up as Seth shoved the bottle in front of him. He took it, twisted off the cork and smelled. "Horses all right, Dalby?"

"Yup. Cain't see 'em too good in the dark, but I could hear 'em snortin' and talkin' to one another in the corral."

Grim took a belt of whiskey and handed the bottle across to the cook. "Here ya go, Barty. This here poison of Seth's will either make yuh a new man or kill yuh."

Barty laughed again and drank. Seth settled down on a flat stone beside his sleeping hound and belched. "Little cool tonight."

"I was just tellin' Barty, here," Grim said, "that I got me a hell of an idea. 'Course Barty thinks I'm loco, although he ain't sayin' it out loud. But the more I think of it the better I like it. Now that we got the Parkin horses, I got me the notion I'd like to have the whole damn farm. Always wanted to settle on a farm, and here's one that's just settin' there waitin' for me."

Seth wrinkled up his face and stared at Grim. "Did yuh say 'take the farm'?"

"Yep, that's what I said."

"How in hell yuh figger on doin' that, Herm?"

Grim shifted his hindquarters around to get more comfortable. He grinned across at Seth. "Well, here's my plan, and I might say it's on account of you that I'm gonna be able to do it."

"On accounta me?" Seth said.

"Yeah. On accounta you havin' blew out Jim Parkin's lamp. Now, Mrs. Parkin, she ain't got no husband no more, right? An' yuh know how damn tough it is fer a lady to run a farm by herself." Grim paused and shrugged his shoulders. "Of course she's got that kid a hers. But I'll wager she'd be mighty tickled to have herself a brand new, good lookin' husband like me to take care of all that farmin' and them chores."

"Like you?"

Grim stared hard at Seth. "Does that trouble yuh somehow, Dalby?"

"Oh, no, Sir. No, it don't, not a-tall. But I ain't sure I killed Parkin. Maybe I just winged him."

"Yuh killed him," Grim declared. "I rode past and took a good look before we left. He was dead, ain't no doubt."

Grim's eyes drifted up toward the sky, and Seth thought he saw a sort of vacant, far away look in them.

"I'll wait a spell 'til the grievin' lets up some," Grim went on. "But not too long, o'course. Wouldn't want some other feller to get the same idea. Then I'll ride in like I'm a drifter lookin' fer work and she'll hire me. Then I'll turn on the old charm and marry myself right into the farm."

"Doggone, Herm," Barty said, "the more I hear the more I like that idea."

"Sure," Grim said. "We could get our horses elsewhere and run 'em into that farm and fix the brands right there. It'd be a lot easier workin' where we got a good barn and water and a house and the comforts of home."

Seth felt himself grinning. "Say, I like that idea," he chirped. "We could turn this thing into a big operation."

"Just one thing botherin' me about all that, Herm," Barty said. "Ain't yer new spouse gonna complain about yer brandin' stolen horses on her farm? Or maybe that kid of hers might find our doin's a mite unusual, don't yuh think, and maybe blab to the Sheriff?"

"Well, Barty, bein' you ain't never been married, I reckon you wouldn't understand how them things work. Yuh see, there's an indoctrination period follerin' the weddin' when the husband reaches an understandin' with the new spouse and kids, if any, about who the boss is gonna be in the family." Grim reached across and twisted the bottle from Barty's hand and took a drink. He handed the bottle to Seth. "That ain't bad whiskey, Dalby."

"No, it ain't. Ain't bad a-tall."

Grim turned back to Barty. "Like I was sayin', ya gotta explain, very careful-like, that what you do as the man of the house ain't nobody else's business, and if what you do happens to get blabbed around, it'll be the last blabbin' done." Grim showed Barty his big, gnarled fist. "Know what I'm gettin' at, Friend?"

Barty laughed. "Yeah, sure do, Herm, sure do!"

"But I been considerin' somethin' else, too," Grim went on. "Wouldn't it be tolerable excellent if we had somebody in with the law who could keep tabs on the Sheriff so's we'd know if we was to fall under any kind of suspicion? Somebody that could throw the law off our track if he had to, or let us know if they was on to us?"

"Yeah, reckon it would be," Seth said. "Who yuh got in mind?"

"You."

"Me?"

"Sure. You can hire on as a deputy sheriff. 'Deputy Dalby!' Don't that have a dandy ring?"

Dalby's jaw dropped open and stayed that way while the dandy ring bounced about inside his head. Camp fire smoke came over and smothered him, and he blinked and dug his knuckles into his eyes. "Hell afire," he said finally, shifting onto another rock. "I ain't no lawman! I always try t'ride clear of them fellers."

Grim smiled. "Freddy Rankin — you recollect old Freddy, don't yuh? Well, Freddy lived in these hills up 'til last year or so. He was here when General Custer and the Seventh Cav came a few years back checkin' out the rumors of gold. An' he was still here last year. In fact, back in '75 when they first declared Custer a real genuine town, old Freddy voted with the Yanks to call her Custer. The Rebs that lived here wanted to name her Stonewall, but Freddy's bunch voted 'em down."

Seth lifted his hat and scratched his head. "Don't rightly see what that's got t'do with—"

"Well, hold on, Dalby. I'm comin' to it. When I ran across Freddy up in Deadwood last month, he told me about this here region. He said it ain't got a whole lot of gold in it, and there's lots more to be had up around Deadwood. But them fellers from the East just keep flockin' in here like sheep a-followin' one another, an' all they want to do is look fer the yellow stuff. Ain't none of 'em wants to be lawmen, hardly, and the county people have trouble keepin' a sheriff here and twice as much trouble keepin' any deputies at all."

"Do tell!" Seth said.

"Now you, Dalby, yer kinda the deputy type." Grim leaned forward, his eyes sparkling. "You could go to that Sheriff feller and tell him what a damn fine citizen y'are and how yuh hate outlaws and hoss thieves and yuh always wanted to be a deputy, an' yuh ain't interested in pannin' fer gold. Maybe he'll hire yuh. They don't know us up here. Far as they know, we're as innocent as...as that dumb old hound dog of yers!"

Barty Hardwise leaned aside and waved as the smoke left Dalby and came over to him. "Yuh don't reckon anybody — goddammit, Herm, how come that smoke never wanders over yer way, anyhow?"

"It ain't got enough guts. Would you, if you was smoke?"

Barty dug his knuckles in his eyes. "No, reckon not."

"All right, then. What was you sayin, Hardwise? Yuh don't reckon anybody what?"

"Yuh don't reckon anybody from the Parkin Farm could recognize us do yuh?"

Grim shook his head. "Ain't no way they could. Our faces was covered good, an' nobody down here knows us. Now, Dalby, I think yuh ought to hightail it to Custer. If yuh get there in time for the funeral, join the good folks in the chapel. Get a shave and some new duds. Let a few tears run down durin' the service to show what a carin' feller y'are. An' take that damn bloodhound with yuh."

"Take m'dog in the funeral parlor?"

Hermund grinned and shook his head. "Sure, why not? His face is ugly as hell, but it's still prettier'n yers, an' he'll add some respectability to yuh."

Seth Dalby sat back and thought about what Grim had said. And the more he thought, the more his insides lit up like he had swallowed a firefly or something. He grinned. "Me! A deputy sheriff! By God, Herm, I like the idea. An' y'know what? They got an election comin' in November,

Maybe I could even get m'self elected sheriff!"

"Damn right!" Grim said. "With you bein' the Sheriff and me and Barty runnin' the stock operation, we'd be livin' high on the hog in no time a-tall!"

All three laughed uproariously and passed the bottle around.

Chapter Three

The funeral service was held at Baklanov's Mortuary in Custer City that Thursday. Egor had managed to smooth the look of pain off Jim Parkin's face and push his eyelids shut, and he appeared to be resting peacefully in the silver casket in the front of the room. Casey noticed that most of the townfolk and a good part of the countryfolk were there, many who had traveled some distance to honor his dad. Casey's Uncle Bart delivered the eulogy, speaking of Dad's military contribution to his country, the high regard the community held for him, and what a great loss his parting was. It was an impressive speech, interrupted only once when a tall man with a pale, frightened face got to his feet and hurried up the aisle and out the door, followed closely by a big red bloodhound.

Casey suffered mightily during the next few weeks. Piled atop the grief for his dad was the agony shown by his mother. She went about each day doing her housework and the cooking and gardening and milking without saying more than a word or two, then so faintly and weakly that Casey could hardly hear her. He did his best to assure her they would not lose the farm, then set about working from daylight to dark and on Sundays too, to convince her of that. He had to use Bacon, their cantankerous brown mule, to pull the plow because the big white work horse was among those taken by the thieves. Bacon worked hard most of the time, but he had stubborn spells where he would simply turn and drag the plow off the field and take to eating grass, and there was nothing Casey could do to stop him. He was obliged to wait until the animal was personally ready to go back to work again.

Finally, in desperation, he spent his saved money on a new plow horse, and then he began to show progress. He tilled the corn field from dawn until sunset, even on Sundays. He thought too that if he worked hard he would not have time to dwell upon his loss. But holding the big iron plow down one row and up another hour after hour led to monotony and he found himself playing a game inside his head where he pretended to be with Dad at the fishing hole, sometimes catching the fish, sometimes swimming among them. Sometimes they were off hunting deer, and Dad would be showing him how the Winchester and the big Sharps rifles worked and teaching him to shoot with skill. Sometimes Dad even let him shoot bottles off the tree limb with the brand new Colt Peacemaker revolver. That was the one Dad dropped in the dirt when he drew his last breath. That was the one Casey had picked up and hid under his mattress. Maybe the rustlers would return and he would have to use it.

They talked often, he and Dad, about life and philosophy and the good sense of going to school and working hard with the three R's. During the cold winters on their ranch in Iowa when Casey was little, Dad often hitched up the frisky red mare to the buggy and drove him to the little school house a couple miles away where Bonnie Sue Graham taught four or five children. Then when Dad came for him in the afternoon, he always asked Casey what he had learned.

"Nothin'," he would answer, but Dad always made him think hard and remember what Miss Graham had told the class that day. The afternoons were extra cold in the open buggy, and he had to pull his big sheep-wool collar up over his ears and duck his chin under to keep the icy wind out. Sometimes teacher had taught them a song to sing, and he was surprised to learn that usually Dad knew the song too, and so they would sing it together on the ride home, and their breaths formed puffy little clouds as the buggy skimmed over the snowbound trail.

His very first memories of Dad were of a handsome man arriving home in a Union Army Officer's uniform, swearing never to leave again. Birk MacDoughall, Dad's friend and neighboring farmer, came home from the war then too, and a few years later married Casey's teacher, pretty Bonnie Sue

Graham. Miss Graham kept on teaching the children, except then they called her "Missus MacDoughall," and it was hard to get used to that.

When Casey was about fifteen, Dad and Birk MacDoughall hit upon the notion they might get rich in the Black Hills of Dakota. Lots of folks had found gold there, they heard, and now, under a new treaty, the Sioux Indians relinquished their claims upon the area. So they both sold their Iowa ranches, bought Conestoga prairie schooners, and in March of 1877 set out across the wild plains of northern Nebraska, Dad's wagon rumbling along in front of Birk's. Casey, then sixteen, looked with pride upon their eight big horses and the magnificent wagon they pulled. The schooners looked like big canvas-covered boats, high at the front and back so things wouldn't fall out going up hills and down. They could even be used like boats if needed, Dad told him. They could take off the wheels and float them across deep rivers, although they never had to.

Dad's and Casey's saddle horses trotted along behind the wagon on tethers, seldom ridden. Sometimes Dad climbed up on one of the draft horses, but most times he was busy afoot tending the teams and keeping them moving. Casey preferred to walk, too, but Mom usually rode in the wagon where she kept things clean and orderly. "Keeping it shipshape," she joked.

After the new treaty, the U. S. Government told the Sioux Indians to allow white folks to cross the reservation to the Black Hills without bothering them. Dad remarked he hoped all the Indians got the message. It was not long after they had crossed into Dakota Territory that a dozen braves, some armed with repeater rifles, trotted their ponies out of the foothills and moved toward the wagons. Dad stopped the horses, and Birk did the same behind. Dad dug in the box for his buffalo rifle, then tossed it back in. "I think we'd be better off without the weapons," he said to Birk. "Just hope they aren't hostile."

Cold shivers invaded Casey's spine at the sight of the fierce looking warriors loping toward them. He ducked around behind, climbed into the wagon, and pulled shut the flap. He dug Dad's Remington revolver out of the box and peeked out. Dad stood smiling alongside the horses and held up his hand in greeting. The first Indian, a big, mean-looking fellow, raised his hand and reined in a few feet from Dad. The others stopped behind their leader, their Winchester rifles held with stocks resting on thighs and muzzles upward. Casey's hands trembled as he held the revolver cocked and ready. If any one of the braves aimed toward Dad, he'd shoot him, and as many others as he could, starting with those with the rifles. Then he noticed that Mom crouched beside him, the buffalo gun snugged to her shoulder and her eyes sparking fire.

But there was no need. With sign language the braves told Dad they had a camp in the hills and were hungry and cold at night and needed food and blankets. Dad gave them flour and sugar and blankets, and Birk provided extra coats and an antelope he'd shot. They smiled and nodded as they took the offerings, turned, and rode back into the hills. Casey drew a deep breath then and waited for his heart to stop pounding.

When they arrived at Custer, Casey was surprised to find dozens of empty buildings. Many disillusioned pioneers had gone elsewhere and left stores and homes vacant. However, a good number of these returned after finding things no better in the area of Deadwood City to the north.

Casey accompanied Dad and Birk to the streams during the first few days after their arrival, working the soil in his mining pan. They realized early that the chances of finding enough gold to survive on were poor, and they settled for the vocation they knew best — raising crops like hay, alfalfa and corn, and dealing in horses and cattle. Even that was less lucrative than it had been in Iowa, for the early folks in the Black Hills were too migrant to stay put long. So now, after three years on these farms in the Hills, the Parkins and the MacDoughalls were not at all rich. Eventually Casey and Dad would have improved and enlarged their farm, he felt sure, if only Dad hadn't been gunned down and the horses stolen.

When he'd plowed the last of the big corn field, Casey quit early for the first time since the funeral. He gave the plow horse a rubdown and oats and bedded him down in the barn stall next to Ebon, his big black saddle horse. He went in and sat at the kitchen table.

"You're early, Casey," Ma said.

He grinned through his fatigue. "Yep, I am. I finished the corn field. I'll get 'er planted, and we'll be in business."

She lifted a pot onto the stove. "Will soup suit you again today, Honey? I just haven't felt up to cooking much since—"

"Soup's fine, Ma. Just fine."

"Get yourself washed, now. I'll have your supper ready in no time at all."

Casey splashed water on his face at the basin. He was tired, but he didn't mind the feeling. It was a good tired. With it came a whole heap of satisfaction for a plowing job well done.

"That's sure a good horse, Ma. He never let up even once. He just kept on goin' and goin'."

"You kept going too, Casey. You've done a fine job."

When he sat down to his soup, she sat across from him and watched him eat. "You surely look like your father, Casey."

He smiled. "Thank you. Dad was good lookin'."

"Can you keep this up all summer? You're working all day every day and half the night."

"Well, we don't have much choice, do we? There's more'n we can do here. You've been workin' day and night too, Ma, doin' the house cleanin', the vegetable garden, milkin' the cows, and taking care of the pigs and chickens. A lot of the things Dad and I used to do."

She rose slowly and poured herself a cup of coffee and sat back down. "We can't keep it up, Casey. We have to hoe the garden or it'll turn into a weed patch. The old milk cow's going to calve soon. Somebody will have to look after her. The corral needs mending. We'll need to be putting up firewood soon. We're going to have to hire somebody to help us, and pay them with the corn money when we get it, if we can find somebody who will be agreeable to wait for their pay."

Casey nodded but said nothing. When he finished his soup, he stood up. "I don't know anybody who'd do that, Ma. I don't even know anyone who's free to be hired, do you? Seems like most men just want to hunt for gold, don't it?"

"Seems that way."

Casey moved his chair away from the table. He got his guitar from the bedroom and sat back down and picked out chords for "Silver Threads Among the Gold."

"Oh, my!" Ma exclaimed. "You haven't played since—"

"No, reckon not. Haven't felt much like it, I guess."

With that he sang the song softly as his fingers played the chords.

Darling, I am growing old
Silver threads among the gold.
Rest your head upon my brow today
Life is fading fast away...

Ma closed her eyes and sat motionless. When she opened them there were tears. "I do love it so, Casey. Please play some more."

"All right. But is ain't very good without Dad's fiddle."

"It's very, very good. It's soothing to the soul. Keep playing."

She moved to her rocking chair and closed her eyes again as Casey sang softly. He was elated that Ma was showing signs of recovering from the grief. He loved her mightily, and he prayed often for her recovery.

At last she rose and picked up the dishes from the table. "When we go to church this Sunday, let's both pray for your father's soul. And also that the Lord will send somebody to help us with the work. To kind of take your Dad's place. Not that anybody ever could."

Several days later when Hermund Grim showed up, it was like the Lord must have heeded Mom's prayers. He was a giant of a man with a good looking face, black curly hair, and a square jaw. He rode a big red gelding, and the saddle scabbard held a Winchester Lever Action Carbine. He toted a Remington revolver on his hip. He rode in one day out of the high country and knocked on the door. Casey jumped up from the table where he and Ma were having their noon meal and opened the door and there he stood, smiling as if he were an old friend.

"Howdy, there," he sang. "I see yer in the middle of fixin' yer corral out there. Need any help? I'm purty good with them long poles."

"Well, I can handle the corral mendin' all right," Casey said. He turned. "Ma, man here lookin' for work."

She came to the door. "Hello," she said. "What kind of work are you looking for, Mister..."

"Name's Grim, Ma'am. Hermund Grim. I been traveling clear across the territory from the Missouri River. Ran low on grub and figured I'd find some work in Custer. I'd be glad to help yuh just fer somethin' t'eat. I had some deer meat couple days back, but ain't had no luck huntin' since."

"Well, we could use some help here," she said. "But we can't afford to pay much. My husband was killed and we don't have much."

"Shucks, Ma'am," Grim said. "Like I said, I'd be glad to help yuh some just for a spot of grub. What's yer name, Ma'am?"

"Annabel Parkin. This here's my son, Casey."

Casey and Grim shook hands. "Pleased to meet you, Sir," Casey said.

"I'd sure be much obliged fer a bite er two, then I'll give yuh a help with that corral. Them poles is pretty dern heavy."

Ma hesitated a moment, then stepped back. "Yes, yes, please come in. Casey and I were just having a snack, and you're very welcome to join us."

Casey felt some discomfort as the stranger washed his face and hands at the basin and took the chair Ma pointed to. There were all kinds of men out there — no way to tell which kind this one might be. Maybe today would be Casey's first test at being the man of the house. He hoped not, for Hermund Grim was several inches taller and many pounds heavier. He dug into the spuds and beef like a hungry man, and when he was done he stood up and slapped his stomach.

"My soul, I do swear, Mrs. Parkin, that was a mighty grand feed! I feel like I can lick my weight in agitated grizzly bears after that. Casey, let's you and me git out there an' show that old corral a thing or two, what say?"

Casey grinned and nodded. He grabbed his hat and the two hit for the corral. Hermund Grim proved to be a good worker and knowledgeable about skinning the bark from pine poles and chopping notches and binding them together with wire. They worked steadily in the hot afternoon sunshine, and the side of the corral was back up strong and sturdy long before Casey could have done it alone. The only time Grim stopped working was when he spotted Ma toting a heavy slop pail from the house to the pig pen, holding one arm straight out as she struggled. He threw down the pole he was holding.

"Mrs. Parkin," he called, running toward her. "Is that bucket fer the pigs?"

She stopped and set it down. "Yes. It's the kitchen remnants for them."

He snatched up the pail, hurried to the pig pen and poured it in the trough between two black porkers. He returned and handed her the bucket. "If yuh got any other heavy chores, tell me, Ma'am. Don'tcha go a-hurtin yer back doin' somethin' like this as long as I'm about."

There was soup at the supper table that evening, but only a small bowl for each of the three of them. An appetite teaser, Ma called it. Then came beef steak, mashed potatoes and gravy, and fresh garden peas and carrots. The whole thing was topped off with apple pie. Casey was aghast. Ma hadn't cooked like this since the tragedy. He guessed company was what she needed. Something different. Somebody to cook for, to impress. Something to think about besides her great loss.

Hermund Grim made a grand to-do about the supper, declaring he couldn't remember when he'd ever eaten such savory steak and tender peas. And the apple pie! Oh, my! Casey could see a new gleam in Ma's eyes. Only he didn't know whether it was a good thing or not.

"What brought you to this country, Mr. Grim?" she asked.

He tore a hot biscuit in half and spread butter. "Well, reckon I heard somethin' about reachin' down an' pickin' up gold nuggets right off the ground here. 'Course I know better'n to believe that, but I thought I might give prospectin' a try. It's better than just drifting like I been doin' since my poor wife died of the smallpox. An' this is sure a breathtakin' part of the country. Seems a shame to start diggin' it up like so many fellers are doin'. Now that I'm here, I don't rightly know what I'm a-gonna do. Fer tonight, though, can I spend it in yer hayloft?"

Casey spoke before his mother had a chance to. "You can sure enough do that, Mr. Grim. We can give you some blankets." He was afraid Ma might offer the spare bedroom, and he didn't trust this stranger quite that far.

"Thank you, Casey. I won't need the blankets, though. Got m'own tied to my saddle."

Casey lay awake longer than he wanted to that night, thinking about the stranger, thankful that the corral got repaired, yet apprehensive about who or what the man might be. He was still tired when the rooster announced dawn, and he climbed into his clothes slowly. He moved to the window and looked out. Hermund Grim was at the pump, splashing water on his face and threading it through his black hair with his fingers. Casey watched him as he dried his face on a towel, threw it over his shoulder, and sauntered back to the barn. Hard to tell what the man might be thinking or planning. Maybe he'd talk about it at the breakfast table.

At breakfast, Grim settled in wearing his wide grin. "Sure slept good," he said. "Extraordinary fine loft in that barn."

Ma took a chair across from Grim. As Casey sat down at his left, he felt a surge of discomfort that Grim was sitting in Dad's chair.

"Sure am much obliged for the lodgin'," Grim went on. "I was just wonderin' — I'd be happy t'help Casey with the corn plantin' in exchange for gettin' some of my duds washed, and I can head on into Custer tomorrow instead of today, an' I'll look a whole lot more decent t'go askin' fer work if I'm sportin' clean clothes."

Ma smiled courteously. "Certainly," she said. "Just bring your clothes in. Casey, after breakfast you fetch in that washtub that hangs on the house outside, put it on the stove and fill it."

"Okay, Ma."

But after breakfast it was Grim who hurried out and filled the tub. "They're my duds," he said. "I can do that much at least."

Grim was a fast worker in the corn field. He dropped in the kernels and covered them in one quick motion, and Casey was hard put to keep abreast of him in the next row over. By day's end a large part of the corn field was planted, and Casey was feeling pretty good about things. He allowed that if they had a hired hand like this, they'd sure be able to keep up the farm work all right.

That evening at the supper table they reached an agreement. Grim would stay on as a hired hand for twenty-five dollars a month and board and Ma would wash his clothes now and then. He'd sleep in the barn loft until he could build a bunk house. He wouldn't take any wages until the corn was sold. Grim shook hands with Casey and Ma to seal the bargain.

The next few weeks saw a grand improvement around the place. The bunkhouse went up in a matter of days, complete with two bunks built right in. The corn field got planted and sprouted promptly with the coming of summer heat. Casey and Grim kept the weeds hoed, and the alfalfa crop was thriving.

Much to Casey's delight, Ma was coming out of her traumatic grief. Her eyes took on the old sparkle, she walked straighter, and the spring returned to her step. Each evening meal was virtually a celebration, with Hermund Grim telling tales of the trail, of bandits he'd encountered and lawmen he knew. Casey had no doubt that her rejuvenation was because of his presence, so he wasn't surprised when she confided in him one day that he had asked her to marry him.

"He asked me just yesterday, Casey," she said, her eyes showing her excitement. "Maybe this is the answer to our prayers."

"Did you say you would?"

"No. I told him I wanted time to think about it. But I wanted to ask you what you thought. It will affect your life too, Honey."

He stood quietly, pondering. Finally he said, "Who *is* he, Ma? He's only been around here a few weeks. We don't know much about him."

"I'm sure he's a sincere man," she said. She moved to the window and gazed out. "He admitted he has been a drifter and never had any reason to settle down since his wife died. Until he met me, he said. He's worked lots with cattle and on farms — well, you can see how he handled the work out there. He surely isn't afraid of work."

He joined her at the window and looked out at the new cornstalks. The sight made him feel good. "Yes," he said. "Mr. Grim is a good worker, no doubtin' that."

"He said he had ideas about more planting and better crops and getting us a herd of beef cattle. He said in a couple years I wouldn't know the place anymore, and we'd build a bigger house and have a maid to help me and hired men to do the chores. Oh, Casey, it sounds so wonderful."

The change in his mother was spectacular since Grim's arrival. What could he say? Certainly, he would not wish to take away her chance at being happy again.

"I won't go against you, Ma. But I have to let it be your decision, not mine. You're the one with the most to lose if he's bad, and the most to gain if he's good."

"You're right," she said. "I should not ask you to make a decision like this for me. I should not put it on your shoulders."

"Do you love him?"

"I...I don't know, Casey. I think love is being compatible. And I think we are that. I think Mr. Grim is a good man."

Hermund Grim and Annabel Parkin were married a week later by the sometimes Undertaker and sometimes Reverend Egor Baklanov in his sometimes mortuary and sometimes chapel, depending upon what kind of service he was called upon to provide. Several of Annabel's friends came to wish them well, including Birk and Bonnie Sue MacDoughall. Casey was taken aback at how skinny Mrs. MacDoughall was. He remembered that when she taught school she was a little on the plump side. Since they arrived at Custer she had come down with a sickness that people didn't openly discuss. "She's got the cancer!" they would whisper. Birk MacDoughall was a fine man, tall and handsome, and a good husband to his poor wife.

He was a square shooter in Casey's eyes, the kind of a fellow who Casey bet would not hit a man that was down and would never shoot anyone in the back. He was glad Birk had come to the wedding.

The newlyweds did not go anywhere on a honeymoon. Hermund Grim declared he was plumb anxious to get to working on their dream farm, and they could go the whole hog later after they were rich.

Casey's first inkling that Mr. Grim was *not* a good man came a few weeks after the wedding. Casey had saddled Ebon, his big black saddle pony, and rode into the western hills to bring in their six milk cows. He found only two of them, Wanda Bell and Bertha. He had hunted so long that it was after dark when he brought the two cows to the barn for milking. Hermund Grim was sweeping a stall by lantern light when Casey put the cows in adjacent stalls.

"I couldn't find but two cows, Mr. Grim." He had never been able to bring himself to call his new stepfather "Hermund." And he would certainly never call him "Dad."

Grim looked through the slats at him. "Don't worry about it." he said.

Casey frowned. "Why?"

"'Cause yuh ain't gonna find 'em, that's why."

"I ain't? Why ain't I?"

There was a silence as Grim made three or four more sweeps with the broom. "'Cause they ain't out there no more."

The smell of booze drifted through to Casey, surprising him. He'd never known Grim to take a drink. He stood and waited while the man swept. Finally, Grim said,

"They ain't out there no more because I sold 'em."

Casey's jaw dropped. "You sold 'em? Why, for Christ's sake?"

Grim whirled and faced him. "Don't you worry yer ass about it, boy! I figured we don't need that many milk cows so I sold four of 'em. You sure as hell don't drink that much milk, do yuh?"

"But, what about the butter Ma churns and sells? What about the cream she sells. We need that money."

Grim stormed out of the stall and glared at Casey. "Listen here, you little bastard! Don't you question what I do, unnerstand? You show me some respect or I'll knock yer goddam head off. Don't you go questionin' everything I do! Unnerstand?" Casey saw rage in his eyes.

"Mr. Grim, I...I don't think—"

Grim's right hand came back, and his fist was clenched. "Don't you gimme no sass, y'hear?"

"Yes, Sir," Casey heard himself say. He pushed Wanda Bell into a stall and snatched the milk stool off the wall. He pulled the flour-sack cover off the pail and sat down. As the milk streamed into his bucket he felt anger and disappointment creeping over him. Grim's eyes had flashed rage and hate and even a hint of insanity in that brief moment. Casey had been afraid of something like this. He had felt from the start that Grim's arrival was too good to be true. Now that the man had showed his true side, it was too late. Grim had the farm, and it looked like he intended to take it over completely.

Wanda went dry and he moved over to Bertha in the next stall. He said no more to Grim and did not even look at him again. He tried to think what he should do. His impulse was to saddle up Ebon and ride out, but of course he could never abandon his mother, especially in light of Grim's true nature. Test time was here. He had hoped Grim was the answer to their terrible loss, but now it was clear that Casey would have to be a man after all, and he'd have to do more than fill the void left by the death of Dad. He'd have to contend with a wild, physically powerful man.

He wondered if Grim had mistreated Ma yet. If he hadn't already, it would just be a matter of time until he flew off the handle at her, too. He had drawn back his fist at Casey. Would he actually strike? The look in his eyes told Casey he would.

The next day he went about his farm chores while carefully avoiding Grim. He did not come in from the field at noon, and it was well after suppertime that night when he dragged himself into the kitchen, hungry and tired. Ma was there.

"You've come in late, Casey. I was worried about you."

"Sorry, Ma." He sat down at the table.

She lifted the cook stove lid and stirred the coals with the iron lifter. "I'll heat up the beans again, and the pork. It's gone cold now."

"That's okay," he said. "I can eat it cold just as good."

She stirred the beans and shuffled them over onto the hot stove lid. "Your step-father's not here right now."

"Where is he?"

"I don't know. He didn't say where he was going. Was he mean to you? Is that why you stayed out?"

"Yep. Has he been mean to you?"

As she looked down at him he saw a new look in her eyes — concern and fear. "He's been drinking some," she said.

"Has he been mean to you?" Casey said again.

"Not physically. But he laid down the law. It was what he called 'Grim's Law.'"

"Really? He wanted you to know he's the boss, didn't he?"

She shook her head, and a tear manifested in her eye. "It looks as though I made a bad decision, Casey. You were right, I shouldn't have consented so quickly. But now it's done, and we'll just have to make the best of it. Can you live with it?"

He was silent as she scooped pork and beans into a dish and set it before him. She got a cup and poured coffee. He didn't know what to tell her. How could he know whether he could live with it? Grim had looked angry enough to kill him.

"I don't know, Ma," he said. "But I'll do my best."

Casey managed to elude his step father two more days. On the second day he finished weeding the last corn row and came in a little before noon. As he strode in from the field, Hermund Grim came out of the barn and met him half way across the yard.

"Where the hell you been, Kid?"

Casey wanted to tell him it was none of his business, but restrained himself because of Ma. Better not to ruffle feathers, he thought. "Just finished the weedin'," he said, chucking his thumb over his shoulder in the direction of the corn field. "Wanted to stay with it 'til it was done."

Grim glared at him, hands on hips. "Is that all you can think about, that goddam corn field? There's other stuff to do around here, y'know. Where y'been at night? Y'ain't been in yer bed a-tall."

"It's been hot, Mr. Grim. I been sleepin' out under the pines where it's cool. I often do that in the summer."

"Tonight you sleep in yer bed," Grim said.

Casey felt anger building up, and a wee bit of self control slipped away. "Why should I, Mr. Grim?"

The man's eyes flashed, and he stepped up close and looked down into Casey's eyes. "Because I told yuh to, that's why. It looks like one thing yuh gotta learn is that I'm yer Daddy now, and you'll do what I say. I thought I explained that to yuh t'other day!"

"No, Sir, you ain't my Daddy and you ain't my boss. I'm nineteen now, and I'm my own boss."

Grim's right fist was so fast Casey never saw it coming, and when it found his cheek bone it was like being whacked by a board. He hit the ground on his back and rolled onto his side. He saw Grim step toward him and bring his boot back. He rolled over and over to avoid the kick and finally stumbled to his feet. He staggered away in the direction of the west hills. When he looked back Grim stood with fists clenched and eyes blazing.

"That's it, yuh little bastard!" Grim shouted. "Get to hell out of here and don't come back 'til yer satisfied who the boss is around here."

Casey kept running until he was past the corn field and into the timber of the hills. He climbed the slope and found a thicket of briar where he could get out of Grim's view. He lay on the ground behind the bushes, gasping for breath, and when it came back, he cried. His world was shattered. He could not possibly exist with that maniac. What would happen to Ma? He stood and peered over the briars, looking for Grim, but he was nowhere in sight.

He sat on the ground and wondered what to do. He thought of Dad. What would Dad tell him if he could talk from heaven? He would say be brave, be calm, don't cry. He'd say do what's right for Ma, the most important person in your life. Do what's right for her, no matter how humiliating it might be, or how self-degrading.

He took off his neckerchief, shook it, and wiped his eyes and face. He didn't cry any more then. He was nineteen and he'd have to be a man. No more crying. He sat quietly in the timber and listened to the sounds of nature. Things began to look better as the afternoon wore on. He'd go back, hat in hand, and apologize to Grim and promise his obedience. It would be, he felt, the best thing for Ma. Right now, at least.

The afternoon shadows stretched across the fields as he strode purposefully back. He looked at the ground in front of him most of the way and tried to appear nonchalant in case Grim was watching him from the house or barn. He didn't want to appear angry. He reached the barn and opened the big door. The smell of warm hay greeted him. "Mr. Grim?" he called. The only sounds were a swish of horse tails and a stomp of hooves from the stalls. He strolled to the house, whistling a tune and even smiling a bit. He would try to look his best. He opened the front door and peered into the service porch. It was quiet. He entered and opened the door to the kitchen.

No one was there.

It was as if everyone had gone, for he could hear nothing except a pot of soup bubbling on the stove.

He moved to the dining room and found that the table had been set for three places. He heard moans coming from Ma's bedroom, and he burst in and found her on the floor, lying on her back. She grimaced in pain as blood ran from the corner of her mouth. Her brown hair was disheveled and her dress spattered red. He knelt beside her.

"Ma! Ma! What happened?"

She opened her eyes. "Casey!" Her voice was weak. "Help me."

"What happened?"

"Mr. Grim—"

"He hit you?"

"Yes." Tears ran from her eyes. "He struck me...many times. He's...he's a very wicked man, Casey. You best go somewhere.

Don't be here when he comes back. He said he was going to kill you when you returned."

"Where is he, Ma? Where is he?"

"I don't know. I...I think I've been unconscious. I don't know where he went. He hit me very hard, many times, in the stomach and chest. It hurts bad inside. Go quickly! Save yourself from him."

Casey ran to the door and his gaze searched the barnyard and corral. He could see nothing of Hermund Grim. He ran to the barn and peeked in the door. Maybe he had returned.

The barn was empty as before. He slipped inside and found what he frantically hoped he would — the sorrel mare, the one that loved to pull the buckboard. He threw the harness over her and led her out and around to the north side to the rig. "Sure hope you feel like a good run, lady," he said, snapping her onto the singletree. He climbed up on the buckboard and slapped the reins softly on the mare's back. She was off in an instant.

He drove to the front porch, all the while looking about carefully for Grim. His heart was pumping and desperation plagued him. He knew not where he would take Ma, except away from the farm. Away somewhere to safety.

When he arrived back at the bedroom, he found her on her elbow, struggling to rise. "Casey," she said, her eyes wide. "Why did you come back? Run! Run!"

He slipped his arm around her back, lifted her, and cradled her in his arms. He was surprised at how easily he carried her. "We're both goin', Ma! I'm sure not leavin' you here any more."

He hurried and laid her in the wagon bed. He raced back in and yanked the quilts from her bed, spread them on the wagon boards and rolled her onto them. He covered her carefully and pulled up the rear board and fastened it.

"Where shall we go, Casey?" Her voice was weak, and he could barely hear her.

He leaped onto the seat and slapped the reins down. "Giddup!" he barked, and the mare leaped forward. He found himself guiding her up the little-used wagon trail toward the MacDoughall farm. That was suddenly the only haven he could think of. He'd never had to think of one before.

"The MacDoughalls' place, Mom."

He slapped the reins again, a little harder. The mare snorted and her hooves tattooed the earth. Iron tires sparked against stones as the buggy leaped ahead and teetered on two wheels. Casey threw his weight to his right and held it there until the rig settled down. He whirled and looked back at his mother.

"God, I'm sorry, Ma. You all right?"

"Yes." Her voice was faint among the rattles and creaks.

"I'm tryin' to be careful, but it's gettin' dark and the shadows—"

"It's all right. It's all right. Keep going."

He pulled back and brought the animal to a trot. They rounded the cottonwood grove, splashed through shallow Earth Creek and struck out across the prairie. He fought back the urge to let out full. He remembered this trail to Birk MacDoughall's place and he knew there were vicious stones ahead, hard to see in the fading light. Could overturn a wagon. He shuddered as he imagined his mom on the ground with the rig on top of her. They left the prairie and rattled up through the timber to the top of the rise, then down the long hill. At the bottom they passed MacDoughall's windmill and small dike at a trot, skirted the corral and rolled into the front yard.

The door swung open as Casey was hitching the mare to the porch, and the rugged face of Birk MacDoughall peered out.

"Casey Parkin!" he said. "What in the name of the Almighty brings you here at dark, your horse a-puffin' and a-snortin' that way?"

"It's my Mom." Casey choked and fought back tears. "In the wagon. Please help me."

"Good God! What happened?"

Casey ran to the rear and pulled up the back board. "Mr. Grim beat her real bad!"

"Lord God above!" Birk sprinted to Casey's side. "Mrs. Grim! Are you awake?"

She did not answer. Her face was ashen in the twilight.

"Oh, God!" Casey said. "Do you think she's—?"

"No. She's breathin'. Get hold of her on that side, Case. We'll get her in the house."

Bonnie Sue, Birk's wife, appeared at the door. "What is it, Birk?"

"It's Annabel Parkin. Grim beat her."

They carried Casey's mother in through the kitchen, past the small dining room to the bedroom. The lamplight showed blood caked on her face and neck, and the puffy shoulders of her gown were spattered red. They settled her slowly and easily onto the bed.

"Birk, you best get the Doc," Bonnie Sue said. "Hurry along. I'll tend to Annabel."

"Yeah, reckon I better." Birk grabbed his hat, strapped on his six shooter and hurried out into the darkness.

"How long do you think it will take to get the Doctor?" Casey asked.

"Three or four hours to Custer and back from here, I think," said Mrs. MacDoughall. "He comes out now and then to check my sickness." She unlaced and pulled off his mom's shoes and spread a blanket over her. "You pump a bucket of water, Casey. I'll warm it up a bit and we'll get some of this blood washed away."

"Yes, Ma'am." Casey found the bucket in the kitchen. "Where's your pump, Mrs. MacDoughall?"

"Straight out yonder. Take that lantern there by the door."

Outside, Casey heard the clatter of hooves as MacDoughall's mount crossed the bridge at Earth Creek. He hung the wooden bucket on the little iron knob on the pump snout. His eyes found the glow of the crimson sky in the west.

"Oh, Lord," he whispered, "please don't take Mom. Please. She's real good, Lord, and she never does harm to anybody. She only does good." He wiped his sleeve across his eyes and worked the iron handle. The pump squeaked and cool well water poured into the bucket.

He carried it in and put it on the floor by the stove. He sat down at the big oak table in the dining room. Fear crept into his heart, fear that his mother might already be dead, and he did not want to look at her at that moment. He could see Mrs. MacDoughall in the kitchen pouring water into a basin. She lifted the iron lid from the cook stove and poked firewood down the hole. "Won't take a minute," she called. "How come Mr. Grim to beat your mama that way?"

Casey shook his head. "Don't know. He's just awful mean, I guess. Ma never did anything to make him mad. I think he thinks it's fun beatin' folks."

He glanced up. Mrs. MacDoughall was looking down at him from the doorway. She looked pale and gaunt, much worse than last he'd seen her. He wondered about her sickness. Her face mirrored the pity in her heart, and she shook her head.

"Sure is a shame all the trouble some folks make for other folks," she said. "You got a bruise on your cheek there, Casey. Did Grim do that, too?"

He touched his cheek bone and felt pain. "Yeah. He got mad at me for no reason at all. He hit me and knocked me down in the yard, and I got up and ran like a chicken. I shoulda stayed and fought back, I guess. I hid in the hills, and when I got home this afternoon he wasn't around, but I found Ma lyin' on the bedroom floor."

"You poor boy," she said. She turned and carried the hot water into the bedroom. Casey followed her and pulled a chair to bedside and sat down. His mother lay as if asleep, covered to her chin. Mrs. MacDoughall washed the blood from her face. Her skin was pale and cool, and her left cheek bone carried a reddish blue lump.

"How is she, Mrs. MacDoughall?"

She shook her head. "I don't know." Her voice was soft in the quiet room. "She seems to be asleep. She hasn't said anything, but she's breathing all right. I can feel her heart beating. Are you sure it was Mr. Grim that beat her?"

"Yes. She told me he did it."

Mrs. MacDoughall sat silently, her eyes fastened on the injured woman's face. Finally she turned to Casey.

"I know it's none of my business, Case, but I'd sure like to know why she married that man."

He shook his head and stared at the board floor. "Well, I guess it ain't too hard to figure," he said. "Things were getting pretty tough for us on the farm after Daddy...got killed. Hermund Grim came along then out of the hills and asked for someplace to stay a day or two. He slept in the barn and helped with the chores to pay for his grub. He's a good lookin' big man, and can be real friendly and likable when he wants to, and he told Ma if she was to become his wife, he'd turn the farm into a big ranch with a whole spread of cattle and they'd be rich. I guess Ma was desperate without Daddy."

Ma stirred and her eyes opened. "Casey, honey, you're with me."

He leaned and kissed her forehead. "How do you feel, Ma?"

"Awful pain...hurts inside."

"Doctor's coming, Annabel," Mrs. MacDoughall said. "He'll fix you up fine."

Ma's eyes moved to the voice. She smiled. "Bonnie Sue. So good to see you. Thank you for taking me in."

"Hush, now, Annabel. Save your strength. Birk's gone for the doctor."

A trembling hand reached for Casey. "What are we going to do, Son? Do we dare go back?"

He took her hand. "Lord, I don't know, Ma. I don't know what to say."

"I'm sorry." Her voice was a whisper. "I'm so sorry to put you in such a fix. A nineteen-year-old boy shouldn't be put through this. I thought things would be better for us."

"I know. Don't blame yourself, Ma. We'll work something out."

Her eyes moved to Mrs. MacDoughall and back to Casey. "What? What can we do?"

He thought about Mom and the farm. He alone stood between her and the heartless Hermund Grim. He'd have to be a man whether he was ready or not. There was no one else.

"I'll think of something, Ma. I promise."

She turned her head away and fell back into a deep sleep. Her breathing was labored, and Mrs. MacDoughall seemed to have trouble finding a pulse. The hours passed slowly as Casey waited by her side, sometimes feeling that time had stopped altogether and that the doctor would never arrive. His mother lay very still most of the time.

"I hope the doctor gets here soon," he told Mrs.

MacDoughall. "Before—"

She pressed her finger to her lips. "Shhhhhhh! I hear something."

Buggy sounds came from outside and she hurried to the door. A moment later Birk entered, followed by an older, balding man in a black suit, carrying a leather bag.

"She's sleeping now, Doctor," said Mrs. MacDoughall.

The doctor glanced at Casey. "You and Birk wait in the settin' room, Son, while Missus MacDoughall and I tend to your Mama."

"Yes, Sir."

The doctor closed the bedroom door and Casey and Birk settled in chairs at the big table. Casey liked Birk a lot. He was honest and compassionate, and just plain good. He guessed if there was anybody besides his dad he'd want to be like, it was Birk.

"How's your ma seem?" Birk asked.

"Don't seem good. I hope the doc can help her."

Birk leaned back in his chair and studied Casey a moment. "How do you feel, Case? Are you holdin' up?"

"I guess so. I sure don't feel good about it."

"Terrible thing when a man beats his wife. It's a mighty cowardly act." Birk fished his Durham from his vest and rolled a cigarette. "Did them fellers that stole your horses take your big black saddle pony?"

"No. Thank the good Lord I had him in the barn at the time."

Birk hung his cigarette from his lips and lighted it at the top of the kerosene lamp chimney. He sat in silence a few minutes, blowing smoke at the ceiling.

"Miss your dad, don't you, Case?"

"Damn right. We were great pals. We went hunting and fishing and farming and did just about everything together. It's awful hard on Ma, too. She and Dad hadn't been separated in fifteen years, since he came home from fighting the Rebs in '65. I reckon she thought Hermund Grim could take his place."

Birk put his hand on Casey's forearm. "Call me Birk," he said. "You're grown up now, Case. Call me Birk."

Casey grinned. "Okay, Birk, I will. Maybe my body is grown

up, but I'm not sure about my brain. I'm downright confused about what to do now. I don't think we dare to go back home." He flopped his hat down on the table and ran his fingers through his sandy hair. "He told Ma he was gonna kill me."

"You know you're welcome to stay here, both of you."

"Thank you. That's awful good of you. Maybe Ma could stay awhile. I reckon I better go back and face the music and try to straighten things out. Guess I better talk to that sheriff in Custer, the one that took Sheriff Johnson's place."

Birk shook his head. "He's not there. I stopped in the office tonight while Doc was hitchin' up. He'll be gone for a spell."

"I haven't seen him yet," Casey said. "What kind of a feller is he?"

"He's a good man. Kinda old for the job, but I'm thinkin' he's honest and hard workin'. His name's Brand."

"Wasn't nobody in his office?" Casey asked.

"He's got a deputy lookin' after things. I told the deputy about Grim beatin' your mama."

Casey sat up straight. "You did? What did he say?"

Disgust clouded Birk's face. "That man is the saddest thing for a lawman I ever saw. He told me he'd make a record of my complaint, but a man had a right to beat his wife now and then, just to keep her behavin' herself."

"No! Is he gonna do anything about it?"

"He said no, not unless—"

"Unless Ma dies, right?"

Birk shook his head.

The doctor came into the dining room drying his hands on a towel "Let's see," he said, "You're Casey Parkin, aren't you?"

"Yes, Sir. How's my mother?"

The doctor shook his head. "Well, she ain't good, boy. She's got some bleedin' inside. We're gonna keep her right there in that bed lyin' real quiet, and in the mornin' we ought to know more."

"Can I see her?"

"Birk," the doctor said, "You got coffee?"

Birk jumped to his feet and moved quickly to the kitchen. "I'll have some in a few minutes, Doc."

The doctor slid a chair out and sat down at the table. "I'd rather you didn't chat with her just yet, Casey. We don't want to let her emotions ride any higher'n we have to. Missus MacDoughall and I will take turns sittin' with her all night. Best you make yourself comfy 'til morning."

Casey took the lantern out and unhitched the mare from the buckboard. He led her to a stall in the barn and pitched hay into her bin. When he returned, Mrs. MacDoughall led him to the back bedroom and plopped a mattress on the floor. She handed him two Indian blankets.

"I'm afraid this'll have to do you, Casey," she said. "The Doc took the rollaway bed."

"That'll do fine. Thank you."

When she had gone, he lay down and pulled the blankets over him. He said prayer after prayer for his mother, and he wasn't able to sleep until sometime in the small hours.

He awoke the next morning to the clatter of dishes and the smell of frying bacon. He arose and hurried into the dining room. Bonnie Sue MacDoughall was fixing breakfast. Birk and the doctor sat at the table eating hotcakes and fried eggs.

"Set yourself down there, Casey," Mrs. MacDoughall called from the kitchen. "I'll bring you breakfast."

"Yes, Ma'am, thank you."

He washed at the basin and settled in at the doctor's left. "How's my Mom?" he asked.

The doc pushed a forkful in his mouth and spoke between chews. "Holdin' her own so far. Can't say one way or another. But she ain't worse, and that's good news."

"Yes, Sir, thank you."

His eyes met Birk's across the table. "Hold strong, Case," Birk said. "Don't let it get you."

After breakfast Mrs. MacDoughall handed Casey the bucket and motioned in the direction of the pump in the yard. He went out into a bright, warm summer day, where chickens scratched and clucked and pigs grunted their way through the muck of their pen. A large Collie dog lay in the warmth alongside the house and Casey moved over and stroked him.

"Hi, fella," he told the dog. "I used to have a friend like you.

Bet you get a lot of love here, don't you?"

The Collie answered with wags and licks. The doctor's voice came through the window from inside the house. Casey made a move toward the pump, not wanting to eavesdrop, but the doctor's words stopped him cold.

"I don't think she can make it, Birk."

Casey sucked in his breath and stood frozen.

"Oh, God, that's terrible," came Birk's voice. "It'll be awful hard on Casey, having just lost his Pa."

Casey moved closer to the wall.

"Well," came the voice, "maybe I oughtn't say this, but it's probably inevitable. If she lives and goes back, he'll wind up killin' her in due time. I've seen his kind before. Even if she don't go back, he'll likely come looking for her. An' you know the law won't do a damn thing until he's killed her."

"Yeah," Birk said. "You're right, Doc. I wish there was something we could do."

Casey moved to the pump and filled the bucket to the brim. He carried it in and settled it carefully on the table. The doc and Birk MacDoughall were silent as he passed them. He went to the bedroom door and looked in at his mother. She lay on her back, her face pale. She was breathing softly.

He went again into the sunshine. The farmyard was blurred, and he wiped his sleeve across his eyes. He moved slowly to the barn, to the mare's stall. He plucked the harness from the wall and draped it over the horse. He could not think clearly what he was doing, nor why he was doing it, but he felt the terrible need to do something. He led the mare out and hitched her to the buckboard. He climbed up and slapped the reins. The rig took him out of the MacDoughall yard and up the trail he had come down last night. He crossed the wide plain and climbed the long hill, unconsciously dodging boulders and prairie dog holes. Just before continuing down the other side, he turned and looked back. No one was outside at the MacDoughalls'. They hadn't seen him leave.

He was glad they hadn't. The plan forming in his mind wouldn't work if they interfered. He'd have to move fast because Birk would come on the gallop when he discovered him gone.

He thought about Dad's six shooter he'd picked up and put under the mattress. He hadn't told Grim about that, and he hoped he hadn't found it by now.

The trip back seemed hard, for his mind was in torture for his mother. He'd soon be an orphan, it seemed — if not now, then later when Grim caught up with her again. He stopped short of the last rise and climbed afoot to the top. He looked down on the Parkin — now Grim — farm buildings. He waited and watched, and after a few minutes he saw Grim come from the house and go to the barn.

He returned to the buggy and drove down the far side to the trail along the creek, then up past the fishing spot until he was a stone's throw from the house. He hitched the mare and went on foot. Hermund Grim, if still at the barn, wouldn't see him coming from this direction.

His heart quickened as he reached the back of the house. He stood by the door and listened. His breath came hard and he felt weak. From the barn a voice echoed angrily. Grim was out there shouting at the horses.

He tiptoed into the house and went to his bedroom. He slipped his hand under the mattress and felt around but found nothing. His lungs heaved as if he'd been running. Frantically, he moved his arm around under the mattress, first right, then left.

Oh, God! Maybe Grim found the gun!

He shoved his arm in full length and felt the slick metal of the gun barrel. He pulled out the weapon and held it in his right hand, sensing the weight of it. Colt Peacemaker .45 caliber, heavy, awesome. The Equalizer, some men called it. Loaded with five deadly rounds. One chamber empty where the firing pin rested.

He wasn't really doing this. Not Casey Parkin. Casey would never take this heavy, horrible weapon and actually kill anyone with it. He would not really do that at all. He was just imagining that he would — it was only a game he was playing. The game was that he would pretend to shoot Hermund Grim. He would stop the game in a moment and try to make peace. He would beg him, please, Mr. Grim, don't kill my Mom, she's all I got without Dad. I'll do anything you say, Mr. Grim. I won't sass you anymore or anything. He would do that in a moment. But for now he would play the game.

He moved out the front door with the weapon in his hand and crossed to the barn. He stopped just outside and listened. He heard Grim grunt, then grunt again, and again. Pitching hay, he guessed.

He slipped inside and stepped to his right, out of the light of the doorway. He stood silently and waited for his eyes to adjust. He heard his stepdad at the far stalls, stabbing the fork into the hay and dropping it into the trough. He stepped forward, cautiously, quietly. He saw the man's big form in the semi-darkness moving the hay across. He stopped thirty feet behind him and stood waiting, the gun at his side.

Grim carried three more forkfuls across, then straightened up and arched his back. He turned slowly. His eyes narrowed as they found Casey.

"What the hell do you want?" he demanded.

Good. Grim was playing the game too.

"You," Casey heard himself say. He raised the gun and thumbed back the hammer.

Grim lifted an arm and pointed at Casey. "Now you dumb bastard, you put that damn thing down."

Casey felt the smooth trigger on his fingertip, and he put on a little pressure. He held the sights on Grim's chest, right where he figured the heart ought to be. He was beginning to enjoy this game.

"Casey, you put that gun down and get yer ass in the house, or I'll ram the damn thing down yer—"

The roar echoed off the barn walls, and the black smoke billowed out and up toward the loft. The massive lead bullet hammered the man backward into the stall, and the horses reared and whinnied. Grim leaned against the boards a moment, his eyes big and surprised, his mouth agape. He slid down, clutching the pitchfork, until he was seated on the floor. His arms dangled out to his sides, and the pitchfork fell across his lap. His eyes were open, but they saw no more.

Casey lowered the gun. The game was over.

Chapter Four

Deputy Seth Dalby leaned the chair back against the office wall and rolled himself a smoke. It was easier to think with a smoke. In fact, it was easier to do anything you could name with a smoke or maybe a little snort of whiskey. He tucked the paper between his yellowed fingers and poured Durham from the little sack. He wondered how long Sheriff Brand would be gone. A long time, he hoped.

He liked working alone in the office. He had his own damn way with things. He could arrest who he wanted to and let go who he wanted to for whatever reason he wanted to. If a drunk cowboy's lady came and posted bail, Seth would give the man a choice of forfeiting the money or appearing in court. If he chose to forfeit, Seth simply put the money in his pocket. No problem, no fuss, no bother, and it saved the county the paperwork. Being a Deputy was turning out to be even more fun than he'd imagined.

He was plumb surprised how easy it had been to get hired. He got himself a shave and haircut and bought some new duds out of his share of the money from the Parkin horses, and just walked in and said "Howdy, Sheriff, I heered you was lookin' fer a new Deputy." And then he went on and told what a straight shootin' Honest Abe feller he was and how he always wanted to serve the community, and the Sheriff hired him on the spot. And as long as he was all spruced up already, he and Slobbers showed up at Jim Parkin's funeral so he would look to be the caring type. Anyhow he attended as much of it as he could stand.

Of course there was that damn kid the Sheriff had hired to run errands and make coffee and such. His "office boy," he called him. Sammy Bents. Sammy might be inclined to mention to the Sheriff some of those little things Seth did like taking the bail money. So when Brand was out of the county, Seth sent the kid home and told him not to come back until the Sheriff did.

He set fire to his cigarette and puffed a cloud at the ceiling. He stood and moved to the wall and squinted into the mirror. His beard had grown a day and was stubbly and dark, and he had a big ripe pimple on his chin. His eyes were bloodshot from drinking a whole bottle of booze down at Alfie's Gold Mine Saloon last night and it resulted in not opening the office until damn near noon. He didn't look near as duded up as on that first day, but that's okay — he was the Sheriff as long as Brand was out of town. He could look however he damn well pleased.

Sheriff Brand never gave Seth Dalby any respect. The old buzzard only left him by himself in the office because he never had a choice, being it was necessary to ride to Livermore and help round up a couple fellers who had held up the Custer Bank. Seth knew damn well the Sheriff had told Sammy Bents to keep a close eye on Seth and report anything peculiar that went on. That damned old dog!

Brand was always sending Seth after drunks and disorderlies, and men that beat on their wives and stuff like that. Just last night that MacDoughall feller had came in telling Seth about old Herm Grim slapping the Parkin widder around. Hell, he wasn't about to go out there and try to tell Grim what to do and not to do with his new wife. That would be suicide, pure and simple. It was easy to just tell MacDoughall there wasn't nothin' could be done unless the lady died. Of course if she was to die, he would have to go out there and make a show of investigating. Naturally, he would never arrest Grim. That would *really* be suicide. He would simply declare the death an accident of some sort. And that would be that.

His mind returned to Sheriff Brand. The old coot never sent Seth after anybody important. Brand arrested a bank robber not long ago and wouldn't even let Seth come along. It made him feel like the townspeople figured he was a dolt, or inept, or maybe a little musty in the attic, or anything except an upstanding man of the badge. Oh, sure, his past was tainted a bit, but that was then, and this is now. The Sheriff was afraid Seth might get better than him and get his sheriffing job away from him. The old fossil was right, by God! He just might get lucky and make some real serious arrests and come next election he'd throw his hat in the ring and beat Brand right out of his job. Wouldn't that please ol' Herm Grim! With the Sheriff out of town like this, he stood a damn good chance of making some important pinches.

He studied his countenance in the looking glass. He had forgot to comb his hair. Didn't matter. He would wear his hat if he went out anyway. Brand had put up this damn mirror and said, "I want you to look good fer the citizens of this here town, Seth, so take a look in this glass now and then. Make sure you're presentable and not lookin' like a bum." What a stupid sheriff! Gave Seth a hell of a headache.

The front door opened and Seth grabbed his hat and crammed it on his head. Birk MacDoughall entered with his spurs clanking. He pulled off his hat and wiped a sleeve across his brow.

"Mornin', Deputy," he said. "I don't suppose the Sheriff has come back yet."

"No, he ain't. He's gone plumb to Livermore. What do yuh need?"

MacDoughall's brow furrowed. "Any chance I could get a wire to him?"

"No, I don't reckon yuh could. He's not right in town, y'see. He's lookin' fer bank robbers in the hills."

"Oh. Too bad." MacDoughall moved to the window and looked out at the big red hound dog on the porch. "Too bad. I was sure hopin' to talk with him. I got kind of a touchy situation."

Seth stood silent and waited. MacDoughall strolled to the bulletin board and scanned the wanted posters.

"Well," Seth said, "what's yer problem? I can handle it fer ye."

"Gotta talk about a murder."

Seth raised his eyebrows. "A murder? Did Grim's old lady die?"

MacDoughall turned back and faced the Deputy. "No. It's kind of a special case, with special circumstances. I was hopin' to tell Brand. He's real understanding of these things."

"Well, try me, Mac. I'm the Sheriff right now. Let's have it, dammit. Who was murdered?"

"Hermund Grim."

Seth almost fell out of his hat. "No! Old Hermund hisself? Who did it to 'im?"

"Well, I expect it was Annabel's boy."

"The boy killed 'im?"

"Yeah, it looks that way. You remember last night I told you the boy brought his mom to our house after Grim beat her? Well, the boy disappeared this morning. I figured he'd gone home, so I rode over. I found Grim dead in the barn, shot through the chest. The boy wasn't there. He must have hightailed it."

Seth felt his insides light up. This was important stuff. Herm Grim, murdered! And it wasn't like he would have to solve the case, already knowing who the murderer was. All he would have to do was find the damn kid! He moved to the desk, sat down, and made notes on a pad. "What's the boy's name?"

"Casey Parkin."

"How old?"

"Nineteen. Pushin' twenty."

It took Seth some time to write the information. He hadn't had the luxury of much schooling. "What's he look like?"

"Well, he's a slim boy, got sandy hair and a few freckles. A little under six foot. Skinny kid. Couldn't hold his own against a big fella like Grim."

"What's his horse look like?"

"His ma says he probably took the big black gelding. I didn't see a black horse in the barn with the others, or in the pasture, so he must have took it."

Seth laboriously wrote down *black horse*. "Has his horse got a brand?"

MacDoughall thought a moment. "Yeah, I reckon. Their brand is a crooked T."

That was easy for Seth. He wrote down T and he didn't have to make it crooked. It just naturally came out that way.

"Well, I'm gonna ride out fer a look-see, MacDoughall. Is the lady t'home?"

"No, she's still at our place. She ain't up to travelin'. But I'd like to suggest if you talk to her, go easy. She's in pretty bad shape. Doctor ain't sure she'll pull through."

Seth stomped his cigarette out under his boot. "Don't worry, friend," he said, "I know how to handle folks. Is the corpse still in the barn?"

"I didn't touch a thing. Left him right there."

"Okay." Seth moved to the rifle rack and unchained a Sharps .50 caliber buffalo rifle. From the desk drawer he pulled a bandoleer bulging with cartridges for the big weapon.

"Another thing, Deputy," said MacDoughall. "Casey's a damn good boy. I'm sure he was afraid Grim would kill him or his Ma sooner or later. It might even have been self defense. Please — go easy on him. Don't hurt him."

Seth turned to MacDoughall and put on his most official face. "We never hurt nobody less'n we have to, Friend," he growled. "But if this kid draws down on me, I'll have to kill him to protect myself." He slung the ammo belt over his shoulder and opened the door.

"I'm lockin' the office now."

MacDoughall went outside and Seth closed the door and locked it. He looked down at the hound dog. "Come on, Slobbers," he said. "We got us some huntin' t'do."

The dog followed as he hurried down to Egor Baklanov's Mortuary, next door to the livery stable on the same side of the street as the Sheriff's Office. The place had one big window in front with a silver casket displayed. The casket was pretty fancy for this neck of the woods, he thought. Most folks hereabouts had to settle for a pine box, although Mrs. Parkin had managed a nice coffin for her husband.

The mortuary was one place Seth kind of liked to stay shy of. He didn't mind shooting a man dead, but he felt ill at ease being in a place like Baklanov's where the dead folks hung around in spirit form even after their bodies had been put in the cemetery. He could feel the presence of ghosts there among the coffin displays and the dark hallways and the pulpit and the benches. The place even smelled like death. It was all he could do to go to James Parkin's funeral. He had sat in that little chapel with the open coffin a few feet in front of him and felt the bony fingers of Parkin's ghost brushing his face and neck. He had to get up and leave right in the middle of the eulogy, or that ghost would sure as hell have done something terrible to him.

A bell tinkled over the door when Seth entered, and the short, bald Russian mortician in his black suit scurried out from the back. "Good afternoon, Deputy. How can I help you?"

"Got a corpse fer ye, Egor. Got yer hearse oiled up?"

"Certainly," said Baklanov, blinking his eyes rapidly. "Who passed to the great beyond?"

"Hermund Grim."

Baklanov looked up and blinked at the ceiling. "The name's familiar. Who is...er, *was* he?"

"He's the one that married the Parkin widder. Lives out past Sawtooth Gap. You did the marryin' yerself."

Baklanov shook his head. "Oh, yes, of course, of course! And I prepared poor Mr. Parkin for his final journey a few weeks ago. How did Mr. Grim pass on?"

"Git yer hearse-horse limbered up, Egor, and let's stir some dust. Tell you about it along the way."

Baklanov shook his head. "Yes, yes, of course, of course." He turned and shouted toward the back, "Alena! I'm off with the Deputy to pick up a customer. Be back soon."

Seth and Egor traveled to the Parkin place, Seth on his saddle horse with Slobbers padding alongside, and Egor in his little one-horse, shiny-black hearse with the round glass windows. As they cleared the city limits, Seth dropped back alongside.

"This feller Grim was gunned down in cold blood by his step son," he said, throwing his shoulders back a bit and stretching up as tall as he could. "Soon as I make my investigation at the barn, I'm goin' after 'im."

Egor looked up and squinted at the bright sky. "Do you know where to look for him?"

"Nope. But I'll find 'im. Ain't no place he kin go that old Slobbers cain't find 'im, y'kin bank on that."

They found Hermund Grim on the barn floor, leaned against

the stall, staring vacantly, with the pitchfork across his lap. Seth reached down and pulled open the blood-soaked shirt.

"Bullet went in right there," he said.

"Yes. Directly through the center of the heart, I'd say," mused Baklanov.

The Mortician took the head and the Deputy the feet, and they half carried and half dragged the big corpse outside and rolled it into the hearse.

"Thank you, Deputy," Egor said, climbing up. He touched the brim of his stiff black hat. "See you in town." He slapped the reins down and was off at a trot.

Seth's investigation inside the barn was nothing more than a brief glance around, followed by a hasty exit out into the daylight. It was likely Hermund Grim's spirit would linger in there awhile before flitting away to wherever spirits flitted, and Seth would as soon not waste more time than he had to inside.

This sure put the kibosh to their plans for a big horse ranch, he mused. But, hell, he didn't really give a hoot. The thought of becoming sheriff was a darn site more fun. In fact, he was kinda glad old Herm was gone. He always worried that someday the big man might turn his wrath on Seth himself. He wondered what Barty Hardwise would do now. He hoped the wimp would keep himself scarce from the vicinity of the Sheriff's office.

He hunted around the place and found lots of pony tracks. To the northwest lay large hills and valleys, and he guessed if he was a boy wanting to hide, he'd head that way. He loped out a couple of miles and zigzagged a few times and picked up a trail in the soft earth. It led him toward the hills, but dusk settled in and made the marks hard to see. Besides, he was hungrier than a hind-tit calf, so he wheeled about and rode back to the farm. He was glad nobody was home. He entered the unlocked front door, went to the kitchen, and filled up on grub and fed the dog. Both he and the dog spent the night in Annabel Parkin's bed.

Next morning he rummaged through the Parkins' closets and dressers. He found Jim Parkin's clothes, washed and folded neatly in a drawer. He figured he might be needing a change along the trail, so he took a shirt, pants, and underwear. He would also need something of the kid's for Slobbers to get the smell from. In Casey's closet he picked out a pair of pants that needed washing, wrapped them in a pillow case, and carried them out with him.

He found a brown mule in the pasture and haltered him and loaded him down with Annabel's grub and a bedroll. He stuffed Casey's pants in his saddle bags. He climbed up on the sorrel and nudged her along after the dog toward the hills, tugging the mule along behind. When he got to the horse tracks he had found last night, he brought Slobbers over and stuck his nose in them.

"This is it, old dawg," he declared. "Git yersef a good sniff a that horse. That's the one we want, boy. That's who we're a huntin'."

The hound held his nose to the track and sniffed long and deep, three or four times. His back leg quivered, and his snout came up to the sky.

"Oooooowwwwwwwrrrrrr!"

"Good boy, yuh got it now, ain'tcha?"

"Oooooowwwwwwwrrrrrr!" the dog said, and headed toward the hills, his nose to the earth, his long ears flapping and his tail straight out behind.

Seth spurred his horse after the hound. He sat up real straight, his chest out, his Stetson square on his head. He felt the presence of the silver star on his vest and the .50 caliber Sharps rifle under his knee. He was Deputy Sheriff Seth Dalby, a man of the badge, and he was on the trail of a vicious, dangerous killer. He was a mighty important hombre in Custer County, Dakota Territory, by God!

Chapter Five

Casey Parkin sensed the big black gelding slack a little as they scrambled up a steep incline well into the Bourbon Hills. He leaned in the saddle and slid his hand along the neck under the mane. "Hate to push you like this, Ebon, old friend," he said. "Don't have any choice, I guess. Sheriff's deputy's bound to be after me by now, and I just don't know how much start I got on him."

They topped the rise into the sunshine again, but they wouldn't have it long. More ridges, even higher, loomed ahead. It would be tough going, and the horse was tired. He guessed he would have to make camp, even though the thought gave him the jitters. He felt he must keep heading north, on and on, to stay ahead. But the Deputy would have to sleep too, would he not?

Part way down into the next valley he came upon a series of crags, and in one he found a small cave, not much more than a depression. It offered some shelter from the night breezes and he wouldn't be out in plain sight. As he swung down from the saddle, his dad's Colt Peacemaker tugged heavily at his side. The sensation was strange, for he had never before worn a weapon. Now it hung in Dad's holster from his hip. He had made a couple of extra holes in the gun belt so it would fit snugly and tied the holster down to his thigh with the thongs. Dad had taught him how to shoot the revolver — how to hold it steady on the target, how to breathe right and squeeze and not yank the trigger. He felt a little better wearing the six-gun. He had brought the old Sharps .45 caliber rifle simply because he hadn't been able to find the Winchester repeater. Maybe Grim took it.

If the Deputy caught up with him, he would just have to surrender, he guessed, because he could never shoot at a lawman. But he might need the sidearm to ward off bears or maybe even renegade Indians, although that was unlikely because Indians seldom came to these hills since the new treaty. He had never seen any around except an occasional one on the streets of Custer and now and then a halfbreed. An old timer once told him that because of the sudden violent thunderstorms with their intense flashes of lightning, the Indians thought evil spirits lived in the Black Hills, and many of them shied away.

He located a grassy area just below the cave and staked Ebon out to graze. He rounded up a few dried branches for a fire, then thought better of it. The glow might reflect in the tree tops. He settled back against the wall and washed down his biscuits and dried beef with canteen water. He would make coffee later in a safer place. He spread his rain slicker on the ground, arranged his bedroll upon it, and snuggled in.

He lay awake a long time despite his tired, aching muscles. He couldn't believe he had really murdered a man, and for a moment or two he wondered if it were only a nightmare. Then the vision of Grim's horrible, vacant eyes, staring at him in the barn, convinced him it really happened, all right.

Hermund Grim had hurt Mom pretty bad. Doc said she might even die. Worry, homesickness and the memory of his Dad left him near tears. He said prayers as Mom had taught him when he was little. He asked forgiveness for his crime and begged that his mother would recover. He heard the breezes rustle the pine branches. An owl hoot drifted through the darkness that covered this vast, endless wilderness. A great loneliness weighed on him, fostering hopelessness and despair.

One evening last winter, when snow covered the world, they — he with Mom and Dad — sat near the pot-bellied stove after supper, and he picked chords on his guitar. "When I get old," Mom said with a smile, "I want to sit back in my rocker and listen to you play my favorite old tunes."

Would he ever play for his mom again? Would he ever see her again? For a moment he toyed with the idea of returning home and taking his medicine. He thought of the gallows then, and decided that wasn't the medicine he would want.

THE KID FROM CUSTER

He awoke the next morning to the raucous cries of magpies and to sunlight filtering through the pines. He jumped to his feet and scurried about the camp gathering his possessions. In a few minutes he was astride Ebon, slipping and sliding down the hillside into the canyon. A large rock dislodged and bounded down the slope, crashing through the brush and trees. He hoped the Deputy wasn't close enough to hear it.

He tried to reason sensibly about the Deputy. Maybe he wasn't even coming after him. Maybe he didn't know Hermund Grim was dead yet, or maybe he hadn't picked up the trail, or maybe he was busy with something else right now. There were lots of maybes.

He reached the bottom of the canyon and filled his canteen in a small, clear stream. An antelope bounded a few yards across on the other bank, then halted and stared back at him. He yanked his Sharps out of the scabbard, then slid it back in. Venison would taste good, but he dared not take time to dress and prepare the meat. Besides, the Deputy might hear the shot. Had to keep moving.

He wasn't at all sure where he was going, but by the sun he held to the north. He hurried along all that day, spent that night by another stream, and continued on the next day until dusk. He began to worry, then, about food. He hadn't brought much, and it was almost gone. He still hadn't made any coffee, and he loved coffee. He decided he was going to have to shoot some game if he expected to eat.

He arose the next morning and rode out of the hills across a wide prairie. As he approached the foothills of the next range, an antelope bolted from his right and bounded gracefully across in front. He hadn't seen it until it moved, and he wasn't ready. He grabbed the Sharps from the scabbard and fired a quick round, but missed. He cursed the limitations of the single shot weapon as the animal disappeared into the timber.

"Damn!" he said aloud. "I gotta keep my eyes open."

He reloaded the rifle, but this time he balanced it across the saddle in front of him where he could bring it into play sooner. He cantered easily to the foothills and up into a gradually sloping canyon. A movement caught his eye, and he looked to his right. An animal of some kind, fifty yards away, disappeared in the brush. He reined in and studied the hillside a few minutes. He saw nothing more. Maybe he had imagined it.

He continued on to the shallow ridge and down the other side. Another long prairie spread out for six or seven miles. As he left the slope and loped onto the grassy plain, the movement caught his eye again. This time he saw the animal, a canine, gray, maybe a coyote. No, too big. Maybe a wolf. It trotted a parallel course two hundred yards to his right, and when he stopped, it stopped too. It sat on its haunches and looked at him, tongue hanging out, panting. It looked hungry, he thought.

He moved on, and so did the animal. As it trotted it moved a little closer, and he saw that it was not a wolf, but a large dog. He stopped, dismounted, and slipped the rifle back in the scabbard. He hunkered down, whistled softly, and held out his hand.

"Here, boy!" he called.

The dog sat and studied him, but came no closer.

"Here, boy, here! Come on, fella!"

He thought he saw the tail move, and called again softly. The animal sat motionless.

"All right for you," he said, finally. "Have it your own way." He mounted and loped along through the sweetgrass and sage brush. The dog moved with him, coming closer inch by inch. He had gone another mile when a jack rabbit rose from the grass and bounded in great leaps ahead of him. He gave a shrill whistle, a trick his Uncle Bart had taught him, and the rabbit stopped. It sat straight up, appearing to be listening. "They're curious," Bart had said. "They'll usually stop a spell if you whistle."

He swung to the ground and slipped the Sharps rifle out of the scabbard. He pulled back the hammer, went down on one knee, and took careful aim. About a hundred yards. Not a bad distance for a Sharps .45, but a pretty small target. He put the sights on the animal and carefully squeezed the trigger. The big rifle roared. SLAP! went the bullet as it hit. The rabbit catapulted into the air, flip-flopped and lay still.

He reloaded the Sharps, stuffed it in the scabbard, and moved forward. The bullet had torn away most of the hare's underside, but the back and legs looked okay. He held it up a moment and let blood drain out, then tied it to the saddle strings. He looked for the dog but saw nothing of it. The bellow of the rifle must have frightened it.

The sun had moved almost due overhead when he arrived at the foothills of the next range. He found a level spot in a glade well sheltered by trees and hitched Ebon to a stump. He built a roaring fire of dead branches and let it burn down to coals and rigged a spit of forked pine limbs over the top. He skinned and cleaned the rabbit and washed it with water doused from his canteen. He tied it to the spit and set it to roasting. He put a pot of coffee on to boil.

The aroma of the roasting rabbit soon teased his taste buds, and his stomach reacted with retching hunger pangs. He wanted to be sure the meat was well done, though. He wasn't sure how safe jack rabbits would be to eat in June. He busied himself by moving Ebon to the other side of the clearing where sun had given life to the sod, and clumps of grass thrived. He hobbled the gelding and left him to graze.

Back at the fire he sat and stared at the meat on the spit. It sputtered and steamed as the juices burst out and turned the surface golden brown. He rotated the stick again and again. Each time the smell of it drove him closer to insanity.

Then the moment arrived when he knew if he waited any longer, he would surely expire. He jogged across to his horse, got a tin plate from his saddlebags, jogged back, and laid the plate on a flat rock near the fire. He lifted the spit off the upright sticks and eased the morsel onto the plate. It was well done, and the fork slipped into the back meat easily. He tore away a forkful and nibbled at it, stretching his lips back away from the searing flesh. Never, never, in all his nineteen years, had he tasted anything so heavenly. He nibbled again and again, until finally the meat was cool enough not to burn his lips.

Then he remembered his coffee. He lifted the lid and smelled. The aroma of fresh boiled Arbuckle's told him he must be near the promised land. He put the tin plate of roasted rabbit on the flat rock and hurried across the clearing to his horse. His sudden move startled the hobbled Ebon, and he reared and almost fell down.

"Easy, boy!" Casey said. "Easy. Everything's okay, pardner." He patted and hugged the silky neck. "Just wanna get this here tin cup outa this saddle bag." He slipped the cup out and turned back toward his camp.

That dog was the fastest thing Casey had ever seen. It flashed across the clearing, snapped up the roasted rabbit in its teeth, and disappeared into the timber. He stood with his mouth agape a moment, then flung the cup at the place where the dog had disappeared.

"Damn you son-of-a-bitch mutt!" he screamed. He grabbed his hat and slammed it into the dirt. He stood a moment, lips stretched back, teeth gnashing, fists clenched. He stormed back to the horse and grabbed his Sharps. He ran into the timber in the direction the mutt had gone. He kept running, looking this way and that as the anger mounted.

"Damn you!" he screamed. "Get back here with my goddam rabbit, you cur bastard!"

His shouts echoed through the trees. A magpie answered. A breeze rustled the pines. A chicken hawk circled above. He moved dejectedly back and shoved the rifle into the scabbard. He strode to the campfire and stood with his hands in his pockets, glaring at the empty plate and feeling the hunger pangs. He looked down at the coffee, still bubbling. He turned and shook his fist at the timber. "Why the hell don't you come back here and steal my coffee too, you goddam thief!"

He stood until his dander cooled a bit, then brushed off his Stetson and put it on. He picked up the coffee pot and realized he didn't have his cup. Where the hell was it? What did he do with it? Oh, yeah, he had thrown it at the mutt.

He found his cup near the edge of the timber and returned to his fire. The coffee was hot, and he burnt his lips and tongue, but by God, he had his coffee at least!

He went into the timber again, carrying the Sharps, and looked around for something to shoot and eat. He looked up in the trees. Anything! He would even take a magpie, he was so damned hungry. For several minutes he scouted, but found nothing. Head downward, feet kicking at the scrub plants, he returned to camp. He looked at Ebon, munching grass. He wondered how grass soup would taste.

He wondered if any cowboy ever ate his horse.

He packed up his coffee pot, cup, and dish, carefully covered his fire with dirt, and rode on.

At dusk he found an almost level spot among evergreens on a hillside and rolled his bedding on the ground on top of his rain slicker. He dropped Ebon's saddle on the sod and crawled under his blankets. He was bone weary, but he lay awake a long time listening to his stomach grousing and fretting. He finally fell asleep, but promptly slumped downhill out of the blankets. He woke up cold, got up, and moved his bedroll so his head was uphill. Sleep came again, but in about an hour he awoke and found he had slid down and his clothes and bedding were in disarray, and he was shivering in the cold, damp air. He arose, straightened his blanket, and got back under it just as the rain started.

Chapter Six

Seth Dalby scrambled after the hound over hills, along ridges and through canyons, the whole time wondering if the critter was tracking a horse or maybe an antelope or something. One thing that kept his hopes up, though, was that every now and then they would hit soft earth and he could even see horseshoe marks. He just hoped it was still the right trail.

He spent the night in a ravine. At dawn the next morning he built a fire and cooked up some bacon and coffee and fried spuds. After his belly was full he felt pretty good about things. He was sure he was on the trail of the killer. He packed his bedroll and frying pan and coffee pot on the mule and poured dirt on the fire. No Deputy worth his salt would be careless with a campfire.

The hound led him over more hills and valleys and across wide plains. In the afternoon they topped a high ridge, and about half way down the other side the dog cut to his right. Along the bottom of a series of crags he found a depression, sort of a cave. Slobbers howled once, ran in several circles with his nose to the ground, then sat back on his haunches and moaned to the sky.

"What's the matter, Slobbers?" said Seth, dismounting. "What is it, boy?"

"Ooooooowwwwwwrrrr!"

The dog sniffed along the grassy ground to the cave and stopped. He made long, concentrated whuffing noises with his nose buried in the tufts.

"That's it! That's the right spot, boy. That's where the bastard slept. The grass is bent down where he laid, by God!"

Seth pulled the dirty pants from the saddle bag and stuffed the dog's nose in them.

"Whuff! Whuff!" went the hound, sniffing deeply. He threw

back his head, took a deep breath, and said, "Whuh, whuh, whuh, waoooooooooowwwwwrrr!"

Seth giggled. "That's it, ain't it, boy? Same damn smell, ain't it? Good boy! Good boy!" He grinned widely and clapped his hands. "We're gonna catch 'im, Slobbers. We're gonna catch up to 'im, and when we do...wham! We're gonna get 'im!"

They spent the night there. Seth allowed there wasn't that all fired much of a hurry. He felt he was gaining on the kid. There was even a grassy place to stake out the horse and mule for the night.

After he'd eaten, he spread out his bedroll and settled in. He lay awake awhile listening to the crickets and seeing the glow of his dying campfire against the pines. He thought about the kid. He would be desperate, for sure. He decided to take no chances with him. Why should he? Wasn't no sense risking his life just to bring in a worthless kid alive. Besides the kid might do some trick and get Seth's gun and shoot him or something. Or maybe he wouldn't surrender without a fight, and maybe Seth would lose the fight. Wasn't likely, but you never know how them things are gonna work out. Wasn't no use taking that chance. When he got close he would be extra quiet and careful and sneak up on him and put a bullet in him. Save the county a lot of trial money, and they would be so grateful they'd elect him Sheriff. Wouldn't be the first man he had killed anyway. Hell, wouldn't them gullible folks in this county turn plumb green if they knew the horse thief that killed James Parkin was none other than their fine Deputy Sheriff, Seth Dalby?

He drifted off to sleep with a smile on his face.

Chapter Seven

Casey Parkin jumped up at the first spatter of rain and rolled up his bed and set his saddle on top. He crouched on the ground, leaned against the saddle, and pulled the slicker over his head. He struggled into his boots.

The rain came heavier now and beat a roaring tattoo on his slicker. It turned the woods pitch dark. He peered out but saw nothing until lightning flashed and showed Ebon standing a few feet away, his head low, drops cascading down his sides.

"Damn!" he said aloud. "This is just what I needed! Half dead tired and near starved to death, and now I'm gonna drown, I guess!"

Thunder crashed and the rain fell harder. Rivulets of water trickled down the slope under the slicker and seeped into his bedding. He felt the wetness on his hip, and the cold and dampness invaded his body. He began to shiver. He peered out at the dank, depressing shadows and smelled the wet pine wood.

"D-d-d-damn that dirty fice dog!" he said through chattering teeth. "I hope that rabbit was poison."

The rain stopped after a half hour, but he did not get up. He stayed as still as he could because to move meant to shift to a cold spot under the slicker. He sat until the grey, dripping dawn appeared, then stood slowly and stretched his legs. The saddle and its blanket were still somewhat dry, but by the time he had put them on the wet horse, they were wet too. He thought about that rabbit he had roasted, and tears came to his eyes. He craved a cup of coffee, but it would be nearly impossible to get a fire going in all this wet. For a fleeting moment he saw himself lying dead on the ground, a victim of cold, hunger, fatigue, and drowning, and maybe being found there by a grinning deputy. He quickly tied the soggy bedroll and slicker on behind the saddle. He felt a wave of pity for his poor, soaked, hungry pony. He wrapped his arms around the black neck and hugged. Then he climbed into the saddle and was on his way.

An hour later he rode out of the timber and across a prairie toward a long row of cottonwood trees three or four miles distant. He hoped he would find a stream there where he could fill his canteen and maybe make some coffee. The sun was peeking through behind his right shoulder. The warmth felt just fine. Now if he could only find something to eat.

A jack rabbit jumped up at that moment and bounded across in front of him to his left. He whistled and reached for the Sharps. But this hare did not stop as the other had done. It loped easily across the prairie until it was out of his sight.

Where there's one, there's more. He kept his eyes scanning the terrain in front but saw no game until he was almost to the trees. Another rabbit, this one a cottontail, hopped out from a thicket and stopped. He climbed down slowly with the Sharps in hand. He kneeled on one knee, pulled back the hammer, and took aim. He squeezed the trigger slowly, and the roar surprised him and the kick sent him reeling back. He regained his balance and looked. He could see no sign of the rabbit.

"Damn!" he said. "Reckon I missed."

He moved to the spot and saw streaks of blood on the ground. A few feet farther and just short of the river bank he found the rabbit. Most of the front end was blown apart, but he still had the back and the hind legs.

He pulled the hide away and washed the meat in the swiftly moving stream. Birds, scattered by the Sharps report, now returned and added their music to the sunshine. He felt the warmth and a lifting of the spirit. He found a secluded spot upstream between the bank and the willows. He fixed a fire and spit as he had before, and put the rabbit on to roast.

He unsaddled Ebon and staked him out in a grassy area a few yards away. He peeled off his wet clothes and hung them on a branch. He rummaged in his saddle bags and found a chunk of strong soap. The cold water took his breath away as he waded into the clear, shallow creek, but in a minute he was used to it, and it revitalized him greatly. He soaped his body and his hair, and when he washed his face, he discovered he now had a pretty decent beard. He had never grown one before, and it gave him a strange feeling of manhood. He liked the sensation.

The air felt warm as he left the chilly stream. He dropped more dry branches on the fire and turned the rabbit a quarter turn. The aroma of cooking meat combined with exhilaration from the cold bath had turned on his hunger pangs in earnest. He rummaged around camp in the buff, rinsing his coffee pot and filling it from the stream. He put in the Arbuckle's Fine Coffee and set it on a rock within the searing coals.

He thought about the Deputy maybe being close behind, and he got his Sharps from the scabbard and leaned it against the tree within his reach. He wondered what he would do if he had to confront the lawman. He could never shoot a man of the badge, even if it meant his own life. As a boy he had adored policemen and deputies and marshals, and hoped he could be one some day. It would be dreadful, he thought, if he killed the Deputy. If he could just keep running and lie low, maybe eventually the man would give up and not hunt him any more. But if he killed the lawman, others of the badge would hunt him forever.

He glanced at the rifle. He would not use it except for game.

Every little while he grabbed a handful of clothes to see if they were dry. He put on his underwear even though it was still damp. He sat and watched his rabbit cooking and smelled the smells and heard the crackling and saw the juices sizzling, and he almost lost his senses. When the coffee had boiled a few minutes, he took it off the fire and set it on the ground to cool a bit. His clothes were dry then, and he dressed. It felt marvelous to be clean again.

Finally came the wonderful moment when the meat was roasted to a golden brown. He slid it off the stick into his plate and pried off a chunk of thigh with his fork. He teased the hot end between his teeth and bit, and it tasted so good it brought tears to his eyes. In a minute the meat was cool enough to take bigger bites, and he found himself wolfing it down.

"Whoa, Casey," he said. "Lets enjoy this here feast and make it last a little." He poured coffee and carefully sipped. Wonderful. Life was looking better already. As he lifted the fare and tore off a piece with his teeth, he thought about the dog who had stolen the last one. He instinctively glanced about, and he nearly dropped the rabbit. There, fifty yards downstream, sat that very same mutt, watching him.

"Well, I'll be!" he muttered under his breath. "So you came back, did you?" He laid his rabbit carefully on the plate and grasped his Sharps. "Think you're gonna steal my dinner again, do you, thief? Well, I've got a surprise for you. You stole your last rabbit, you dirty fice dog!"

He raised the rifle and put the stock to his shoulder. He lined up the barrel and squinted down the sights. The dog sat with his tongue hanging out one side of his jaw and panted. He looked straight at Casey. He licked his jaws and smacked, then stood and hunkered down on his front legs, looking up almost from the ground. He uttered a short, high whine and gazed with brown eyes soft and pleading.

Casey put the sights dead center on the animal's forehead and began the trigger squeeze. It was bigger than he thought, even as big as a grey wolf. It looked somewhat like a wolf, maybe mixed with one of those large police dogs. He held the aim steady, waiting for the report and the kick. Then he saw the tail wag and heard the whine again. The body wriggled and the tail made wide sweeps and the whines got louder. He lowered the weapon.

"Christ!" he muttered. "How in hell can a man shoot something that looks as pitiful as you. All right, you thief, I'll let you live 'til the next time you steal food from me."

He leaned his rifle on the tree and returned to the rabbit. He took two or three bites and looked and the dog was still there, except he had moved a few feet closer and whined again. Casey looked at his rabbit, now about half gone. He looked back at the mutt. He took another bite, but it didn't taste quite as good. He tried to think about his situation. Where was he going next? Maybe he would wade the horse a ways upstream and make it hard for that Deputy to stay on his trail. He wondered what kind of a man he was. According to Birk MacDoughall, he was a simpleton of sorts. You could never figure what a man like that would do.

The dog whined again. He had moved still closer, and his tail was wagging faster. Casey watched him a moment, then looked again at his rabbit.

"Oh, all right, for Christ's sake. I know you're hungry, dammit. Here, I'll give you some, all right?"

He tore a hind leg off the rabbit and walked forward, holding it out. The dog trotted away a few feet, then turned back and sat down. Casey moved closer, and the animal retreated again. He put the meat carefully on a flat rock and returned to the fireside. "Okay, you thief, it's yours. Go ahead. Take it, dammit."

The dog slithered forward, took the meat, and wolfed it down. Then it sat with eyes wide and ears erect, watching Casey as before, except now the whines were louder and more pathetic.

Casey took a large chew of rabbit meat and thought about home again. He had a dog once when he was ten years old. It was an old mongrel that came to the farm all hungry like this one. He'd spent a good hour convincing his dad and mom he should keep him and that to turn him away would be inhumane and cruel and he would be sure and feed him and take care of him and he could eat scraps from the table and could sleep in the barn and wouldn't be any trouble at all. He won the battle and kept the dog for the next three years until it died of old age. He had cried at old Boney's funeral services, which were held out back of the barn where he is buried to this day.

"Rowwwwwer, rowwwwwer!" the dog squealed, extra loud. When Casey looked up, the mutt moved up off his haunches and wagged his tail so hard the whole back half of his body moved with it. His eyes were glued on Casey's rabbit, and his ears stood straight up. His tongue snaked out and licked his jaws.

Casey stood and moved toward the dog, tearing a chunk of meat off as he came. He put the meat on the rock, and before he got back to the fire, the beast had wolfed it down already.

"You ain't only a thief," muttered Casey, "you're a hog, too."

He finished the meat and drank coffee amid squeaks, howls, and tail wags. He threw the bones toward the dog. He put on his clothes, now dry, and shook out his bedding and rolled it up. He washed his dishes in the stream and filled his canteen. He brought Ebon over and tied stuff on. He would like to have spent the afternoon lying by this babbling brook in the shade of a cottonwood, but thoughts of the Deputy made him uneasy. In a few minutes he was on his way, and the dog trotted along behind.

Chapter Eight

Seth Dalby moved quickly over the next range where he found soft soil and good tracks from the Kid's horse. These led him to a recent campsite, and from there to a wide prairie, damp from a recent shower. Slobbers lost the scent in the wet grass, but the tracks held up good, and after a few miles the hound picked up the trail again.

Seth felt the excitement building. A euphoric feeling swelled in his chest and his face stretched into a grin when he thought about catching a murderer, and he couldn't help but burst out in little snickers every now and then. When that happened he would look down at his shiny silver star and consider what a damn great feller he was. Them folks in Custer County was going to be damn lucky some day to have Seth Dalby for their Sheriff!

He was almost to the other side of the prairie where the trees started again when he felt the mule's lead rope pull. He looked back. The mule had stopped and was pulling back. It dug in its hooves and skidded a little and forced the pony to halt. It dropped its head and began munching on the thick grass. Seth gave the rope a yank.

"Come on, mule, let's shake a leg. We're hot on the trail now."

The animal kept right on eating, and next Seth knew, his horse was eating too.

"Come on, you two mangy critters," he said, yanking some more. "We gotta keep a-movin' or we're gonna lose 'im. Come on, dammit!"

The mule ignored him.

Seth swung out of the saddle. He yanked hard on the rope, and the critter raised his head a moment, then went back to the feed. Seth grabbed the rope in both hands and pulled as hard as he could. The brown neck stretched out toward Seth, but the hooves moved not a bit. The moment he slackened his grip, the mule went right back to the grass.

"Dammit!" he bellowed. "What I gotta do to get yer ass movin', anyhow?" He glanced about and found a tree branch four or five feet long. He picked it up, stomped over, and whacked the mule across the withers. The animal snorted and jumped aside, then turned and faced him. It was the first time Seth had ever seen a mule look mad like that. His long ears folded back and his eyes squinted and his jowls wrinkled all up and his lips curled back showing his big teeth. Then came the loudest, angriest snort Seth had ever heard, and the critter charged straight at him.

"Aaahhhhhhhh!" screamed the Deputy, leaping aside. But he was too late. The mule's teeth cinched down on his right shoulder and bit out a good sized chunk. Seth took off running a hundred yards or so, and when he looked back, the mule was standing in the same spot staring at him. Seth grabbed his shoulder, and his hand came away bloody.

"Goddam you rotten son-of-a-bitch, you!" he screamed. The blood gushed down his arm and chest. He slipped off his neckerchief and dabbed at the wound. He held his arm up and, although it hurt like hell, he could move his fingers and hand okay, so he guessed it wasn't as bad as it felt. He put the wadded-up kerchief tightly on the wound and held it there. When he looked again, his horse and the mule were back grazing at the good grass.

He took out his .45 Colt Revolver, pulled back the hammer, and aimed at the mule's head. He just wished — oh, how he wished! — that he could shoot the ornery bastard! But if he did, he would be in a hell of a spot, with no way to tote his gear. He allowed he would just have to cool down and baby the critter along. He let the hammer down and holstered the weapon. He moved slowly back and stood a few feet from the mule and cleared his throat.

"Still mad, ol' buddy?"

The mule kept eating.

"All right, Pal, you jist go on ahead and fill up yer gut, hear? We got lotsa time. I'll jist stand right here and wait while that murderer goes all the way to Montana, all right?"

He approached the mule and carefully slipped Jim Parkin's shirt out of the big roll tied across its back. He held the wadded-up kerchief to the wound and wrapped the shirt around the shoulder as tightly as he could and tied it. It was a pretty messy job one-handed, but the best he could do. He would fix it better when he camped next.

If he could get the mule moving, that is.

He climbed up in the saddle and tugged on the mule's rope. The critter pulled back.

"Nope, reckon yuh ain't ready yet, ol' friend. We'll jist wait a bit fer ye."

Seth rolled a smoke and inhaled deeply. He looked at the high pine-covered hills ahead of him and wondered whether he would ever catch the kid. For that matter, would he ever catch his hound dog? He wriggled his fingers again. He sure didn't want anything to lame up his shooting hand any. He was going to be needing it.

If he could get the mule moving, that is.

He glanced back. The animal calmly ripped up mouthfuls and chewed, like he didn't have a damn thing to worry about.

"Yuh wanna know somethin', Mule," said Seth, grinning. "Yer such a nice feller. Tell yuh what I'm gonna do fer you, soon as this is all over an' we're back home again. I'm gonna take this here Sharps rifle and blow yer damn brains right out onto the ground. Won't that be fun, though?"

A half hour went by and Seth got to thinking about his situation. Sure was funny how things worked out sometimes. He'd been on the lam from Saint Louie for robbing a bank and killing a teller feller. Wasn't his fault, of course. The man was reaching for more money under the counter and Seth thought he was going for a gun, and he shot him dead. Wasn't really murder, just a case of misunderstanding. Anyhow, he had come across Hermund Grim and Barty Hardwise, two fellers who had been falsely accused just like him, and together they went to pulling bank jobs except for that time when Grim was busy sweet-talking that woman into giving him her money, and after that they started confiscating horses. And when he killed Jim Parkin, that wasn't his fault, neither. Parkin was stupid and came running with his six shooter, and there wasn't nothing Seth could do but shoot him dead. And the funny thing was, now Seth was chasing after Parkin's nineteen-year-old kid, and was going to kill him, too, because the kid had killed his step dad, who was none other than old Hermund Grim. Sure was a small world!

Another half hour went by before the mule raised his head again. When it did, it moved a couple steps toward Seth and waited. Seth squeezed his knees into his horse, and they were on their way again. The mule stepped along lively behind him.

He moved over the next range of hills and spotted his hound trotting back toward him across the wide prairie just beyond. He guessed Slobbers must have wondered what the holdup was. As he drew close, the dog wheeled about and took up the scent again.

Near the foothills of the next range ran a river of some kind, he could tell by the row of cottonwoods. The dog disappeared among the trees, and a minute later Seth heard him baying. He was on to something.

When he got there, he found a clear, cool stream. He moved upriver toward the shrieks and howls and found Slobbers sniffing about a recent campsite. The coals from the fire were not much more than cold, he figured. He couldn't be more than half a day behind.

He staked out the animals and let them graze while he washed up the mule bite and wrapped it better. He sat and ate and thought about Seth Dalby's wonderful world.

Chapter Nine

The hills were bigger now, almost mountainous, as Casey kept heading north. In some places the forests were so thick he had trouble telling where the sun was so he could keep his directions. He found another delightful stream tumbling along through a canyon, with a trail of sorts alongside. He decided to stick to the canyon for a spell. He was becoming less worried about being pursued now. He could not imagine the Deputy being able to follow his tracks this far. He had waded up creeks and stuck to hard ground, and lots of places he had left no trail at all. He began to think about trying to find a place to settle in. He would have to have a cabin against the cold winter that was four or five months away, and some grub stored up. He would have to find a town of some kind to buy supplies. He would have to locate where he could have a garden spot. Lots of things to think about and to accomplish, and not much time.

His thoughts were interrupted when a white tail deer bounded up from the creek bed and stopped on the trail a hundred yards ahead. He reined in and slowly, carefully slipped out the Sharps. He brought the barrel up and fixed the sights on the neck and squeezed. The animal leapt forward just before he fired, and its hindquarters lurched aside as the bullet struck. It staggered a few yards, then regained its footing and scrambled up the side of the canyon into the timber. The dog barked once and raced after it.

Casey kneed his mount through the brush up the hillside. A moment later he saw the dog farther up with his nose to the ground, moving at a trot. He saw nothing of the deer. He followed as fast as he dared through the thick woods and in a few minutes gained the top of the ridge. Now he had lost sight of both dog and deer. Thick timber stretched out to his left as far as he could see, covering ridges and valleys. He sat still a moment, not knowing where to go.

The sound of barking and snarling echoed through the timber from his left. He nudged Ebon down the gradual slope and a moment later came upon the animals. The deer was down against a large tree trunk, struggling to rise, and the dog was snapping at its throat.

"Down!" shouted Casey. "Down, boy, down!"

The dog swung its head around. Blood covered its mouth and chest.

"Down!" rasped Casey, this time with anger in his voice, and the dog backed away.

He drew his Colt revolver and killed the wounded animal with a shot to the head. He said a little prayer of thanks that it had not escaped wounded to die a slow death. He tied the deer behind his saddle and rode back over the ridge to the stream. He looked down at the dog that trotted beside him.

"You belong to somebody, don't you, boy? By God, if it hadn't been for you, I never would've found this deer. You don't look like a huntin' dog, but I bet you'd make a damn good one with a little training."

He found a level spot on the bank of the stream among pines and larches, and set up his camp. He built his customary large fire and let it burn down to coals while he dressed out the deer. He decided against putting the whole thing on a spit because it was too much and would take too long. He cut off strips of side meat and some from the thighs and tied them onto the spit pole.

He sat awhile, watching the meat cooking. The dog stood attentively, and each time Casey looked at him, he wagged his tail. Casey cut a strip of meat from the carcass and held it out. The dog stood up and moved to within a few feet and stopped.

"Well, come on, fella, take it. It's yours."

The dog moved forward, a step at a time, and stopped, ten feet away.

"Well, do you want it, or not? Come on, boy. Come get it."

He came forward again, slowly. He stretched his neck, took the meat, and backed away to his ten foot mark. There he devoured the meat in two or three gulps. He resumed his pose of watching Casey, his ears erect, his eyes soft and pleading.

"I can't figure you out, dog," Casey said, cutting another slice from the carcass. "You act like you belong to someone. Sure wish you could talk, fella."

He proffered another strip of venison, and the dog moved up without hesitation and claimed it. It occurred to Casey that this was about as good looking a creature as he had ever laid eyes on.

"Well, if you're gonna stick with me, I reckon you better have a name of some kind. Fido? Rover? Naw, those aren't no good names." He sliced more raw meat and gave it to the animal.

"That first day you stole my rabbit, you earned the name I'm gonna give you. *Thief.* I reckon you were hungry that day, and I guess I can't blame you none for stealin'. But now you're 'Thief,' and it's a good name for you."

When the meat was done on the spit, he shared it with Thief, and a durable bond formed between the two. The animal, with his wags and licks and whines, eased the emotional burden a bit for young Casey and helped take his mind off his formidable woes.

That night he slept soundly in his bedroll beside the stream. Curled up less than an arm's length from him, slept Thief. The dog was a great source of comfort, for Casey had heard that such dogs slept with one eye open and nose at the ready.

The boy and his dog traveled north for the next two days, following the stream through the hills and canyons and across wide prairies. Each day the bond between them strengthened, invigorated by the love that rose from the need of each for the other in a lonely wilderness. By the second day Casey was stroking the rich, silver fur, and Thief responded with licks to the hand and wags of the tail. On the trail Thief most often trotted ahead, sniffing the air and the ground.

On one occasion Casey found himself on a plateau high above and to the right of the canyon he had been following. He felt a need to stay as long as he could with the creek that tumbled down that canyon, its waters being sweet and cool and the game plentiful. He was separated from it now by a sheer cliff, and it appeared for a moment he might have to backtrack to reach the stream again. But a quarter mile farther he found a precipitous, winding trail down the face of the bluff that took Ebon a half hour to traverse. At the bottom he waded across the steam to a small meadow where he dismounted and staked the horse to graze. He laid his saddle-weary body flat on the river bank, and the music from the brook lulled him to sleep.

A noise foreign to the gurgling of the water awakened him and he sat up and listened. It came to him again, very faintly, mixed with the river's rushing. It seemed like a howling, as if from a hound dog. Thief sat to his left, ears perked.

"I don't know what that was, Thief," he said. "Probably nothin'. Maybe an animal of some kind."

He climbed back in the saddle and rode on.

Chapter Ten

Seth could tell by the way Slobbers sniffed and snorted along the ground that the trail was getting hotter. The old hound stopped, buried his nose in the soil and sniffed real loud. His back leg quivered and he lifted his snoot and howled to the heavens.

"Gettin' close, ain't we, boy?"

Slobbers was off on a fast trot and Seth had to hurry his horse and mule along to keep up. The trail took them along the creek on his right through cottonwoods and willows and into the hills again where the pine and cedar and fir flourished. He followed Slobbers onto a plateau above the creek and along the bluff top where he could look left and see the stream trickling through the canyon well below. He had gone about a half mile along the top of this break when he spotted a movement far down on the trail next to the water. He almost fell off his horse. There the kid was, just kind of moving along slow on that big, black gelding, his bedroll tied down behind the saddle, his battered black hat pushed back on his head and a lock of sandy hair sticking out in front. A grey dog trotted along behind.

"Baaah Gawd! Baaah Gawd!" whispered Deputy Seth Dalby, glaring wide-eyed at the rider several hundred yards down in the draw. "If that damn hound ain't one hell of a tracker!" He never really thought he would catch up with the kid, way back in his mind. And he had trouble believing it now, looking right at him. He saw then that Slobbers was waddling down the trail in the side of the cliff, winding to and fro on a steep, narrow path. He reckoned it would take several minutes just to get the horse and mule down that trail to the creek, and by that time the boy would be far away. He calculated his chances of shooting from this distance. Probably not good, but what the hell? Worth a try! It would at least give the kid something to think about.

He dismounted and slipped the Sharps from the scabbard. He rested the barrel against a pine trunk and took careful aim. He lowered the stock a tiny bit to allow for the drop, and put the front sight on the kid's shoulders. He squeezed the trigger slowly. The rifle roared and kicked his shoulder, and a searing pain shot through the mule bite. A cloud of acrid black-powder smoke billowed up. A moment later he saw the boy slouch forward and slide from the saddle to the ground. His horse shied aside, spun about, and backed away.

"Hee! Hee! Hee! Hee!" the Deputy chortled, grinning widely. "That there was a damn fine bit of shootin'!" He stuffed the rifle in the scabbard and swung up. "Come on, you two mangy critters. Let's go get 'im."

In spite of his injured shoulder hurting like hell from the rifle-kick, he spun the horse around and headed down the cliffside trail. He tried to see the kid from the trail, but trees and foliage got in his way.

Casey heard a bell ring, loudly and agonizingly, like someone had held it to his ear and hit it with a hammer. He felt himself strike the ground, and the bell rang again and again. The tree tops above him whirled against the sky and clouds, and he fought nausea and dizziness. He lay on his back, arms out to his sides, and between the clangs he heard Thief's whine. The dog licked his face and sniffed the wound on the top of his head.

"My God!" Casey heard himself say. "My God, what was it?" He moved his hand up and felt warm, sticky blood running down through his hair. He looked at his hand.

"Oh, My Lord! I been shot! I been shot! Who...?"

He struggled up onto his elbow and looked about. He saw no one. The bell rang less intensely now, and the dizziness let up some. He carefully felt the wound in his scalp. Couldn't tell much about it except that it was bleeding pretty bad. Whoever shot him would likely be upon him in a moment. He sat up and saw that his pony stood a few feet away, waiting patiently. He would try to get back into the saddle.

A long, low growl from Thief took his attention. The dog's eyes were riveted on the trail behind. His ears stood erect, lips curled back, hackles bristled. A big, red hound dog, its nose to the ground, plodded up the trail toward them. It stopped just short of Thief, raised its head and bared its fangs. It half howled, half snarled, and lunged forward.

Thief met him in midair, and his fangs snapped at the red throat. The two dogs twisted and rolled in the grass and fallen pine needles, snarling and slashing with bared teeth. Casey saw one moment the red back of the hound, and the next the silver mane of Thief. The battle paused momentarily as Thief backed away and stood hunkered down, ears laid far back and fangs gleaming. He did not growl nor bark, but stood frozen, his eyes burrowing into the hound. The red dog licked at blood oozing from his shoulder, then snarled and charged. Thief met him in midair again, and this time the fangs found their mark. The hound reared back on its haunches as Thief's momentum carried him up on top. His teeth ripped, and a gash opened up in the hound's neck. Thief grabbed a new bite on the throat, clamped down, and held on. It was over in a moment, and the great red tracking dog lay gasping while blood from his juggler pumped out and stained the pine needles.

Casey struggled to his feet and staggered the few steps to Ebon, expecting at any moment to feel the shock of another bullet. He found the reins, looped them up, and pulled himself into the saddle.

"Go, boy, go!" he said to the horse.

Ebon swung about and galloped up the canyon as if knowing haste was crucial. Casey surmised his wound was bad because the bell rang again and the trees ahead wavered across his vision. He felt he was going to black out. He could see Thief racing alongside, and he felt relief at that. There was blood on the dog's face and front quarters.

"Thief!" he cried. "Thank God you're still with me."

He felt weak and figured he might fall again. He didn't want the shooter finding him helpless. He slowed Ebon to a walk and moved off the trail into the thick timber and kept going until he came to the bank of the creek. Ebon stopped, and Casey slid to the ground. He crawled to the water's edge, fearing he would be unconscious soon. He splashed water into his face and saw the red stain swirling away with the current. His awareness waned, and he lay back on the bank.

The darkness came and covered him.

Chapter Eleven

Claudia Morton drew the curtains across the north and west windows so the bears couldn't see in if they were of a mind to come snooping around her little cabin during the night. She didn't really mind the bears — they had never run after her or anything like that — but she wouldn't feel comfortable if she thought they were peeking in at her. Especially with John not around.

She glanced up at her Winchester '73 that hung above the door. If one ever really got after her she would have to shoot it, she guessed. She would hate to, though. They had become almost like neighbors, padding up to the house every now and again like they were visiting. When she was outdoors and they sidled up a little too close for her comfort, she fired the Winchester in the air a couple times and they skedaddled.

It was summer in the mountains. The sweet smells of crocus and lilacs reminded her of her love for this place and of the love she had shared with her husband. Even the frigid Black Hills winters had smells that told her this was home. The wind that blew icy from the lake brought sensations of frost and cold pine needles, and they seemed like smells to her. When the snow came heavily and smothered everything and made the world quiet, that's when the loneliness was the worst. That's when she longed the most for the wonderful evenings with John in the warmth of their little cabin. He had given her the love and fulfillment she so intensely craved. He had helped her develop a love for this beautiful place. But now, without him, the evenings were barren and lifeless.

She turned quickly and looked at the bedroom door. It was closed. She stood silently and gazed at it, pretending he was there waiting for her. She held to the fantasy as long as it remained real in her mind, then set about bathing herself in the round tub with water heated on the cook stove.

She curled her white legs under her and splashed water on her belly. Again she thought of moving into town among the people, but the idea of leaving her hidden utopia appalled her. In Rapid City, before she met John, had she not been the object of ridicule because of her natural penchant for men? The self-righteous old bags of the church society gave her a pain in the ass. She would rather be lonesome out here with her animal friends and her little garden and her beautiful lake than to suffer the daily wrath of those loose-tongued gossip-mongers in town.

In the night as she slept he was beside her in her dream, so handsome and loving, and he gifted her the exquisite pleasure she yearned for. In the morning she awoke and, finding it but a dream, wept.

Chapter Twelve

Seth Dalby pushed the mare down the cliffside winding trail as fast as he could without letting go of the mule, but it wasn't fast enough. When he got to the spot he found only his dead hound dog.

"What the hell?" he exclaimed. "What happened here?"

He dismounted and kneeled beside the hound's body. He couldn't believe that other dog could have done that to his big tracker. Why, old Slobbers had stood off rampaging bears, for Christ's sake. And where the hell was that kid? He knew he had hit him. He could tell by the way his body jerked just before he fell off the horse.

He looked around and found blood a short distance ahead where the kid had lain. So he was wounded! Well, by God, he would get him, then. He couldn't be far ahead. He mounted his horse, took a farewell look at his dog, and moved up the trail at a trot. He would like to have galloped, but he could never get the damn mule to trail along that fast. But he would catch the kid anyway. It was just a matter of time. He would likely find him dead a little farther up.

He tried to see a trail to follow, but found nothing. He hoped to see blood spatters, but didn't find that either. He didn't want to take the time to get down off his horse and look at every little spot that might be blood. To do that would give the kid too much time to get away. He would just follow this trail that nature had formed along the stream, and sooner or later he would find him.

A mile or so farther on, the natural trail left the stream and meandered off to the left. Seth kept on it, every once in a while scanning the ground for any sign of hoof marks. But the ground was rocky and hard here, and he saw no sign of anything. The country was hilly — almost mountainous — and he reckoned there was a whole bunch of places the kid and his horse could hide.

He wondered about that damn dog. He didn't recall anything about the Parkins even having a dog. He hadn't seen one when he had shot Parkin that day they took his horses.

For a moment the idea crossed his mind that maybe this wasn't the Parkin kid he'd knocked out of the saddle, but some other feller instead.

"Oh, hell, yes. Sure it was. Hell yes, that was him all right!" he said out loud to his horse. He turned and looked back at the mule. "That was him, all right!" he said to the mule. "Yuh couldn't miss that damn big black gelding."

He rode several miles up a deep canyon that seemed to be a gap through the mountains. The way got rocky through the pass, and when he reached the other side he found himself gazing far out across the plains. For a moment he thought about turning back. Maybe the kid had hid somewhere along that trail and he just missed seeing him. On the other hand, maybe he was out on this big prairie somewhere, riding through a gully, and that might be why Seth couldn't see him from here. He allowed he would ride on a few miles at least, and maybe spot him. He would hold to northward as the kid had done all this time.

Five miles out on the plain he found a solitary tree with a few scraggly leaves. It was the only tree for a spell, at least until the mountains he saw ahead. It made a little shade, so he sat under it and ate his hardtack and jerky. The sun was getting low in the west and he didn't want to spend the night out in the open. He calculated he must be half way to the mountains ahead and decided to keep going. Maybe he would find another of the kid's campsites.

It was dark when he reached the foothills, and he made a camp at the edge of the timber. In the morning he scoured the area but found no sign of a campfire nor of any horse tracks or droppings. Keeping the sun to his right, he rode north into the hills for several miles. The terrain became so rough that he had difficulty keeping a northern course. He had to change and go west sometimes, then east, and once he even had to double back and ride south to get around a big, wide canyon with a blue lake in the center. He hadn't heard anything about a beautiful lake being up in this area of the Black Hills. It was almost like it was hidden, and he came upon it only because he rode back south. If he had gone north he would have missed it altogether. This valley, with tall pines rustled by soft afternoon breezes, and the sounds of birds and wild critters, and the clean blue water of the lake gave him a feeling of peace he couldn't recall having come across before.

He rode down the slope to the shoreline and looked out across the water. He guessed it was four or five miles to the other shore. He dismounted and threw a couple of rocks in, then he flung a couple more flat ones so they skipped along the surface. Like when he was a kid. It gave him a strange feeling of joy.

He mounted up and rode along the shoreline. He didn't have much hope of finding the kid here. He had found nothing to indicate it. He rounded a bend in the shoreline and came to a clearing in the thick timber. He reined in suddenly and his eyes bugged. There, a hundred yards ahead among a grove of cottonwoods stood a log cabin. Beside the cabin was a garden, and hoeing weeds in the garden in bib overalls and a slouchy hat was an honest-to-God female woman.

"Baaah Gaawd! Baaah Gaawd!" he mumbled, clutching his hat. "Somebody livin' way up here?"

He sat still, watching. The woman was about thirty-five, he reckoned, with golden curls sticking out from under the hat and a slim body under the bib overalls. It stirred the juices in him, seeing her kind of half bent over working that hoe, and the well-washed denim stretched across her bottom that wriggled so tantalizingly when she stepped to the next row of carrots. He looked around for somebody else. She must have a man about, it would seem. Pretty woman don't come way out here in these mountains, settle down, build a house and raise a garden all by herself. He looked toward the small barn out near the back of the clearing, expecting to see somebody. For a moment he thought the kid might even be here. Maybe that was it! Maybe the kid was hiding out with this woman.

The mule stomped and farted, and the lady whirled. Her eyes were wide and startled, her mouth agape. "Who...who are you?" she gasped.

"Howdy, Ma'am," he said, suddenly remembering he had a scraggly growth of beard. "I'm Deputy Sheriff Seth Dalby from Custer County." He pulled his star outward toward her, stretching his vest fabric. "This here's m'badge, Ma'am. Sure didn't mean to give yuh no fright."

Her face relaxed. She moved forward and stood beside his horse, looking up. "Sure didn't expect to see no lawman up here," she said. Her voice was high pitched and hard. "Fer that matter I didn't expect to see nobody a'tall come ridin' in. We ain't had no visitors fer over a year."

"Yer husband home?" Seth asked.

"No, he ain't right now. He went out to get us a deer this mornin'. He'll likely be ridin' in most anytime now. What's that blood on your vest there? Get hurt?"

Seth looked down at his right side. The blood had dried, but it was still obviously blood. It had spattered and run down his arm and got his shirt and vest bloody. He dismounted and stood beside the lady. She was six inches shorter. He wondered what it was like, being her husband and living on this beautiful lake and hunting deer. Then he thought about the kid.

"Ain't nobody in yer house right now, Ma'am?"

"No, there ain't. Not 'til John gets home from huntin'."

"How about in the barn?"

She shook her head. "No, Deputy, ain't nobody here right this minute."

"Mind if I take a look? I'm on the trail of a murderer, and he bushwhacked me a ways back and shot me in the shoulder. He could be waitin' in yer barn to do it again, and you wouldn't even know he was there."

"All right. Go ahead and look. But I was out there not ten minutes ago, and ain't nobody there."

Seth ran to the barn, scattering squawking chickens on the way, and peeked in. It wasn't big enough to hold many horses and cows. He saw two horses in stalls. He drew his six shooter and slipped inside. He checked the ground space then went up into the loft. He was satisfied the kid wasn't there. On his way back he yanked open the door to the outhouse. The kid wasn't there, either. At the garden spot, the lady had resumed hoeing.

"Ma'am, I'd like yuh to tell me if you've seen a young man go by here yesterday or today. Young, just a kid. Ridin' a big black gelding, wearin' a black hat."

"No, I ain't."

"Mind if I check the house?"

She looked at him and frowned. "I'd rather you'd wait until my husband gets home."

"Why is that?"

"Just don't like nobody in my house when John ain't home, that's all."

"But I'm a lawman. I ain't gonna do yuh no hurt. I'm paid to protect yuh, and that's what I aim to do. I'm tryin' to lay hands on a cold blooded murderer, a kid that killed his daddy." Seth figured it would sound more serious if it was the daddy killed rather than the step-daddy.

"Well, all right then, go ahead. I'll be out here in the garden. I'll keep a watch for John so's he won't think you're a robber and blow you apart with his shotgun."

"Yes, Ma'am. You do that."

Seth stepped up on the front porch step and it creaked loudly. He jumped back. If the kid was in there, he probably heard that. He stepped over the board this time and entered and checked the place carefully, even under the bed. The kid wasn't there, and he figured the lady was telling the truth. It was a three-room place, but one room was just a big closet and pantry. A '73 Winchester rifle hung over the doorway just inside. He went outside and found a hinged trap door that led under the house. He went down, six shooter first, and searched a root cellar with jars of fruit and vegetables but no kid. When he came up, he saw the lady coming toward the house carrying carrots and beets in her arms.

"See anything of yer husband yet?" he asked.

She stopped near the corner of the house. She wasn't especially pretty, but had a wholesome quality in her features. He took notice that her skin was clear and inviting, and her eyes an unusual light blue.

"No, I ain't seen nothin' of him just yet," she said. "I expect he'll be along about dark, a little before maybe. Depends on what he shoots."

"Huntin' must be good here. I saw lots of game on my way up from Custer."

She shook her head. "Yes. Pretty good. We don't often butcher any cows. We eat plenty of venison. Now and then John heads out fer the prairies and bags us some quail."

Seth moved up and stood before her. Her lips were full, and her nose turned up a trifle at the end. He wondered what her husband was like.

"Mighty fine lookin' carrots there, Ma'am."

"Yes, they grow quite well here where the timber's been cleared away to let the sun in. I...I wonder whether you might stay for supper."

He wondered whether she would ever ask. "Sure would be much obliged if I could, Ma'am. Ain't had home cookin' since m'wife died several years ago."

"All right, then, settle your horse and mule in the barn if you're a mind to. There's a couple empty stalls and some hay in that far bin there. Couple hours yet 'til supper time, so if you want to do some lookin' for that murderer first, you can."

"Reckon I've looked enough fer today, Missus...eh...'Scuse me, I guess I never heard yuh say yer name."

"Oh, I'm sorry, Deputy. It's Claudia. Mrs. John Morton." She smiled. "And yours was...?"

"Deputy Seth Dalby, Ma'am."

"All right, then. Take care of your animals and come in the kitchen and set and tell me about the man you're seekin'."

Seth tipped his hat. "Thank you kindly, Missus Morton." He turned and led his horse and mule to the trough and pumped some water for them. When they had drunk, he led them into the barn, quartered them in stalls and forked hay into their bins. He pulled the saddle from the horse and the pack from the mule and propped them along the wall. He slipped the Sharps rifle from the scabbard and carried it over his shoulder to the house.

"Come in, Deputy Dalby," called Claudia. She was teasing firewood into the cook stove. He stepped over the squeaky step and entered a cozy room that served as both kitchen and sitting room.

"Sit down there, please. I'm fixin' soup and a steak of venison." She turned and looked at him. "My, my, that looks like a bad wound you've got there. Have you treated it?"

"Ain't had a chance to do it proper," he replied. "I ought to wash it out some, I reckon."

"Well, I should expect so!" she said with a toss of her head. "Lands sake, you could get all kinds of infections." She plopped the iron lid down on the cook stove and strode over.

"Set yourself right down there, Deputy, and we'll tend to that shoulder. Take off your vest and shirt." She dippered some water from the bucket into a pot and set it on the stove to heat.

Seth was embarrassed to disrobe, even a little bit, in front of this lady. Then another thought left him feeling a mite worried. "Eh..." he muttered. "Yuh don't s'pose yer husband might come home and not understand right away what we was doin', do yuh?"

She grinned. "Reckon I could explain it quick enough, before he let loose with the shotgun. Leastways, I sure hope I could."

The thought of her husband with his shotgun made the hair rise up on Seth's neck. Slowly he peeled off the vest and unbuttoned his shirt. She pulled back the extra shirt that was wrapped around the wound.

"Land's sake!" she said. "This here looks more like a bite of some kind than a bullet hole. What kind of gun did he shoot you with?"

"Revolver, I reckon. Didn't see it too close. He was shootin' from ambush, y'see."

She moved to the stove and tested the water with her finger. The venison steak had begun to sizzle, and she probed it with a fork. She saturated a cloth with warm water and washed the wound in Seth's shoulder.

"Sure looks like a bite," she said. "I'll wash that shirt and vest for you after supper."

"Naw, naw, ain't no need fer yuh to go to all that fuss. I don't want to be no burden to you er yer husband."

"Ain't no trouble a-tall."

She tore a strip from a sheet, made a bandage, and wrapped the hurt shoulder. "There, now," she said. "Good as ever was. How's it feel."

"Jist fine, Ma'am," he said. He slipped into his shirt, hurriedly.

"Sure you don't want me to wash that shirt and vest?"

"No, thankee kindly. You've done too much fer me already."

Seth had nothing against clean clothes, but he figured it was just as well he rode back into Custer with blood on his shirt so his story about the kid shooting him would pack a little wallop. He fully meant to tell the Sheriff and the folks in Custer that very tale.

Claudia Morton moved about the little cabin getting supper ready. The aroma of venison sizzling in the pan awoke the hunger in Seth's belly. He allowed it would be cozy and homey sitting at the table with this fair lady and eating good, hot food. He sure hoped her husband wouldn't get home anytime soon. He'd not be much at ease if that happened.

"John and me will have to be headin' over to Pine Valley for supplies one of these days," she said.

"Pine Valley?"

"Little town about twelve miles east. Did you see the wagon road?"

"Didn't notice one."

"Well, it ain't very plain. Only use it ever few months when we go get salt and flour and sugar."

When supper was cooked, she motioned him to a chair at the table. She put a plate of potatoes, vegetables, a steak, and baking powder biscuits in front of him and poured coffee.

"Gracious me!" he said. "Sure been a spell since I've had vittles like this. I'm much obliged, Ma'am."

She sat down across from him and buttered a biscuit. "Ain't often we have company up here, especially a lawman. Tell me about this murderer you're chasin'. Think he might be hidin' around here somewhere?"

"Could be," said Seth, cutting his steak. "I ain't been able to see the trail last few miles, so I ain't real sure I'm still on it. But I'm right sure he's wounded. When he ambushed me, I returned fire and nicked 'im, I believe."

"Must be difficult followin' a trail through all that timber," she mused.

"Downright impossible, almost. I had me a good huntin' hound, but when he ambushed me, he shot my dog too."

"He must be a terrible man!"

"Yes, he is. He's a dang well dangerous hombre. I got to catch up to him before he murders more folks. He's a born killer, y'see."

"Yes," she said. "I do so admire you lawmen. You're so fearless in the face of danger. You stake your lives on keepin' us honest folks safe."

"Yes, 'um." said the fearless Seth, popping a biscuit in his mouth. "We do our best."

He stole glances at her now and then. She wasn't a raving beauty, but she wasn't difficult to look at neither. She wore a man's kind of shirt, and it didn't take him long to notice a hint of a ripple across the bosom when she moved just so. It had been quite a spell since he had known a woman, and he became most aware of that fact as he watched Claudia Morton. She arose from the table and lit the coal oil lamp with a stick ignited from the cook stove. The light brightened and illuminated her face as she adjusted the wick. Her skin was smooth and clear and inviting as she smiled down at him.

"You're welcome to sleep in the barn loft tonight if you'd care to," she said. "I can give you blankets."

"Right kind of yuh, Ma'am," he said. "I have blankets in my pack, though. Ain't no use usin' yers." He wondered again about her husband. Here it was getting dark, and no sign of him.

"Y'think yer husband might be upset if I sleep in the barn?"

"Not a-tall, Deputy. Don't think he'd mind a-tall. Lotsa hay in that loft you can throw your blankets on."

"What do yuh reckon's keepin' 'im?"

"I ain't worried," she answered. "He sometimes stays out overnight when he's huntin'. He'll be along. He could pop in anytime during the night or tomorrow morning."

Seth finished his steak and potatoes and stood up. "Reckon I'll be turnin' in, Ma'am," he said. "It's been a long ride and I'm a mite tuckered out." He would like to have stayed longer and watched her move about the kitchen, but the vision of a jealous husband with a shotgun kept him on edge.

"All righty," she answered. "Take this with you." She pulled a lantern from the cupboard, lit it, and handed it to him. "If you're a-needin' anything, give a holler. When you get up in the mornin' I'll fry up some bacon and eggs if that's to your likin'."

"Mighty kind of yuh, Ma'am. Much obliged." He put on his hat and tucked his rifle in the crook of his arm. "I bid yuh good night and thank yuh again."

"You're welcome. Always happy to help a lawman. Good night."

He made his way out to the barn in almost complete darkness. He felt uneasy, like someone might be watching him from the timber. Someone with a shotgun, maybe. He was almost tempted to blow out the lantern so he wouldn't be such a target. He felt relief when he reached the building and slipped inside.

When he bedded down in the soft hay, he realized how exhausted he was from the long trail. He didn't let himself drift away, though, until his mind had gone over every inch of Claudia Morton's tempting body. If it weren't for the prospect of her husband and his shotgun, he could dang well find a way to enjoy that body more than just imagining what was under them denim overalls. He bet she'd be willing to wrestle a mite with a good looking deputy like Seth Dalby if she didn't have a husband around.

Claudia set about washing dishes and cleaning the stove and table. It was fun having someone besides herself to visit with, and even more exciting that it was a man. Not a bad looking man either, she'd bet, under the whiskers and trail dust.

She put away all the dishes and wiped the cupboard doors clean. She dusted and swept and mopped. Wouldn't want her visitor to think she was sloppy or unclean. Not that *he* was clean. He was typical of a man of the trail whose mind isn't often bothered by thoughts of bathing or shaving or washing his clothes. All the same, when he had stripped off his shirt and peeled back his underwear so she could tend to his wound, she had felt a bit short of breath, especially when her fingers brushed his chest.

She wondered about the outlaw he was chasing. The thought of a murderer lurking about out there was worrisome, and it occurred to her that such a criminal could be looking in her window this very minute. She quickly drew the curtains and closed the door. She wished she could have the Deputy stay in the house; she'd feel a lot safer. But of course that would never, never do, at least not by the standards of those stuck-up ladies in town. Her ire rose a speck as she thought of them. Always so prim and proper and righteous, as if the thought of making love with a man never entered their perfect brains. She would bet that if you could peek inside their craniums, you'd find as much or more hankering for what a man can give as held by any of the ladies they defiled with their malicious gossip. She despised their phony facades.

She had told the Deputy a small lie, that her husband was expected home. To do otherwise would have left her at his complete mercy, and she had no wish to be at anybody's mercy. It would do no harm to let him continue thinking it for as long as his visit lasted or as she thought prudent.

She heated water on the stove and poured it into her round washtub on the floor. She stripped off her clothes and stepped delicately into the water and sat down, curling her legs under her. She splashed the warm water onto her belly and thought about her visitor sleeping out in the hayloft.

Chapter Thirteen

The next morning Seth Dalby got up just after daybreak and washed his face at the pump. Smoke puffed from the chimney pipe on the house, so she must be up. He guessed her husband hadn't come home because he would have put his horse in the barn, and he would have heard him. He went to the door and found it open. He saw her inside at the stove, and he smelled the bacon cooking. She turned toward him.

"Good Morning, Deputy," she sang. "Come in. Breakfast will be ready in a quick. Sorry John didn't get home last night. I know you're real anxious about meetin' him."

"Yes," he lied, stepping into the room. "Might be he's seen somethin' of the outlaw I'm chasin'." He smelled the coffee bubbling, and in truth he was more interested in that than her husband. She carried a plate of flapjacks and another of crisp bacon to the table. Two plates and cups and tableware already graced the fresh white cloth covering the table.

"My!" he exclaimed. "That do, indeed, smell good, Missus Morton."

She smiled and poured coffee. "Might as well call me Claudia," she said. "Ain't no use bein' formal out here."

"Oh. All right then, eh...Claudia."

"An' set yourself down and dig in."

As he settled in he saw some changes from yesterday. Her face and throat glowed white and soft in the early light as she sat down across from him, and her hair glistened in newly done curls. She wore a freshly laundered brown dress with lace at the throat and puffy shoulders. She was all woman! He had no doubt about that.

He watched her butter her flapjacks and pour syrup, and when she looked up suddenly, he felt embarrassed.

"What plans have you for today, Deputy?" she asked.

"Oh, well, I reckon I better have a look around to see if I can come across the kid's trail. If I cain't, I think I'll head back to Custer and give up the chase 'til another day."

"Kid?"

"Yeah, well, that's what they call 'im, you see, 'cause he looks young. His looks fool people, makes 'em think he's a nice boy or somethin'. But he's a vicious killer, like Billy the Kid or John Wesley Hardin or somebody like that."

She put a forkful of flapjack in her mouth and chewed daintily. "Will you be stayin' here another night? You're welcome to, you know."

"Yes, I might. Much obliged fer the offer. Yer barn's a right nice place to bed down."

"Besides that," she said softly, "it's mighty comfortin' to a lady to have a lawman about when her husband ain't home to protect her."

"Yes, Ma'am. I should expect so. I'll spend the day searchin' fer the outlaw's trail and if I don't find it, I'll come back here fer the night."

He saddled up the sorrel, took his Sharps rifle and, leaving the mule in the barn, rode back up the shoreline. He rounded the lake on the west side and checked the valleys and ridges to the north. He found no sign of the kid. He did see several deer, many of them bucks. He wondered about John Morton. Why did it take him so long to find a deer? They seemed to be everywhere he looked. Maybe he just wasn't in a hurry to get back. Looked like he would be, though, with a little honey of a wife waiting at home.

He returned to the cabin in the late afternoon. Claudia was out again, working in her garden. He reined in next to the carrots and looked down at her.

"Yer sure a hard-workin' gal," he said. "A poor little weed wouldn't have no chance a-tall in yer garden, would it?"

She laughed. "Nope, I don't tolerate no weeds. Did you see any sign of your outlaw?"

"Nope. But I sure saw a heap of wild game out there. Hell a Friday, Mrs. Morton, if yuh need venison, I'll bag yuh a deer quicker'n yuh kin blink."

"All right, if you see a nice buck, bring him in. John will likely bring one in too, but that's all right. We can dress 'em down and salt 'em. You gonna keep lookin' fer The Kid?"

He gazed up at the sky as if the clouds could help him decide. "I ain't likely to keep lookin' much longer," he said, finally. "Maybe a couple more days."

"What signs do you look for?"

"Well, mostly signs of a camp fire, where he mighta spent the night and cooked somethin'. I keep m'eye peeled fer horse signs like hoof tracks and them there round, brown apples, if y'know what I mean." He grinned slyly.

"It's an awful big country, Mr. Deputy."

He leaned his hands on the saddle horn and stretched his back. "Yup. Sure is. An' a feller gits tired ridin'. Tomorra I'm gonna take a look-see down along that there stream that drains down from the lake. He's gotta have water, and likely does his campin' along a creek."

"Yep, I reckon you're right," she said. She turned and commenced hoeing. He watched her a moment, taking note of the curve of her hips as she reached across the rows. Then he trotted his horse to the barn and put her away for the night.

As soon as he and Mrs. Morton had finished supper that evening he made his way to the barn. He would a whole bunch rather Mr. Morton came home and found him there than in the house with his missus.

He spent the next three days scouring the riverbanks. The foliage was thick and darned near impassable in some places. At one site he dismounted and led his horse into the shallow stream to get around dense briars. As he rounded the river bend he heard a shot. He whipped out his six-gun and crouched. A movement near the bank caught his eye and he leveled the weapon. A large beaver swam a few feet toward him, then, with another splat of the flat tail, dove under the surface.

"Damn you, Mr. Beaver!" he said. "Yuh sound more like shootin' than shootin'." He slipped the gun into his holster, feeling ridiculous, and glad nobody was with him to see him get fooled by an animal.

He was becoming weary of looking for The Kid, and he allowed he best be getting back down the trail to Custer. Looked like he wasn't going to find him — the country was just too damned big. But that didn't mean he couldn't run Sheriff Roscoe Brand a tight race anyhow. When the good folks saw he had been wounded and still shot his way out of a tight fix, they would vote him right in. Brand was getting old and slow anyhow.

On that third afternoon, after he had completed a check of the creek for several miles down the mountainside, he returned, put his pony in a barn stall, and went to the house. He decided not to mention the beaver incident to Mrs. Morton. He hoped Mr. Morton would already be home. He'd rather meet the man that way than to be sitting at his table with his missus when he got home with his shotgun. It would be a lot more comfortable. She was preparing supper when he walked in.

"Howdy, Mrs. Morton," he said. "Mr. Morton get home yet?"

She turned from the stove. "No, ain't seen nothin' of him yet. Find yer outlaw?"

"Nope." He hung his hat on a wooden peg near the door and headed for the wash basin.

"John's shavin' stuff is on the shelf next to the wash basin," she said. "How about gettin' rid of that scruffy old beard, Deputy? You look more like a billy goat than a man of the badge."

Seth was taken aback. He never had anybody tell him what to do except maybe Hermund Grim or Sheriff Brand. Mostly he didn't like a woman telling him, but when he started to sass her back, she was smiling kind of sly like, and her eyes squinted up at him and made him squirm. She sure was a forceful lady.

"There's a razor and shave mug and a brush. The strop hangs there on the wall."

"All right," he said. "I'll see to it."

"After you shave, y'might take a little bath in the lake. Make you feel like a new man to get all refreshed. Right down yonder by them three big pines in a bunch — you can see 'em right there — the lake is shallow and the bottom is all covered with them little rocks and makes wadin' around a pleasure. Ain't all that mud and moss you find in other parts. Go in easy, 'cause it's colder'n an old maid's rump. Take a chunk of this here soap with you."

"Uh...all right Ma'am. I'll see to it."

"Name's Claudia. Remember?"

"Yes'm. Claudia."

While Seth was shaving, she bustled about the kitchen, stirring the cook pots and looking in the oven. When he had finished, he looked at his pale face in the mirror and reflected on what a good looking man he was. He allowed he really ought to give the ladies a little more of his time, in all fairness. He turned toward the door.

"Don't be all night in the lake, neither," she called after him. "I got supper dang nigh done and I don't want it gettin' cold."

"All right. Thankee."

At the shore he shed his clothes and waded into the lake. The water was so cold he thought he might expire before he got used to it. But once he did, he swam about and splashed like a kid, and the first thing he knew she was hollering for him from the house.

"Hurry up down there. Supper's on the table. In a minute I'll throw it to the hogs!"

He scrambled out and climbed into his clothes. She was right — he was refreshed and then some. His skin tingled.

They sat at the table across from each other and ate. It was a feast the likes of which he could only imagine. She had prepared a venison roast, baked potatoes, baking powder biscuits with butter, garden vegetables, and custard pie. If John Morton was staying away from home on purpose, Seth thought, he sure must be loony.

"What about yer husband, Claudia?" he asked. "Ain't he never comin' home?"

"Oh, sure. He'll be along directly."

"Ain't yuh worried a-tall?"

"Nope. He's stayed out huntin' longer'n this before. He'll be along in good time. I gotta say, Deputy, you're a right handsome feller without that bird's nest on your face."

He laughed. "An' I reckon I feel like a new spring lamb after that dip in the lake. Colder'n all Friday, that water."

"Yep," she said, grinning. "It'll start your birds t'singin' all right. More coffee?"

"Thankee. Mighty satisfyin' supper, Claudia. Yer a fine cook."

He finished his pie, whittled himself a toothpick from a wooden match, and tilted his chair back. He wished he could undo his top pants button and let his poor stuffed belly out some, but maybe she wouldn't understand right away what he was doing. He wanted a smoke after that fine meal, but he didn't want to get too comfortable nor linger too long. He wouldn't want her husband to come home and find him in the house with her after the sun went down.

He heaved a sigh. "Reckon I'll be gettin' out to the barn," he said.

She stood at the counter beside the stove washing dishes. She looked over her shoulder at him. "Already? What's your hurry, Deputy? Miss your mule, do ya?"

"Well, no, it ain't that exactly. I, eh...I jist don't wanna be a doggone nuisance to yuh, Missus Morton."

"It's Claudia, remember? An' y'ain't no nuisance a-tall. Roll yourself a smoke and lean back a spell. Ain't no reason to rush on outa here."

He rolled a smoke and lit it at the top of the glass chimney of the coal oil lamp. He tilted his chair back again and puffed white clouds to the ceiling.

"I wish you wouldn't go to the barn," she said suddenly.

"What?"

"No need your goin' to the barn. I'd be much obliged if you'd sleep right here in the house. Y'see, I've been worried plumb sick these last few days bein' alone, what with that murderer out there somewhere. I'd sleep a whole lot better if I knew you was right here in this cabin instead of way out there in the barn where you couldn't hear me holler if I needed help. You could sleep on the rollaway bed."

"I could?"

"Sure you could. I'll get the cot."

He watched wide-eyed as she rose and hurried to the pantry and emerged pushing a bed on casters. She unfolded it next to the table.

"What about yer husband?" Seth asked.

"What *about* my husband?"

"What if he comes home in the night and finds me here in bed?"

"Well, he ain't gonna shoot you fer just lyin' on the cot. I'll tell him right away who y'are and that you was protectin' me from The Kid. He'll understand."

Seth thought about that awhile. "Well, I dunno," he mumbled. "Maybe if I slept on the ground outside yer winder, y'could holler if y'needed me."

"An' what if The Kid comes and murders you in your sleep out there?"

Seth gave in finally. He didn't like the idea of sleeping outside anyhow, when he could as well be inside. He stayed up that night until she had gone into her bedroom and closed the door, then he blew out the lamp, slipped off his boots, and went to bed. But every time he'd close his eyes to sleep, he'd think about her in the next room in her bed, and his eyes would open up real wide. Then, when he was about to drift off again, he'd think about her husband and his shotgun, and his eyes would open real wide again.

It was a long night.

The next day Seth rode up and over the ridge to the east, following the faint wagon trail and watching for signs of The Kid. In the afternoon he returned without finding anything, and he guessed he would start back for Custer in the morning. Sheriff Brand would be wondering what had become of him. He shaved again and bathed in the lake, and when he entered the cabin Claudia had supper all ready. He sat down and she placed the usual delicious fare in front of him, except this time it was fried chicken. She returned and got the coffee pot.

"Doggone it, Claudia," he exclaimed, "a man would sure be lucky to have a wife that kin cook like this, and one as all fired pretty as you be!"

As she poured, she held her gaze to his face as if studying him. He dropped his eyes to his plate.

"Them's nice words I ain't heard for awhile, Seth," she said. "They're like music to a lady's ears. You don't mind me callin' you Seth, do you?"

He met her gaze again, and he couldn't remember when he'd ever seen eyes so pretty and soft and limpid, even on some of them lady antelopes he'd seen peeking at him from the forests. A puff of her breath caught his right ear. It made him feel as if little porcupines were scampering up his legs and backbone.

"I...I..." He tried to swallow. "I reckon yuh kin call me most anything y'have a mind to, and...and I won't mind."

She straightened and backed away slowly, then she was back at the stove again. He took a bite of his chicken and chewed. He couldn't taste it. Desire and lust had filled him in that brief moment and chased away his hunger.

"We have apple pie, Seth," she said. "Save space for it. It's hot. I hope you like it hot."

He felt his face flush. "Eh...yes. Yes, I do. Sure do. Like it hot. Apple pie, I mean. I like it hot."

It was dark outside now, and she lighted the coal oil lamp on the shelf. He watched her as she moved about the room drawing the curtains and closing the door. "Wouldn't want your murderin' friend sneakin' up an' shootin' us through the window, would we?"

"No, sure not," he said. "That kid's just the sort that would do a trick like that, too."

"John has some books," she said. "In that box in the corner. Some about deer huntin' and some on fishin'." She laughed. "Even one on philosophy of life, if you're attuned to such. You can read while I'm cleanin' up if you want."

"I ain't a real good reader," he said. "I write pretty fair, though. Good enough to be a lawman. But I ain't figured out how to read the long words. I was raised out in the wilds of Missouri, y'see, and they waren't no schoolhouse there a-tall."

"Sure ain't hard to learn," she said. "If you was gonna be here a spell I could teach you easy enough."

"Well, yes. Reckon I'd like that. If things work out right in

Custer, Claudia, might be I'd come back up chasin' some outlaw or other and yuh could teach me. If yer husband wouldn't mind, o'course."

She turned and looked at him in silence for a moment.

"He wouldn't," she said. "He wouldn't mind a bit."

"Must be a nice feller. Wish he'd get home so I could meet him."

"He'll be here," she murmured, smiling. "In due time."

When she had finished the dishes she slipped into the bedroom and returned with a small book. She slid a chair over beside him at the table, sat down, and opened the book in front of him. He caught a whiff of an aroma. Perfume! Why would a lady way out here a hundred miles from nowhere put on perfume?

"This book is called *From the Earth to the Moon*. Ain't it fascinatin' to think about goin' to the moon?"

"Yes'm. Sure is."

"See this here letter, Seth? That's an *m*."

"I know m'alphabet all right, y'see, Claudia," he said. "It's just I don't know how them letters goes so's they'll make words." He felt her thigh against his under the table, and it was a chore just to think what he wanted to say.

"Well, y'gotta know what sounds they make. *M* makes *mmmmmmmm*, like in *mmmoon*."

"All right. *Mmmmmmm*," he said.

"That's how you learn to read big words, by the sound the letters make. I could teach you to read this very book."

"I ain't never been too interested in readin', but I reckon with you a-showin' me, it might be downright fun."

Her thigh moved against his. "You could read what the moon's like."

"...eh, when I was a boy, somebody said it was green cheese."

She told him about other letters and moved her leg around some more. He felt the great frustration of being drawn in two directions, one of almost insane passion for her soft body and the other an intense fear of a violent husband and his shotgun.

She closed the book and folded her hands on top of it. Her face was less than a foot ruler from him.

"I want you to sleep with me tonight, Seth," she whispered.

He was aghast. He sat staring at her for what seemed a long time, before he realized his mouth was hanging open.

"With...with you?"

She stood up and faced him with hands on hips. "Well," she huffed. "You could do worse, Deputy. I wouldn't bite you."

The room swam around him. He was burning with desire.

"Yuh want me to share yer bed with yuh?"

She took his arm. "I'm offerin' you a bit of hospitality. It's up to you. But maybe you'd rather be with your mule."

"Heck, no. No, 'course not. Yer a mighty pretty little gal, Claudia."

She led him into her bedroom, closed the door, and opened the curtains on the window. In the semi darkness of the bedroom she slipped out of her clothes and stood beside him.

"Well," she murmured, "are you gonna sleep with your boots on an' everything?"

He sat on the bed and pulled off his right boot. "Good Lord, Claudia," he said. His voice was shaky. "What if yer husband comes home with his shotgun?" Light from the open window gave him glimpses of her nude body, white and soft and inviting. He knew he would have to have her if it killed him.

Claudia waited silently in the darkness as excitement mounted within her. She pondered the wisdom of telling Seth that John Morton was dead and would not be returning at all. It would relax him of course, and perhaps their affair would be more satisfying. But she knew a thing or two about men. Once they had made love to a lady they took on the idea that by virtue of her consent and submission, they owned her, body and soul, to possess her and treat her any way they pleased. And, by God, nobody owned Claudia Morton any further than she desired them to! She would not tell him. The specter of her husband would hold him at bay.

"You'll hear him if he does," she whispered. She moved close and unbuttoned his shirt. "If he comes up on the porch you'll hear him and you can slip out this window and hide in the barn."

"Oh, my God!" he croaked, dropping his trousers in a heap

on the floor. "I hope he don't come home."

"So do I," she whispered, and pulled him onto the bed with her.

Seth Dalby took a long ride the next day, all the way around the lake and back, with the breezes cooling his face and calming his nerves. The night with Claudia Morton had been delight beyond anything he had ever experienced, at least until he was spent and his brain cooled down and let him reason out what a hell of a fix he would be in if John Morton came home. He didn't think much of shotguns as lawmen's weapons because they didn't carry far. But he had seen what that buckshot could do to a man from a few yards away. Saw him right in half! So he hadn't slept at all the rest of the night. He kept thinking he heard noises.

On his way back in the afternoon a white tail deer crossed the gully ahead of him, and he brought it down with his Sharps and tied it on behind his saddle. Claudia was all smiles and gaiety when he got there, delighted about the deer and glad Seth was back.

"See anything of yer husband?" he asked.

"Nope. Not a thing. But he'll be along before long. He's stayed out longer than this 'cause he loves the country and plumb enjoys sleeping under the stars."

They dressed down and salted the deer. Before supper Seth bathed in the lake and shaved again at her insistence. He couldn't remember when he had kept himself so well groomed.

He shared her bed again that night. By the time dawn arrived he was haggard and drawn from worry. His bones ached and his eyelids drooped. After breakfast he went to the barn and collapsed in the hay and slept until afternoon.

At supper that evening they had venison steak. "This is your deer, Sethie," she said. "Isn't it delicious?"

"Yes. Eh, Claudia..."

"Yes?"

"Maybe I should sleep in the barn tonight."

"Why? Don't you like me?"

"Oh, no, no! It ain't that. Not a-tall, it ain't. It's just that... well, I'm a mite tuckered out, y'see, an'..."

She laughed. "Am I too much for you? Can't keep up?"

"No, no! It ain't that neither. It's just that I worry about yer husband comin' home and maybe ketchin' us and maybe sawin' me in half with his shotgun."

She took a sip of coffee and licked her lips. "Well, all right then. If you're afraid, you go ahead and sleep with your mule."

"Now, now, Claudia, don't you go gettin' testy. It ain't that I'm afraid, y'see. It's jist that bein' a lawman, I've learned to be careful."

By the time they sat down after supper, and Claudia taught him about the sounds made by three or four more letters, and breathed in his ear and rubbed her thigh on his, he was willing to forget about sleeping in the barn and about being careful, and they went to bed. They hadn't been there more than a few minutes when they heard the squeak of the loose board in the front porch. A shock traveled up his spine.

"Oh, my God!" he whispered. "Somebody at the door!"

"I heard it!"

He listened a second, but heard only his own heart booming. "Damn!" he whispered. He leaped to his feet and felt for his underwear.

She sat up. "I don't know who it could be!" she said.

"Well, dammit, I do!" he whispered. "It's yer husband, sure as Satan!"

Another squeak came from the porch, and then a slap against the front door. His heart leaped into his mouth and he climbed onto the bed and scrambled over the sill and out through the back window into the cool night air, completely naked.

"Seth, come back!" she said.

Just as his feet found the ground, he heard a snort to his left. He whirled and stood face to face with a huge brown bear.

"Aaaaayyyyeeee!" he screamed. He turned and rushed headlong toward the barn. He tripped on something and fell bare-belly down in the grass. He figured this was his final day on this earth, and if the bear didn't get him, Claudia's husband sure would. He crawled on hands and knees a dozen yards before regaining his feet. He stumbled another dozen steps and then heard gunshots. Three or four in quick succession. He fell again, face down. He wondered if he'd been hit. He crawled the rest of the way to the barn. He pulled himself up, entered, and latched the door behind him.

He strained his eyes in the dim light from the single high window, looking for somewhere to hide. He headed first for the loft, but came to a sliding halt. No! That's the first place he'd look. He whirled and raced for the mule's stall and crawled inside the hay bin in front of the animal. He doubled up and lay on his side with his eyes closed tightly. His heart was racing and he was panting like a hound dog. He'd have to be quiet when her husband came in the barn looking for him. He might could hold his breath awhile, but how could he quiet his hammering heart?

He heard the latch rattling on the barn door. Holy Mary and Joseph, this was the end! He opened his eyes wide and turned his face upward. Now he was nose-to-nose with the mule. It stood looking down at him with the same look it had given him back on the prairie when he had whacked it with a stick. Back went the long ears and up curled the floppy lips. Just as Seth heard the barn door squeak open, the mule sank his big teeth into his stomach.

"Eeeyyyyaaaa!" screamed Seth. "Goddam you bastard mule!"

He flailed his arms out and banged his knuckles against the bin. The mule was reaching for another bite, but Seth rapped his nose with all his strength.

"Damn you!"

The animal backed up a couple steps and snorted. Then Claudia was there in her nightgown, reaching through the stall and pushing the mule away from him.

"Hurry up and get outa there while I hold this critter!" she shouted.

He crawled to his feet and stood upright in the bin. Blood ran down his hip and leg. "Where's yer husband?" he panted.

"He ain't here. Hurry up before he bites you again!"

"Ain't here?" He scrambled out of the bin and stood kind of crooked, holding a hand over the wound. "The hell he ain't here! He was shootin' at me, fer Christ's sake!"

"That was me," she declared. "I was shootin' to scare the bears. There was two of 'em. My husband ain't here. There was a bear at the front and a bear at the back."

She was grinning now, looking him up and down.

"What in the name of Mariah is so gul durned comical?"

"You. Just look at you! Y'got dirt and mud all over your belly." She sniffed the air. "Smells like it's more'n just dirt. You must've picked up a little something the milk cow left, too. Your nose is skinned, and your forehead is too." She pulled his hand away from his side. "And it looks like that mule finds you to his taste."

Seth felt tears run down his cheeks and he began to cry. "I cain't stand this no more," he babbled. "I'm goin' plumb crazy around here, worryin' about gettin' caught with yuh. It jist ain't no way t'live, and I'm goin' back to Custer soon as I kin get my stuff together."

"All right," she said, softly. "I'm sorry I laughed at you. But you do look pretty funny standin' there all naked in the barn like this. Come on, lets get in the house and get you cleaned up and fix up that bite."

"All right," he said. He followed her to the barn door where she retrieved the Winchester .73 from where she had leaned it against the wall on her way in. "I keep this rifle in the house special for scarin' away the bears," she said. "There are several regulars that come around lookin' for something to eat. Ain't no use killin' 'em unless I have to. They ain't never bothered me or chased me or nothin'."

His whole body was shaking, and he felt like he was losing his mind. The thought of returning to that house where her husband and his shotgun might appear any moment was almost more than his brain could stand. They entered by the front door and she lit the coal oil lamp and hung up the rifle. She wrapped a blanket around him.

"Sit down. We'll get some water and clean you up."

He sat on the edge of the chair and scanned every inch of the room as if expecting John Morton to be there somewhere, maybe even sitting on the ceiling. He was shaking so bad he almost shook the blanket off.

She washed the dirt spots and bandaged the mule bite. "I likely shouldn't say this," she mused, "but this bite looks an awful lot like that gunshot wound on your shoulder."

"Are yuh done?"

"Yes."

He stood up. "Then let me get my clothes on. Me an' m'horse and that dirty mule is hittin' the trail." He looked down at her, his eyes wide. "Now!"

"Just a minute, Seth. Set down a minute. I got somethin' to tell you." She took his arm and pushed him gently into the chair.

"What?" He wiped his eyes on the blanket. "What yuh got to tell me?"

"Now, don't get mad, Seth. Promise me you won't get mad."

"Well, I don't know how I could get much madder. What is it?"

"I ain't got no husband."

He felt his mouth drop open and his face wrinkle up.

"No husband?"

"Nope."

He stared at her, not believing that he was hearing right.

"No husband?"

She straightened up and picked at the corner of a bandage remnant. "John Morton was my husband, but he died several months ago."

"Several months ago?" he said.

"Yes. He got pneumonia and I couldn't get him over to Pine Valley to the doctor in time. He's buried up on that hill there." She pointed to the south. "I been alone since then, and I was gettin' mighty lonesome when you came along."

"Yuh...yuh...All this time yuh let me think..."

"I'm sorry, Seth."

"Why?"

"Well...at first I just didn't know you. Didn't know who you were or what kind of a man you were. I figured you wouldn't mistreat me or beat me or something if you thought I had a husband."

"Me?" He stuck his thumb in his chest. "Me? Mistreat you?"

"Well, I just didn't know about you then. But now I know you're a fine man and a man of the badge and you wouldn't harm a lady, and I want you to stay here with me."

"Claudia, fer Christ's sake! Yuh shoulda told me. Yuh shouldn't of let me suffer that way."

She looked coyly at him. "Now, Seth, don't you have to admit that makin' love is a lot more exciting when you never know what the next minute will bring? Doesn't it just tickle you to the very core to be having your way with a lady right in the very face of possible death? Ain't it just the most wonderful, exhilarating fun y'ever had, like goin' on a high ride at the carnival?"

He sat with his mouth agape, listening, trying to make sense of what she was saying. He thought a moment.

"No," he said, finally. "It was a mite like hell, I'd say."

"I'm sorry," she said. She leaned down and hugged him and kissed his cheek. "I'm truly sorry. Please forgive me. And let me say that you are an exciting lover, even when you're scared."

"I am?"

"Yes. An' if you would like to stay a spell longer, you're plumb welcome to. You don't have to go hurryin' off."

He felt her breath on his ear. "Oh, well," he said. "Might as well sleep the night and think about what to do tomorra, I reckon."

"That's a good fellow." She headed into the bedroom and he followed.

"Are you sure about that?" he called after her.

"Sure about what?"

"Yer husband is dead?"

Seth stayed with Claudia Morton for two more weeks. By the end of the first week he was pretty well worn out and he began to wonder if pneumonia was what John Morton *really* died of. He had never seen nor heard of a woman like Claudia. She just never ran down, it seemed. Along about the middle of the second week he rode out hunting and took along his bedroll and slept under a big pine tree just to catch up on his rest. At the end of that week he laid his cards on the supper table.

"I'm gonna have to be gettin' back, Claudia," he said, pressing his fingers absently on the mule bite on his stomach. "If I don't show up pretty soon, Sheriff Brand'll likely put somebody else in my place."

She turned from the dish pan. "Can't you just make it a day or two longer? I was hopin' you'd ride the buckboard with me into Pine Valley tomorrow. I'm gettin' low on grub."

"How long a ride is it?"

"Oh, it ain't bad. Eight, ten miles maybe, up over that mountain and across the prairies. You can ask around if anybody's seen your outlaw. If you can catch him, Sheriff likely won't fire you."

Seth's face lit up. "Say, that sounds like a mighty fine idea. Jist might bear fruit, at that."

The more he thought about Claudia's idea, the better he liked it. Could be somebody had seen the kid. He could even be hiding somewhere in the town. If he could find out where the kid was without him knowing he knew, he could sneak up on him and put a bullet in him. He wouldn't just nick him this time.

They ate an early breakfast the next morning and were soon on their way up the trail toward Pine Valley in Claudia's one-horse buckboard.

Chapter Fourteen

When Casey drifted back to reality, he was in bed. He felt the covers over him and wondered if it was time to "rise and shine!" as Dad always said. The tragedies of the past few weeks came back to him then, and he wondered if Hermund Grim and The Deputy were part of a bad dream from which he was awakening.

He opened his eyes a peek. Bright light made him close them again, but in the brief second he saw a face. Mom's? No. Then whose?

He flinched, remembering the river bank. How long had he lay there? Was he alive? He opened his eyes again, carefully, but the face was gone. Before he could focus on anything he drifted back to darkness.

When he awoke next he opened his eyes wide. The face wasn't there but a ceiling was. He tried in vain to sit up. He raised his head and looked around as pain stabbed at his skull and neck. A small bedroom. Family pictures. A dresser against the wall. A small mirror. A straight-back chair. Another chair. He touched his head and felt bandages.

He tried to remember. What was it? Something about a dog fight. "Thief!" he heard himself call out.

The bed shook and Thief popped up from the floor and licked his face. Casey ran his fingers through the thick hair on the neck, and pulled the dog to him and hugged him.

"Thief! Lord, I'm glad you're here, boy!"

The dog wagged and whined and licked. A chair scraped the floor somewhere, and a moment later a girl appeared in the doorway: young, brown haired, pretty.

"So!" she said, smiling. "You're awake. It's about time."

He gazed at her in awe. "Hello," he said. "I...I'm awfully glad to see you." About his age, he guessed, with laughing blue eyes and a full mouth.

"We found you," she said. He heard gaiety in her voice. "So, since finders are keepers, I guess you're ours."

He tried to rise again, but fell back.

"Don't try to get up yet," she said. "You're too weak. You lost a lot of blood." She settled in the chair. "What happened, do you know?"

He thought a moment. "It's hard to remember. I think somebody shot me."

"Yes, it looked like a bullet wound. It creased your scalp. We found you by the river bleeding like all yesterday. We had a terrible time making the blood stop. That's why you're weak. You need to generate more blood to get your strength back."

"Where am I?"

She slipped her fingers under his head, lifted it, and straightened and fluffed his pillow.

"We brought you to our farm, a couple of miles from where we found you. We're the Asters. My mom is Heather and I am Hope. Daddy is Durwin Aster."

"Just you three?"

She raised the edge of his bandage and peeked under. "We've been watching for bleeding," she said. "Lately it's been pretty good. No, there are four of us. Billy is my younger brother."

"What about my horse?"

"That's what brought you to our attention. We saw your horse standing beside the creek and when we got there we found you and your big dog. Your horse is in our barn."

"I'm lucky you found me."

"We found your black hat, too. It was down the canyon a ways. We guessed it was yours. It has a hole in it that matches where your wound is. There was a dead dog in the canyon too."

"Yes. I remember a dog. There was a fight. Thief killed that dog."

He heard a door slam. "Billy!" called Hope. "Our friend is awake!"

A man about Casey's age entered the room.

"Hello," said Casey, smiling weakly. "You must be Hope's brother."

"Hello yourself. You've been doin' a lot of sleepin'. How do you feel?"

"Tired." He noticed a small table by his head, with a water pitcher. "How long have I been here?"

"Couple of days. Mom and Hope patched up your wound. You were lucky. A little lower and we'd have had to bury you."

"Is there water in that pitcher?"

Hope snatched the pitcher and a cup. "Help him up, Billy," she said.

Billy boosted him to a sitting position. For a moment the room spun and he closed his eyes. "I'm a little dizzy."

"Not surprised," Billy said. "Nasty wound."

"We tried to give you water before," Hope declared, holding the cup before him, "but you couldn't do very well and it ran down your chest."

He gulped at the water. He had never been so thirsty. When the cup was half empty, Hope took it away.

"Lets go easy," she said. "I don't know if you should drink the well dry the very first time, do you?"

"No. Reckon not."

"Are you hungry?"

"Don't feel none."

A lock of his hair had tumbled down in front of his eyes, and Hope brushed it back. "We don't know your name," she said. "You didn't have anything with your name on it. If you'd been killed we'd have had to put a blank tombstone on."

He smiled. "Would've been okay with me." He thought about giving a false name, but somehow he couldn't bring himself to lie to these folks.

"Casey Parkin."

"Wanna lie back, Casey?" asked Billy. "Or maybe you'd like us to prop you up with pillows for awhile."

"I'm awful tired," he said. "You've been so good to rescue me and take care of me. I wish I could chat awhile, but I don't think I can stay awake."

Billy settled him back into the pillow. "Go ahead and sleep," he said. "Plenty of time to talk later on."

In less than a minute he was sound asleep.

He awoke at dawn the next day to the crow of a rooster. He felt vivacity now, and hunger pangs. As he stirred, Thief popped up again and washed his face.

"Thief, you rascal!" He patted and hugged the dog. "You're still here with me."

He heard dishes rattling, and a moment later voices came through the thin clapboard walls. The aroma of bacon and coffee told him the Asters were preparing breakfast. He was aware that he hadn't eaten in a long, long time.

"Well," came a man's voice, deep and mature, "we sure as Sunday don't know who he is nor what he's doin' up in here, do we?"

"No, Daddy, but he's a real nice person. Wait 'til you meet him. You'll see."

"You're young yet, Hope, very young. And gullible. You would trust anyone. How do you know who he is? He could even be a murderer."

Casey felt his heart jump.

Hope's voice came right back. "He's not just anyone, Daddy. He's a very nice boy. I know he could never be a murderer."

A screen door slammed and footsteps sounded close by the bedroom wall. "Pa!" came Billy's voice. "Milkin's done."

"All right. Come and eat. Do the cream skimming after breakfast. And look in on that kid, will you?"

As Billy strode in, Casey smiled. "Good morning."

"'Mornin', Casey. How you feelin'?"

"Lots better."

Billy petted the dog. "Fine lookin' animal here. You call him Thief?"

"Yep. That's him. He joined me on the way up. He must've belonged to somebody at one time or other. He's pretty smart."

"How come 'Thief'?"

"He stole a cooked rabbit from me. The whole dang thing!"

Billy laughed. "He sure takes a hankerin' to you. Right at first he wouldn't let us near you down by the river. Sat and growled some. But it didn't take him long to know we were tryin' to help. He's been right beside you the whole time. We've been feedin' him here by your bed."

"Well, I'll be danged!"

"Yep. He's your pal, ain't no argument about that."

"Billy!" came a woman's voice. "There *is* no argument. Don't say ain't!"

A lady in her forties entered and moved to the bedside. "I try hard to teach my children proper grammar," she said, smiling at Casey. "But sometimes they just don't seem to care. I'm Billy's mother."

"Pleased, Mrs. Aster. I'm Casey. Thank you for taking me in. You saved my life."

"So glad you're here," she said. "You're so much like Billy that you seem like you ought to be one of my own children. You even wear a black hat like Billy's. Are you hungry?"

Casey shook his head and smiled. "Yes'm. I'm a mite starved, I reckon."

She held her palm on Casey's forehead. "Seems like your fever is gone. Do you think you can abide bacon, eggs and flapjacks?"

"Yes, Ma'am. I'd be plumb loco to turn down an offer like that."

They all left the room, and a few minutes later Hope returned with a small table and put it over him on the bed. "This is called our sick-a-bed table," she said. "Let's prop you up so you can eat."

She helped him up and stuffed pillows behind him. "Now you wait right here," she said. "Don't go away."

She hurried out and returned a minute later with dishes balanced on her arm. She put them on his sick-a-bed table and laid silverware beside them.

"Ohhhh!" he sighed, smelling the bacon and flapjacks. "This is beautiful, Hope. I'm so hungry."

"We've been feeding your dog table scraps. I hope it's okay."

"Yes, thank you. He eats anything and enjoys it better when he steals it."

She leaned and petted the dog. "He's so pretty. And I'm so

glad your wound is getting better."

"My nose is better too," he said, grinning. "It tells me there's coffee somewhere."

She straightened up suddenly. "Oh, my goodness! I forgot your coffee!"

He watched her whirl and scurry from the room. Her moves were graceful and elegant, even when hurrying. In a moment she was back, balancing a steaming cup.

"Daddy always makes the coffee," she said, setting the cup on his sick-a-bed table. "Now don't spill it on yourself or we'll have to nurse you back to health again. I'll be back after breakfast. Daddy insists we all be at the table."

"All right. I'll be right here."

When he had finished the breakfast he lay quietly and thought about his predicament. Was it the Deputy that shot him? If so, maybe he was hanging around the area looking for him. It might be wise to get on his way the very moment his strength returned.

But why didn't the deputy finish him in that canyon? The bullet had sure knocked him flat for awhile. Maybe the shooter was up high, someplace like on the canyon rim, and took him a spell to get down. Maybe he'd been tracking him with that big red hound that Thief took the measure of. Maybe he wouldn't be able to track him without his hound, so maybe he shouldn't worry.

Durwin Aster, slim and dark haired, came into his bedroom after breakfast and stood a few feet away. "Your name be Casey, that right?"

Casey raised partly up onto his elbow. "Yes, Sir. You're Mr. Aster?"

"I am! What brings you up this way? Bill said you were from Custer City, that right?"

"Yes." Casey felt uncomfortable under the intent gaze. "I'm just out seein' the Black Hills country and somebody took a pot shot at me. Maybe I trespassed on somebody's property."

The man moved to bedside and stared down at Casey. "I'd say most likely the law's after you, that right?"

Casey felt a twinge of uneasiness. "No, Sir." He forced a grin.

"Not that I heard about, leastways. But I sure do appreciate your hospitality and your help. I would've died if it hadn't been for you folks. I'll be on my way soon as I get my strength back."

"That big black horse in the barn. Yours, that right?"

"Yes, Sir, that's Ebon. He's a great horse."

The man stood a moment, quietly gazing at Casey. He folded his arms and stroked his goatee. "You look like a good kid," he said. "Least you would if you shaved off some of that tender grass growin' on your chin. You're a might young for a beard. Must be about the same age as my Billy, that right?"

"I'm nineteen. Be twenty in a couple months."

"What do you do fer a livin'?"

"I live with my folks and I do regular farm work." He reasoned he better not tell him about his dad being dead now, and his mother beaten half to death. In fact, he wished he would stop asking so many questions.

"Well," said Mr. Aster, "Hurry up and get well. You're welcome to stay with us as long as you behave yourself and carry your own load. Soon as you're well you can help with the chores around here."

"Be glad to, Sir," said Casey, dropping back to the pillow. "But I'll be movin' on as soon as I can make it up to you for all the trouble and cost you went to for me."

Mr. Aster moved toward the door, but turned back again. He stroked his chin thoughtfully. "After you're well might be you'd want to stay awhile. We could use a little help around here, and of course I'll pay you. We got a hired man, but he's off to Sioux City for a spell visitin' his kinfolk."

"I'll have to give that some thought," Casey said. "Maybe I could stay a while. When's your man comin' back?"

"Ain't sure. We'll talk about it again in due time." He turned and strode out.

Casey thought about what Mr. Aster had said. His big worry, of course, was keeping away from too many people. If word got to that Deputy that he was here with the Asters, he would be in a bad fix. But he had to stay someplace. Had to have a place to live. Couldn't just keep skulking around in the timber like an animal. Maybe if he stayed he would have a chance to look over the country and secretly build himself a little cabin somewhere in one of the hidden draws so he could ride out the winter. He would have to put in provisions, even a stove of some sort. He decided to bide his time and see how things looked when he was up and about again.

In two days, with Billy's help, he was on his feet. They spent the afternoon hours strolling about the gentle, treeless slope that led from the doorstep to the edge of the west timber. Billy showed him the corral a thousand feet northeast, and the windmill pumping water into the trough, and how one could snag a bucket of cool water for the kitchen. They went by the shed where blocks of ice cut from last winter's frozen lake were stored in layers of sawdust. They peeked in the window of the empty bunkhouse located near the shed. They visited the barn, and when Casey looked in and smelled the hay and warm air and saw the line of stalls, he visioned his stepfather sprawled against the boards, his sightless eyes open, staring. He shuddered.

"What's the matter, Buddy?" Billy asked.

"Eh...nothin'. I'm just a little weak, is all. I'll be all right."

"Reckon you've done too much for one day. Tomorrow you'll be stronger."

The next day Casey was stronger. He was elated at the energy that flowed through his body. He began taking meals with the family. He and Billy strolled about the prairie and moseyed through the timber. He found it exciting to hear the birds again and smell the summer grass and feel the breeze on his now clean-shaven face. He found a stick and threw it. Thief pranced after it and brought it almost back, but not quite.

"Come here, you monkey!" Casey called, reaching. Thief pranced about, staying just out of his reach, and Casey turned his attention elsewhere. It was two days before Thief realized that if he didn't return the stick to Casey's hand, the game was over.

On the fifth day Casey felt almost as strong as before the shooting. After they had their noon meal, he moved out to the prairie with Thief and threw the stick.

"Casey!"

It was Hope on the porch. "Wait. I'll join you."

He took the stick from thief and stood waiting. Hope moved toward him and the breeze tousled her hair and rippled her soft dress against her body. He was hardly aware that Thief was nudging his arm, begging another toss of the stick.

"May I go with you on your walk today?" she said, smiling. "Billy has gone cow hunting."

"Sure, if you want. I'm much stronger now, though, and I can go by myself." He wished, as soon as the words were out, that he had them back.

"Well, all right, then," she said. "Have fun." She turned and headed back toward the house.

"No, no, I didn't mean...I...Hope! Come back here darn it!"

She turned back, her face a mask of mischief. "It sounded like you don't like my company."

"I do! I do! I love your company. I just didn't want to put you to any trouble, that's all."

She came back and stood beside him. She stroked Thief's neck. "I'm only going because I like Thief," she declared. "He likes my company."

"So do I, darn it," he said as they strolled toward the timber line. "Me and my big mouth!"

She laughed and took the stick from Casey. The move put Thief on alert, and he stood with his nose pointing in the direction he anticipated she would throw.

"Fetch!" she called, and flung the stick as hard as she could. Thief was off in a flash, tearing across the prairie. In a moment he caught up and pounced upon the stick as if it were an animal. He came prancing back, tail wagging fiercely, and offered it to Hope. She threw it again.

"That could go on all day," Casey said.

"I know." She smiled and shook her head. "We had a dog until recently. We called him Schooner. He got old and died. It was like losing one of the family."

"Yes, it hurts to lose 'em. I had an old black pooch a couple years back, and when he died, I felt like dyin' too."

"We plan to get another one soon," she said. "We need one to help find and herd the livestock."

"What kind of a dog was yours?"

She flung the stick back toward the house, and Thief was off again. "I don't really know. Just some kind of a mutt. But he had a big heart and lots of love, and we loved him."

They strolled slowly down the path toward the timber with Thief trotting alongside trying to give the stick back to Hope.

"Could your dog follow a horse's trail?" he asked suddenly.

"Oh, my! I should say so. That's one thing we miss. We have to find the stock ourselves. Sometimes we're out there looking all day and then don't find them. Schooner could lead us right to them."

"I wonder if I could train Thief to follow livestock."

She stopped, bent down, and plucked a honeysuckle shaft from its stem. "Of course you could. He's a very smart animal, you can tell by his ears."

"By his ears?"

She tucked the honeysuckle between her lips and pressed out the honey. "Sure. Just look at how he holds his ears, straight and alert. He's a smart one all right. You could teach him in no time at all."

Casey thought about the big red hound that Thief had killed. He felt certain that's how the deputy had stayed on his trail. But that was a hound, and he'd heard they have special noses for picking up the scent. He didn't know whether a dog like Thief could do that, although he had stayed with that deer very well back in the hills.

"Maybe Thief could help you and Billy find the cows," said Casey.

"I'll bet he could."

"If I was gonna be here that long."

She plucked another honeysuckle shaft and handed it to Casey. "Did you ever suck the nectar from these?" she asked.

He took the offering and pressed the honey into his mouth. "Sure did." He smiled. "This one is real sweet. This is the candy Mother Nature grows just for kids. When I was little, we hunted them every summer."

"So did we." She glanced up at him. "Do you plan to leave? You're welcome to stay awhile, you know. Mama loves you. Daddy will too, as soon as he gets to know you."

They walked through the timber silently, and Casey thought about her father.

"I feel your dad doesn't like me much," he said, shrugging. "He seems suspicious of me."

She laughed and tossed her head. "Daddy's suspicious of everybody. That's just his way. He'll find out what a nice man you are and he'll ask you to stay, I know it."

"He already has, but I'm not sure he meant it. He said I could help around the place and he'd pay me. At least 'til the hired man gets back."

She stopped and turned, smiling. "See! He likes you already. I think that's grand, Casey. Can you stay?"

"Just don't know yet. I really would like to."

He reached up and felt his wound through the bandage. There was still pain when he pressed.

"My head feels better every day," he said. "You should have been a doctor."

"We thought about taking you to the doctor in Pine Valley, but we didn't think you could stand the trip. It's a pretty rough road. So we sort of brushed the dirt out of your wound and cleaned it up and put iodine in it. Mama sewed it shut."

"She did?"

"Yes. When she was younger she worked for a doctor and helped him sew folks up."

"Another thing—I've been sleeping in Bill's bed, haven't I?"

"Yes. And you know you're welcome to it as long as you want."

They left the timber and Hope scooped up another honeysuckle shaft and handed it to him.

"Thanks," he said. "And Billy's been sleeping on a mattress on the floor."

"Yes. He wanted to be close in case you had trouble and needed help in the night."

Casey felt a twinge. "I'm never gonna forget that. Bill's what you call a true friend. God bless him! And you've been so wonderful too, Hope. I'll always remember what you've done for me. And your Ma and Pa too. You're a good and thoughtful family. I owe you my life."

She put her hand on his sleeve. "Just seeing you well like this, Casey, has made it all worth while."

She was looking up at him, and for a moment he saw a tenderness in her eyes he hadn't noticed before. Then Thief rooted his nose into their hands, and Hope was flinging the stick again.

Thief, you rascal! he thought. You're still stealing from me.

After breakfast two days later, Casey strapped on his dad's Peacemaker. He set his black cowboy hat carefully over the bandages, then suddenly pulled it back off. The hole had been repaired with a black felt patch and stitching.

"Well, I'll be!" he said. He moved into the kitchen and found Heather Aster doing dishes.

"Mrs. Aster, did you fix my hat?"

She smiled. "Yes. We can't have you gadding about with a hole in your hat, can we?"

"Thank you, thank you. It was very thoughtful of you."

"It just seemed like something I ought to do. You're so much like one of my own. I'm glad to do it for you."

When he got out to the barn, Billy was there, rubbing down a brown pony.

"Hi, Casey. Where you headed?"

"Gonna take a ride around, look over the country," he said. "Wanna join me?"

"Can't this morning. Gotta groom the horses and get a little weedin' done in the garden patch. Sure be glad when Jim gets back."

"Jim?"

"Yeah, the hired hand. He's been gone to Iowa a couple months now. I hope he's comin' back. If he is, he ought to be here any time. If he knew you were here, I bet he'd hightail it back."

"Why?"

Billy grinned. "For one thing he'd probably be afraid you

might take his job here. And for another he's Hope's boy friend, and he'd likely figure you're competition."

"Hope's boy friend?" Casey felt an annoying twinge in his stomach. "How old is the man?"

"Oh, about twenty-three or four. Good lookin' fellow. Been takin' Hope to the dances over at the Seiden's place."

Casey's chest felt heavy. There was no mistaking the sensation. It was jealousy, pure and simple. A feeling of affection for Hope had been growing in his heart, but it had taken this unwitting slap by Billy's revealment to make him aware of it. He looked around the barn.

"Shoot, maybe I better help you with them chores instead," he told Billy. "I can go ridin' some other time."

Billy laughed. "You can help with the chores some other time, Case. It'll be good for you to ride again." He turned and shook his grooming brush at Casey. "But be damn careful, hear? Keep your eyes open."

"I will."

He saddled Ebon and slipped his Sharps in the scabbard. He led the horse outside and climbed up. He loved the power of the strong gelding under him and cherished the free feeling it gave him to be riding again. He loped a half mile, then brought Ebon back to a walk. The horse was raring to go, it was plain to see. So was Thief. He trotted alongside, his tail a perpetual whip.

As he rode, Casey saw Hope in his mind, so pretty and full of life and vibrant. Just being around her had given him a new and beautiful look at his world. Now he would have to stifle that feeling and think about her in a different way. It was one more thing to add to the malaise he suffered because of The Deputy and the fear of discovery. Perhaps it was better this way. Until his big trouble was settled, if ever, he could offer a lady nothing but grief.

He rode down into the canyon and found the place where he had been shot. The carcass of the big hound was gone, probably dragged away by predators. There were still signs of struggle. He examined the terrain around him and saw the edge of the precipice high above the creek on the other side. He felt that could have been where the shooter had stood.

He moved downriver to the spot where he had crossed after descending the cliff. Here he found many animal tracks including canine marks which could have been from the bloodhound or Thief, or even from coyotes or wolves. The trail down the cliff was obviously used often by livestock and wild animals.

He waded Ebon across and up the winding trail. It took him half an hour to travel to the rim, and when he got there and looked down, he was satisfied that was where the shooter had fired from. And he had used a high powered rifle, one at least as powerful as Casey's own Sharps. Now he knew his figuring about his pursuer was close to right. It had to be the Deputy, and the Deputy was hell-bent on killing him. Lord, how he wished he knew what the man looked like. He recalled a man being followed by a bloodhound at Dad's funeral. He had looked at the man only briefly, and now he couldn't recall what he looked like. He wished he had looked more closely.

He had given thought several times to surrendering and taking whatever they gave him. But he would hope for a chance to explain his side. He held no doubt that Hermund Grim would probably have killed him eventually, and might have already killed his mother. Shooting Grim was something he had to do. If it had not been for the threat to his mother; if it had just been him alone, he would have simply left the county. Now he knew he could never surrender to the deputy who was after him. If he tried, he'd be killed.

Over the next few days Casey did a lot of riding. Billy showed him the range the milk cows usually followed and where to find them. It became Casey's job to fetch them on the afternoons that Billy had other pressing chores.

He always took Thief with him, and it was a game for the dog to sniff out the trails of wayward bossies and point out their hiding places. It reached the point where Casey could put Thief's nose in a cow track and the dog would follow that one cow for miles, even though it would crisscross the trails of other livestock. Every time Thief led him to the proper cow, a rousing game of Fetch the Stick followed.

Chapter Fifteen

Casey and Billy stood by the porch and watched Mr. Aster hitch a horse to the buckboard and climb up. Mrs. Aster came out and stood beside him.

"Do you have the list, Durwin?" she said.

He patted his shirt pocket. "Yes. Right here. Are you certain there's nothing else?"

"I don't think so. Don't stay away too long."

"I'll stay the night at Foster's Boarding House," he told her. "Tomorrow I'll head over to Deadwood and see about them work horses that feller's got for sale."

"Dad!" Billy called. "Bring home some candy, okay?"

"I'll bring home a little, but it ain't good for your teeth." He glanced over at Casey. "You fellers get out there and find them saddle horses. And get that damn fence fixed up on the slope while I'm gone. When I come back it'll be all fixed or me and Mom eats all the candy ourselves."

Billy laughed. "Okay, Dad."

"And keep an eye out for that mangy brown bull. He ain't much, but nowadays every head counts."

"Okay, Mr. Aster," Casey said. "We'll see to it."

He said good-bye to Heather and Hope and slapped the reins down.

That evening after supper Mrs. Aster carefully cut and pulled the stitches from Casey's wound. Billy and Hope watched in awe. It brought tears to his eyes, but he held pretty steady.

"It surely is healing up nicely, son," she said.

"You're a good nurse, Mrs. Aster."

"Well, I got lots of practice at this sewing business. I made rag dolls for the children when they were little."

"For Hope," said Billy. "Not for me."

Mrs. Aster grinned. "Oh, yes I did make a doll for you. And it slept with its head on your shoulder, too!"

"Aw, Mom!" growled Billy. "Why do you tell those things?"

"It's nothing to get all red-faced about. Lots of boys have dolls when they're little. I bet Casey did."

"No, Ma'am," said Casey. "I don't believe I had a doll. But I had a little stuffed donkey I slept with."

"See!" Billy's mom pointed at him. "Same as a doll."

When the last stitch was out she washed the wound carefully. "It looks very good now, son. Let's not put bandages back on. It'll heal better. And your hair will grow back soon, but you'll probably always have a part right there."

To celebrate the bandage removal, they held a concert. Billy played the violin, Casey the guitar, and Hope a harmonica. The house was filled with the notes of "Oh, Suzanna," "Old Dan Tucker," "Jeannie With the Light Brown Hair," "I'll take you home again Kathleen," and "Silver Threads Among the Gold." Heather Aster sat and patted her foot and smiled. "Oh, my," she breathed, "the music does so stir the soul. Casey, where did you learn to play the guitar so expertly?"

He laughed. "Mother wanted me to learn so I could play for her when she got old. She sent me to a guitar teacher in Custer. I wish I could play the violin, now that I've heard Billy."

"Yes," Mrs. Aster said with a note of pride. "He does quite well. He plays with the Seiden boys on dance night."

"Where do they live?"

"They have a place about four miles over southeast," Billy said. "Every couple of months they hold a dance at their place and I play my violin. Mr. Seiden plays the piano and Wilmer picks a banjo. Les plays the guitar and so does Dick Furnell. Dick lives in Pine Valley."

"Do you play in the band too, Hope?" Casey asked.

She laughed and looked at her harmonica. "Heavens no! I don't think they like mouth harps, and besides, they would never let a girl play."

"I'm glad for this chance to practice," Billy said. "Our next dance is this Saturday night. Wanna come along with Hope and me, Casey?"

"Uh...well, no, I guess not. I'm not much of a dancer, I'm afraid."

"Oh, I'll bet you are, too!" put in Hope.

"You could dance with Hope," Billy said. Grinning, he added, "If you could stand it."

Hope stuck her tongue out at her brother and turned to Casey. "That's why they put Billy in the band, for gracious sake. To keep him off the dance floor. He steps on the girls' toes with his big boots and breaks their feet."

Billy grinned. "You could likely dance with Hope most of the evening, Case," he said. "Unless Jim gets back by then. If he does, he'll hog her. He always does."

"Guess I better not go," Casey said. "I'd sure enough break some feet." He figured word might get spread that he was at the dance, and The Deputy could find out where he was staying. Besides, he didn't think he could stand to see Hope dancing with others.

"Why don't you come anyway?" Hope asked. "You wouldn't have to dance if you didn't want to. You could drink punch and listen to great music, and maybe they would even ask you to play in the band with them."

"I'm sorry," Casey mumbled. "I guess I'm just not the partyin' kind. I don't like to be among a lot of people. Please excuse me if I don't go."

"Certainly," Hope said. "I understand."

Casey had been there three weeks already, and he was glad that before Mr. Aster left for town, he assigned him to specific chores for which he would be paid. It became his duties to milk half the cows every morning, to keep the beets and squash areas clear of weeds and to alternate with Billy in chasing down the cattle and horses in the wilderness. These chores kept him so busy he didn't have time to dwell upon his troubles. He also hadn't found time to work on the broken fence until three days after Mr. Aster had gone.

On that morning he pulled open the big barn doors, and the

smell of warm hay brought back the vision of Hermund Grim sprawled against the boards. He would have to keep working hard, he allowed, or that memory would likely drive him crazy. He found the team he wanted — the big grey in the stall next to Ebon, and the sorrel mare in the corral — and hitched them to the farm wagon. He found cut posts stacked neatly behind the barn and loaded a dozen of them in the wagon along with a shovel, a crowbar, a hammer and a saw. He included a roll of wire from the barn, and in the bunk house he found nails and pliers. Mr. Aster would be pleased to see the weak place in the fence fixed when he got home.

Chapter Sixteen

The sun was high when Seth Dalby and The Widow Morton drove into Pine Valley, Dakota Territory. It was a little place, nestled in a small valley, with one dusty street running through. Commercial business houses stood along the street, and residential houses and shacks were scattered around pretty much at random on the hillsides.

Being the gentleman that he was, Seth took the reins from Claudia and did some of the driving. He handed them back when they entered Pine Valley and hopped off in front of the only saloon in town. She drove on toward the millinery and general store another quarter mile down.

The saloon was pretty good size, almost bigger than the town, Seth thought. It even had a piano, although nobody was playing it. Two cowboys sat at a table playing cards and tipping glasses. The portly bartender polished the bar with a rag, but his eyes were on Seth as he approached, and Seth wondered what he thought when he saw the deputy's star. Seth nodded as he reached the bar. "Howdy," he said.

"Howdy. What brings the law to Pine Valley, Marshal?"

"I ain't a marshal," Seth said. "I'm Deputy Sheriff Seth Dalby from Custer County."

"Saints! What brings you way up here?"

"Well, I heard yuh got the best whisky in the Black Hills, so I rode up to see if it was just a rumor."

The bartender laughed. "You heard right!" He reached across a chubby hand and Seth shook it. He plunked a glass on the bar and poured it full of amber liquid. Seth laid down a dollar, and the bartender pushed it back. "It's on the house, Deputy."

"Well, thankee, friend." Seth tipped up the glass and drank half. It was, indeed, good whiskey.

122

"Looking fer a feller that did a murder in Custer County," he said. "Thought you mighta seen 'im or heard of 'im."

"What's his name?"

"Goes by the name of Casey Parkin. Looks and acts like a timid kid, but he's a cold blooded killer. Shot his daddy dead, he did. Got mad 'cause his daddy wouldn't let 'im have his way about somethin' and jist cut 'im down while he was pitchin' hay in the barn."

"Young fella, y'say?"

Seth drained the glass and slid it back toward the barkeep. He pointed his finger at it and the barkeep refilled it.

"Yup. Young feller. Kinda brownish sandy hair. About nineteen or so I reckon. Wears a black hat and rides a black gelding."

"Wouldn't a been wounded, would he?" the bartender asked.

Seth's eyes opened wide. "Yeah, believe he was. We had a gunfight and I think I nicked 'im. Why? You see 'im?"

The bartender went back to polishing. "No, he ain't been here, but Durwin Aster was in here tellin' me his kids found a young feller with a head wound along the creek in Forsythe Canyon. Said the kid almost died, but they doctored him and brought him through. Aster said he's stayin' there with them, least fer now."

"Well, baaah gaaawd! Baaah gaaawd! About time I got me a lead on 'im. Where does this Aster feller live?"

The Bartender pointed. "Got a little farm about fifteen, twenty miles southwest a here. About two miles above where they found the kid."

"That fits!" Seth exclaimed, grinning wide. "That's the man I'm huntin' all right. When did Aster tell you this?"

"Just yesterday. He left outa here for Deadwood this mornin'."

Seth tipped the glass and drained it and plunked it on the bar. "Thanks fer the help, friend," he said. "And thanks for the drinks. It's true what they say about your whisky. It's first fiddle!"

He turned and strode out and looked down the street.

Claudia's buggy was in front of the general store, and he hurried down there. He found her at the counter buying flour. He moved up and whispered in her ear.

"Hurry up, Claudia. I found out where The Kid is. Some family found 'im wounded and took 'im in."

"Good," she said. "Tell me about it when we get outside."

He stood about with hands in hip pockets awhile, then went outside and paced up and down the board walk. A half hour went by and Claudia was still in the store picking out groceries and brushes and linen and hardware, and Seth thought he would go out of his mind. He strolled back out to the buggy and climbed up and waited awhile. Then he went back inside and tried to hurry her along.

"Just you take it easy, Mr. Deputy," she said to him. "I don't get to town more'n once in a season, and I'm gonna take me the time to do my shoppin'. Why don't you get yourself back up to the saloon and sop up a little more firewater."

"I don't know how long that damn kid's gonna stay put," he growled. "I don't wanna miss 'im."

"Just relax. Life's too short t'fret an' carry on." She lifted a long dress from the rack and studied it. "My, my, it's been a long time since I've been anyplace where I could wear something like this. Do you dance, Seth?"

He was impatient, and growing more so with each passing moment. "Only when somebody's shootin' at m'feet."

"I reckon if I want you to dance with me, I'll have to shoot your feet, won't I?"

Seth gave her a disgusted look. He spun around and strode out front and climbed in the buggy. He crossed his arms and tried to be calm.

When she finally came out he was so mad he wouldn't speak to her. She put her merchandise in the buggy bed and climbed up and took the reins.

"Don't you think we ought to get a bite to eat before we start back?" she asked. "We won't get home 'til late afternoon, and we'll be hungrier'n them old bears that come around."

He turned his head slowly at looked at her. He stretched his lips across his teeth and doubled up his fist and showed it to her. "Git a-goin', woman," he said. He was glad she didn't give him any sass, because he would have popped her right in the nose if she did.

They headed back across the mountain as fast as she dared go over the rough, seldom-used trail. After an hour she pulled up under a large cottonwood tree.

"What we stoppin' fer?" he demanded.

"For nature, that's what," she said. She climbed down and turned back to him. "I bought some sandwiches at the general store. They're in that basket in the back, and there's some milk there with 'em. How about gettin' 'em out while I attend to nature?"

He got the stuff out and put it on the tail gate, and when she returned from the bushes, they ate. He felt a little more relaxed and not quite so ruffled now that his stomach had some grub to mix with the whiskey.

"Reckon I got a mite short with yuh, Claudia. Sorry. I jist don't want to miss my chance, that's all."

"It's all right," she said. "I understand how you feel." She put the basket away and climbed up on the buckboard. "Better take a pee, Seth, so we don't have to stop again."

After Seth had peed and took his seat, she handed him the reins. He slapped them down and they were on their way again.

"I ain't gonna miss the kid this time," he said. "I ain't gonna give 'im no chance to get away again. Soon as I put eyes on 'im, I'm gonna cut 'im down."

Claudia looked at him sideways. Deep furrows creased her forehead. "Cut him down? You mean you're just gonna shoot him? Ain't gonna say 'stick 'em up' or nothin'?"

"Nope. I reckon you don't know this killer, Claudia. He's plumb rotten to the core. Before I could even say 'stick 'em up,' he'd have that six-gun out blazin' away at me. Nope, I ain't gonna give 'im that chance." He looked at Claudia to see what effect his words were having. "Sure hope I see 'im first, 'cause if I don't, I'll be dead."

"My, my!" she sighed. "Looks like if he's that mean and dangerous, you'd have another deputy along to help you."

"Don't need none," said Seth with authority. "I kin handle it."

They arrived at the cabin two hours before sundown, and Seth hurried to the barn and began rolling up his blankets and tying supplies on the mule. After Claudia had moved her purchases into the house, she joined him in the barn.

"You're not going tonight, are you?"

"Yep."

"It'll be dark soon," she said. "And you're tired from all that buggy-bouncin' we did. Why not wait 'til tomorrow and start out real early?"

"Ain't got no time t'waste," he declared, tying his bedroll to the mule's back.

"It'll be dark, and you'll just get lost in the timber."

"Hell, no, I won't. Dern near a full moon tonight. Just like daylight out there."

She moved up close behind him and reached around his waist. "Aw, come on, Sethie, don't go." She stood on tip toes so she could reach his ear with her mouth. She nibbled on the lobe and let her breath drift into his ear canal. He stopped tying in the middle of a knot.

"Claudia, d-d-d-don't do that. It makes me all shivery."

"Stay home just one more night," she whispered. "Just one more night with little me won't hurt you a bit." She kissed his neck. "How about it, handsome Deputy?"

He pulled his bedroll down off the mule and they went into the house. It was a sublime way to spend a night, without the worry of a husband and his shotgun.

The next morning at sunup he tied the mule behind his sorrel and rode away from Claudia's house. His jaw was set in determination, and his eyes flashed a contemptible, villainous gleam. He felt the powerful Sharps rifle under his knee.

He rode hard that day and well into the moonlit night. He made camp for a scant time and was up early and on his way again. Later that second day he was forced to acquiesce to the mule's hunger, and he wasted a whole hour fretting while the critter munched the tender grasses.

He ate some hardtack and jerky at about noon while still in the saddle. He rode down a long draw and saw landmarks and signs he remembered from the way up. He was becoming more and more excited as he approached the fateful valley, and he carried a strong feeling that he would succeed this time.

By the time he had pushed his tired sorrel down the last long slope that led into the canyon where the kid had got away from him, he was becoming mighty tired himself. He allowed he ought to stop for a breather before trying to pick a route to the Asters' place. He nudged the pony to the left and in a few minutes found himself on the rim of a cliff at the west bank of the creek. He looked down at the water trickling among the willows, and he wondered how he might get down to the bank. He kept along the rim for another half mile until he came to a spot where the cliff was only about thirty feet high and sloping much less severely. He had just headed the sorrel down the side when he saw a big red bull coming through the trees from downstream with a rider behind it. He reined in, led his horse quickly back up to the top, and hid himself among the bushes.

The rider drew closer and Seth blinked his eyes a dozen times. He couldn't believe what he was seeing. There, moseying along driving the bull was the kid in the black hat on the big black gelding!

"Baaah Gaaawd! Baaah Gaaawd!" he huffed under his breath. "I knew I'd find 'im."

He snatched his Sharps rifle from the scabbard and braced it against the tree. He would not miss this time, by God! He couldn't miss from this distance. He put the sights dead center on the boy's chest and pulled. The big rifle roared, and the kick jarred him back. A cloud of black smoke from the breech blinded him for an instant, and he stepped to one side to see better. The kid's hands flailed out to the sides, and he spun out of the saddle to his right and landed heavily behind the side-stepping horse.

"Got 'im!" yelled the Deputy. "Baaah Gaaawd, they don't git away from old Deputy Dalby, they don't!" He led his sorrel and the mule down the bank to where the kid lay flat on his back.

Blood pumped from a savage hole in his chest. He was dead, there wasn't any doubt about that. The bull stopped and turned to eye Seth a moment, then moved a few feet and stopped where the grass was long enough to eat.

Seth felt like jumping up an down, he was so happy to bag the murderer. He could hardly wait to see old Sheriff Brand's face when he saw him riding in with the kid over the saddle. He stood watching the blood pour out until it slowed a bit, then he rolled the body over so the rest could run out.

It occurred to him suddenly that someone else could have been with the kid, and he looked around carefully. There was no sign of anyone. He was glad he didn't need to go to the Aster's place, because then he would have had to take the kid into his custody since others would be present. Of course he'd never have delivered him to Custer alive because that would have meant a trial where anything could happen, possibly including the revelation that he'd shot the kid from ambush on the way up.

He was glad the kid was wearing a six shooter. He'd need an excuse for killing him, and he could say the kid refused to surrender and drew down on him and even winged him in the shoulder and in the side. He guessed he'd tell them the kid fired four shots at him, and even though he was wounded, he returned fire and killed the kid with one shot. He looked down at his vest. The mule bite in the shoulder looked good because the shirt was stained with dried blood there. But there was no stain, nor even a hole, in his vest and shirt at his side because he'd been naked when the mule did that one. He allowed he'd have to fix that.

He drew his Peacemaker, stuck the barrel inside his shirt, turned it so it aimed away from him, and fired a round through the shirt and vest from inside to outside. It made a dandy bullet hole, he thought. He bent over the dead boy, wiped his fingers in the chest wound, and smeared blood on the vest and shirt, inside and out. He was proud of the result. That would sure convince them he'd been nicked by bullets.

How many bullets? Two out of four ought to do it. He took the kid's six-shooter from the holster and fired four rounds into the ground, then replaced it. He hoisted the kid's body up across the black gelding face down and tied him onto the saddle. He was pleased to see the Sharps rifle in the scabbard. He would keep that one for a spare. He untied his bedroll and equipment from the mule and secured it on the black horse behind the saddle. He slipped off the mule's halter and tied it to the saddle strings. When he turned back, the ornery critter was trotting away into the timber.

"Go ahead and run, yuh mangy bastard," he called after him. "Shore glad to be rid of yuh!"

He climbed up on his sorrel and moved down the canyon toward Custer City, leading his prize behind him. He hurried along until he had passed the place where the first shooting happened. He didn't find his hound's carcass, but he knew it was the spot. When he left the high ground and started across the wide prairies he slowed a bit and rolled himself a smoke. He never felt better about things. Once he got this murderer back and word got around that Seth Dalby had beat him in a fair gunfight, the sheriff job was in the bag. He drew the smoke in deeply and puffed it high over his head. He would miss Claudia Morton, of course, but when he was the famous Sheriff of Custer County he could pick most any woman he wanted.

He looked back at the kid tied in the saddle. His head bobbled and jerked side-to-side as the mount stepped along. He had freckles on his clean-shaven face. His eyes were open, and this gave Seth's heart a little jump. When he had put the kid across the saddle, his eyes had been closed. He wished he'd close 'em and look dead like he ought to. Made a feller feel plumb uneasy.

He had ridden ten or twelve miles when a canvas-covered wagon drawn by a team of horses appeared on the prairie to his left, and he headed over that way. He was curious about who it was, and, anyway, he sort of wanted to show off his prize. When they came abreast he stopped and held up a hand that said "howdy" to the driver, a man in his fifties, and his woman beside him. The man smiled.

"Howdy, Marshal," he called.

"Howdy, there," Seth said. "Only I ain't a Marshal, I'm a

sheriff's deputy from Custer. Name's Seth Dalby. Where you folks headed?"

"Got some relations in Pine Valley," said the man. "We're takin' our time travelin' up there, though. We're spendin' a little time tryin' our luck pannin' gold along this stream here. My name's Alex Hemming, and this here's m'wife, Olga. Is that a dead man on that black horse there?"

"Yup. He's a cold blooded killer. Leastwise he was 'til he got the idea he could kill me. He drew on me before I knew what was happenin' and winged me twice before I could reach for my gun. I got 'im, though, right through the middle!"

"My heavens, Deputy!" said the lady. "Have you had medical attention for your wounds?"

"No, not yet," Seth declared, looking as stoic as he could. "But I'll be all right 'til I get to Custer. They ain't too serious."

"All the same, you ought to have them looked into."

"Reckon I will, Ma'am. Right now I better be headin' on. It's a few more days' ride and this outlaw can't get nothin' but riper."

"Well, all right, Deputy," Alex Hemming said. "I wish yuh a good trip."

"When yuh git t'Pine Valley," Seth said, "tell that bartender in the saloon I got my man."

"We'll do that. Good-bye."

Seth waved and was on his way again. He sat up real straight, his chest out, his Stetson straight on his head. He felt the presence of the silver star on his shirt. He was Deputy Sheriff Seth Dalby, a man of the badge, and he had rid the world of a vicious, dangerous killer. He would be a mighty important hombre in Custer County, Dakota Territory, when he got back, by God!

Chapter Seventeen

Casey located the damaged fence uphill a half mile and just over the rise. Billy had told him of propping up the fence along that stretch as a makeshift measure. He saw that it was still holding, but not well. If it gave out, the stock could slip out and the Asters wouldn't know because the place was out of sight of the house. He dug fresh holes, put the posts in and tamped the dirt all around. He hammered boards to the new posts, and when he stepped back and admired his handiwork, he was proud of himself. Maybe someday he would have a farm of his own, and maybe even a pretty wife like...well, maybe someone like Hope Aster. He thought of his plight then, and clenched his jaw hard. A hundred times a day, it seemed, he was somehow reminded that he was a murderer, that the law was seeking him, and that an unscrupulous man with a badge wanted him dead. But a man had to keep hoping, and that's what Casey vowed to do.

On the way back he saw that Mrs. Aster and Hope had spent the morning scrubbing clothes. The lines alongside the house were filled with shirts and dresses and stockings and long john underwear and Levis and bedding, billowing and fluttering in the breeze. All these things they had done in a round metal tub, same as he had seen his mom do so many times, boiling the heavily soiled clothes on the stove top and fishing them out, scalding and steaming, with a wooden stick and rubbing them vigorously together. He knew it was a sizable chore for them because he, himself, had on occasions helped Ma with the washing.

He dared stop a moment and watch Hope pinning things to the line. How graceful her slim, white arms as they reached upward, and how round her hips as the breezes tugged at her frock. She was a delicate flower reaching for the sun.

When he put away the equipment and unhitched the team, he saw that Ebon was no longer in the stall where he had left him, but Billy's pony was there instead. When he arrived at the house, Mrs. Aster was in the kitchen.

"Hello, Casey," she said. "I'll fix you something light, is that all right?"

"Gosh, yes. Thank you."

She pulled dishes from the kitchen cupboard. "Billy took your horse to go look for livestock. He hoped you wouldn't mind. He got up the canyon a couple of miles this morning and his pony went lame so he came back."

"He *did* take my horse, then?" Casey hated the dark feeling that crept up his spine.

She paused and looked at him. "I told him he should go up where you were fixing fence and ask you, but he said you wouldn't mind. Will you be needing him today? Billy didn't think—"

"Oh, no, no, I won't need him. It's all right that he took him."

He moved to the small wash room off the kitchen and splashed the fence dirt from his face. He couldn't figure why the cold malaise gripped him. After all, it was an awful big country out there. Seemed he worried too much sometimes, when there really wasn't anything to worry about.

That evening after supper Casey and Thief wandered out and down the slope to the edge of the timber. He squinted in among the tall, straight pines. Billy ought to be riding in on Ebon any time now, driving the Aster livestock to the home pasture. He would be glad to see the fence was fixed. Casey found a wagon-sized boulder and climbed up. It was high enough for him to hang his legs over and swing them like when he was a little boy. It was an hour yet to sundown, and the evening breeze was comforting.

"Casey!"

He turned. Hope was skipping down the slope, holding her long skirt above her ankles. She was smiling, and his heart skipped a beat or two.

"What are you doing?" she asked.

"Oh, nothin'. Just kind of enjoyin' the evening."
"Can I join you?"
"Sure. Pull up a rock and sit down."

She found a flat spot near him and climbed up. "This is a fine rock," she said. "It reminds me of the one Billy and I played on when we were children back in Indiana."

"I can see where you'd have had fun on a rock like this."

The breeze tousled her hair and she brushed it back from her face. "We surely did. Some of the neighbor children came over and we played cowboys-and-Indians. The boys chosen to be Indians galloped around the rock shouting "bang! bang!" at the cowboys hiding behind the rock." She laughed and tossed her head. "I always had to be an Indian. Isn't that silly?"

"No, not silly at all. You were an Indian Princess, I'll bet."

She laughed. "I pretended that's what I was, but the boys insisted on calling me a squaw. Billy loved to tease me."

They laughed together, but Casey's laugh ended sooner than he had wanted, and the sudden sobering hinted of his malaise. Her smile faded, and she said, "What's wrong, Casey? You seemed troubled."

"I'm a little worried about Billy, I guess. It'll be sundown soon and he's not back yet."

"Oh, is that all it is? Poosh! Don't worry about Billy. He often sleeps out when sundown finds him far from home. He'll be along, if not tonight, then in the morning."

They strolled back to the house, and Casey left many important things unsaid. But as the sun dropped behind the mountains, a silent specter crept into his consciousness time and again — a vile lawman and his powerful rifle.

He spent a restless night on the floor mattress where he had been sleeping since he recovered from the wound. He tried not to think about the fact that he and Billy looked so much alike, that Billy wore a black hat too, and that Billy was riding Casey's black gelding with the Crooked T brand right on it, and that somewhere out there in the Black Hills rode a vicious man with a compulsion to kill such a person. He awoke several times in a sweat, and by morning a knot occupied his stomach and his hands shook.

He got up at daybreak and dressed. He strapped on Dad's six-gun and went out and stood in the yard. A moment later Hope, a blanket thrown over her nightgown, joined him there. The sun was an orange ball, just peeking over the eastern hills.

"Casey! What are you doing?"

He shrugged. "Oh, God, Hope! I don't know what I'm doing. I want to go looking for Billy, but I don't have a horse."

She stood close and looked up at him. "I don't understand. Why are you so worried? I told you Billy often—"

"I know! I know! But you don't understand, Hope. You don't know how things really are!" He hadn't meant to say that, but it blurted out. And the next thing he knew he was telling her about The Deputy and about his mother being near death, and his killing of Hermund Grim, and his flight that ended when he was shot. He looked into her eyes and took her hand.

"I'm scared crazy, Hope. I always think that deputy is out there somewhere, and Billy and I are about the same size and he's ridin' my black horse, and I don't think that man would know Billy from me. Lord, Hope! I can't hardly stand it."

A mask of concern and pain covered her face. "Oh, my God, Casey, I had no idea what trouble you were in. I'm so sorry. You poor man! What are you going to do?"

"I don't know. If I had a horse, I'd go looking for Billy."

"You're more worried about Billy than about your own problems. You shouldn't be. I'm sure the Deputy has left this area by now, wouldn't you think? And it's a big country. I doubt whether their paths would cross."

He lowered his head and closed his eyes. "I suppose you're right. But I can't help worryin'."

"Don't fret about it, Casey. Come back in the house and we'll have breakfast."

When they returned, Mrs. Aster was in the kitchen.

"Good morning, Mom," Hope said.

"What in the world are you doing out in your nightie, Hope?"

"I...I noticed Casey outside and went out to see what was wrong."

Mrs. Aster dippered water into the coffee pot. She turned to Casey. "Well, is anything wrong, Casey?" She stood holding the pot, waiting.

"Yes, Mrs. Aster, I'm afraid there is."

Hope put her hand on his forearm. "Casey...don't..."

"I have to tell your mother, Hope, and let her do or say what she will. I can't hide this from her. She's got a right to know. I had no right to hide it." He felt tears in his eyes.

"All right," Hope whispered. "Tell her what you told me."

He blurted out the whole horrible story, as he had for Hope earlier. "And now," he told her, "that deputy is hell bent on killing me without even givin' me a chance to surrender. I've carried the fear with me that he might still be in this area. And he doesn't know exactly what I look like, except my black horse and maybe what clothes I wear. And now, with Billy gone looking for the livestock, ridin' my black horse, and wearin' his black hat, that insane deputy might mistake him for me."

Mrs. Aster gasped. "Oh, my Lord!" Her face turned ashen, and her eyes filled with terror. "And Billy didn't come home last night. Oh! Oh, my Lord!"

"I don't think we should become alarmed, Mother," Hope said. "It's a big country out there, and Billy probably wouldn't ever just happen across that deputy. I'm sure he's still hunting the stock. Let's not worry ourselves sick."

Mrs. Aster stared at her, open mouthed. "My God!" she said, and the tears came.

Casey strode to the window in frustration. He smashed his fist into his hand. "If I only had a horse," he said. "I'd go lookin'."

"What if you came across the deputy?" Hope asked. "Then you'd get shot, wouldn't you?"

"I'd take that chance to find Billy."

"There are horses in the pasture!" Mrs. Aster cried, almost shouting. "There's your pony, Hope, and that little pinto, too."

"Where?" Casey said. "What pasture?"

Mrs. Aster pointed. "Down near the lake. Just north of the lake.

They usually hang around there because the grass is good."

"I'll show you," Hope said. "But please, let's eat breakfast." She took the coffee pot from her mother and put in the grounds and set it on the cook stove. In a few minutes she had flapjacks and eggs ready. Mrs. Aster went into the bedroom, and her sobs came back through the thin walls. Casey sat down and picked at his plate.

"Come on, Casey," Hope said. "Please eat. You'll need the strength to hunt Billy."

"I shouldn't have told your mother."

"No, you probably shouldn't have until we knew something for certain. But it's done now. I wish Daddy was home. He could help us look for Billy."

Hope put on a pair of Billy's Levi trousers and rolled up the bottoms. They hiked quickly to the north pasture, found both ponies, and led them back to the barn.

"You take my horse, Casey," she said. "I'll take the pinto."

"I don't want you to go, Hope. Just in case."

She gave him a stern look. "Sorry, Casey. I'm going. I know the country good, and I know where to look."

He reckoned that one thing he had learned in his young life was when not to argue with a woman, and this was one of those times. He threw Billy's saddle up on Hope's piebald mare and cinched it. "Sure wish I had my Sharps," he muttered.

"Billy's got a Winchester. Want that?"

"Scabbard, too?"

"Yes. I'll get them." She ran for the house.

Casey slipped the bridle on and slapped the horse on the neck. "Looks like we're partners awhile, Madam Pie," he said. "I hope you can move good."

Hope returned quickly with the Winchester. Casey buckled the scabbard on under the left stirrup fender and drove in the rifle.

"What about cartridges for the carbine?" he asked Hope, who was cinching her own saddle on the pinto.

"Right there," she pointed. "That's Billy's saddlepockets on the hook. He keeps a couple boxes of shells in them."

Casey tied on the saddlebags. He found two boxes of Winchester cartridges inside.

"I need a bedroll," he said. "Maybe Thief will pick up a trail. I want to be ready to travel if he does."

"All right. What shall I get?"

"Couple old blankets. Maybe some your mom don't care about."

She raced back to the house and returned with a bedroll. He tied it on behind the saddle.

"Mom is fixing some food for us to take," she said. "Some biscuits and jerky and salt pork and stuff that'll keep awhile."

"Bless her."

"I have binoculars, too."

They led their ponies out through the barn door to the front yard. Hope wore a brown cowboy hat with a string under her chin. Thief tagged along and waited patiently beside his master's horse. Mrs. Aster came out and stuffed wrapped bundles into the piebald's saddlebags. Her eyes were red and her cheeks puffy.

"Thank you for the food, Mrs. Aster," Casey said softly.

She looked at him and her face wrinkled and she wept. She threw her arms around him and hugged him and sobbed. "Casey, please be careful. Please, please. You're like my Billy. You're my son, too. I don't want to lose you."

"I'll be careful," he said. "I promise."

She backed away, dabbing with a handkerchief.

They mounted and moved toward the timber. Hope looked back. "Don't cry, Mom. I'm sure we're worrying for nothing."

They rode to the north first and checked the hollows and draws and hillsides where Hope remembered the stock having wandered previously. They moved south over the mountains in the afternoon and searched the plains with binoculars. They found some of their cattle on the southern plains, but no sign of Billy. Thief followed several trails, but each time they faded out or led to some of the stock.

"We have to keep an eye on the sun," Hope said, nudging her pinto alongside Casey. "I don't want to be out here in the dark."

"Okay. But this is mighty rugged country. We could have missed him easily."

She shaded her eyes from the sun and scanned the hillsides. "We could have, but I doubt it. Let's try up on those slopes."

"Okay. But look at Thief. He's on to something."

The big dog buried his nose in the sage and moved slowly uphill, sniffing loudly. They nudged their mounts along behind him to the top of the rise, and just beyond that they found a ragged brown mule yanking up tufts of grass and chewing.

"Good Lord Almighty!" Casey exclaimed.

"Goodness!" Hope said. "It's a mule!"

Casey pulled Pie to a halt and sat frozen in the saddle, his eyes wide and his chin dropped. "I...I can't believe it—"

"What, Casey? What's the matter?"

He looked at Hope, then back at the mule. He blinked his eyes rapidly. "That ain't just any old mule, Hope. That's *my* mule!"

"Really? It is?"

"Yeah. It's old Bacon. I'd know him anywhere. And, see that brand? That's our Crooked T."

"How do you suppose he got way up here?" she said.

Casey slipped off his hat and wiped his brow. "I'll bet that half-witted Deputy brought him."

"Would your mom have let him take him?"

"I don't think Mom is at the ranch. She was beat pretty bad. The Deputy probably just took him. I wonder how Bacon got away from him, and where he was at when he did, if that's what happened."

"Can Thief follow a trail backward?"

"Don't see why not."

Casey dismounted and fashioned a halter from his lariat and slipped it over Bacon's head. "Come on, you old rascal," he told the mule, "you got some explainin' to do." He gave Hope the lariat. "Hold on to him 'til I can get Thief started right."

He whistled. "Thief, come!" He took the dog to the trampled grass and pushed his nose into it. "Okay, boy. Show us the way."

Thief smelled the tracks, turned about, and sniffed his way back to the mule where Hope was holding him. Bacon backed off a few steps and bared his teeth at the dog.

"No, Thief, No!" shouted Casey. "The other way, dammit!"

He gripped Thief around the neck and pulled him back to the trampled area. He moved him along the bent grass trail a few feet and let loose.

"Go, boy, Go!"

It worked. The dog sniffed his way back over the rise and down the slope.

"Looks good." Casey said, swinging into the saddle. "Can you handle Bacon all right?"

"Sure, I think so."

They spurred their ponies over the rise, and Bacon trotted along behind Hope's Pinto.

"He must have his belly full," Casey said, "else he wouldn't come along so easy."

Near the base of the slope the trail turned suddenly to the left and wound down into the canyon. They rode alongside a small brook, and there in the soft earth they found hoof marks. Casey dropped to the ground and studied them.

"Look, Hope. This here's a bull's track goin' up that way, and these right with 'em are tracks of a shod horse. Might be Ebon's."

She alighted and stood beside him. "Could be, all right. Maybe Billy is driving our lost bull."

They rode up the canyon another mile to a larger creek which bubbled down a canyon to the southwest. Above the fork they came to the place where Casey had been ambushed. A half mile above that they found an open meadow, and in the meadow grazed the Aster's missing bull. "I wonder if that's the bull that made them tracks we saw," Casey said.

"I don't know," Hope said, squinting. "If it is, then where is Billy?"

Suddenly Thief howled. It was the most mournful sound Casey had ever heard. He turned and saw the dog sniffing a large black stain in the grass.

"What's the matter with him?" Hope asked.

"I don't know. He's found something."

Casey swung to the ground and kneeled next to Thief. He looked up at Hope, still in the saddle. "It's blood," he told her.

She slapped her fingers to her mouth. "Oh, my God, Casey! No!"

"And look over here. Tracks of a shod horse. They look the same as them we just saw."

He stood and moved a few steps south. "Here's tracks of another horse. There's two sets of tracks here. And here's a boot track, right here in the dirt. And it ain't Billy's."

Hope sat in the saddle, her eyes riveted on Casey. "Maybe it's that...that—"

"That damn deputy!" said Casey. "I hate to say it. I hate to even think it, but I'm afraid it might be The Deputy. And all this blood, Hope. I'm afraid..."

"Oh, my God!"

Thief moved down a few yards and sniffed the tracks of the horses, both going southward into the canyon on the right. He put his nose to a flat stone, and Casey saw that there was blood on it.

They led their ponies down the canyon a hundred feet. Here the ground was softer and barren of grass, and the tracks were plain. So were the blood spatters that appeared alongside the hoof tracks every few feet.

"Thief, come!" called Casey.

The dog turned and trotted back.

"What is it?" Hope asked.

"There's spots of blood every little ways alongside them horse tracks." He frowned deeply. "Like as if something on one of the horses was dripping blood. And that big patch back there. It's a lot of blood, maybe a day old. This ain't good, Hope. It ain't good."

"Oh, God, Casey! What shall we do?"

He sat quietly, thinking. Finally he turned to her and spoke with a tremor in his voice. "I'm goin' to take up this trail. Maybe I can catch up to him, if that's what it is. Can I take this piebald of yours to Custer City?"

"Yes, of course."

"All right, then, I'm on my way. I've got to hurry. He's probably got a whole day's lead on me."

She moved close to him and tugged at his sleeve. She was trembling. "Please, Casey," she said. "Please don't go after him. He's sly and vicious, and probably older and more experienced than you. He might ambush you again."

"I have to go. Ain't got no choice that I can see. If I can catch that Deputy I'll put a bullet in him — just like he tried to do me."

"Please, no. Don't go." Tears came to her eyes and she gripped his hand. "It's too dangerous, can't you understand that? If you catch up with him, he'll kill you this time. We can go to the local Sheriff instead and tell him everything."

"But I have to go after him! I owe it to Billy. If it hadn't been for me he wouldn't have been out there on my horse."

She stood, head down, clutching his hand. "Don't blame yourself. We're just guessing at what happened, anyway. He could have shot a deer and put it on the horse."

"Maybe so. But I must find out. Go home, Hope. Tell your mother I'll get word to her as soon as I know anything."

"All right." Her eyes held to his for a long moment. "I can see you're determined. And I know how you must feel. I'll be praying for you every moment. Write to me as soon as you learn anything."

"All right. How shall I address the letter?"

"Just Hope Aster, Pine Valley. Daddy picks up the mail in town."

He mounted up and rode a few feet then turned in the saddle. "Hope, could you take old Bacon up to that good pasture? Maybe he'll stick around and I can get him later. He's ornery as can be, but I love him anyway."

She smiled through her tears. "Yes. I'll take both him and our bull to the home pasture."

He whistled for Thief and trotted the horse down the canyon. Thief took up the scent trail and hurried along ahead. Casey turned once. She was still standing, watching him go. She raised her hand and waved. He wished very much that he could go back and tell her how he felt about her.

Thief held steadily to the trail for several miles. They crossed a flat, treeless plain, and just as they headed into the timber again, a faint cloud of rising campfire smoke caught Casey's attention a quarter mile ahead on his left.

The Deputy? Most likely not, he thought. He would have been farther along by now. No sense taking chances, though. He spurred the piebald up the slope and came around to the left so that he was above the source of smoke. He dismounted and led the horse down a hundred yards and moved about until he could see between the trees. A covered wagon stood along the creek. A man about fifty and a woman knelt beside a campfire. He looked about sharply, but saw no one else. He led the pony down, and when he neared them, the man looked up.

"Well, hello there!" he called.

"Howdy," Casey answered with a wave. "Where you folks headed?"

The man stood up and met Casey with a handshake. "Well, we're headed toward Pine Valley, but right now we're takin' us a little vacation and pannin' a little gold while we're restin' up. I'm Alex Hemming. This is m'wife, Olga. Join us for some supper?"

Casey tipped his hat to the lady. "No, thank you. Got to be hurrying along. Tryin' to catch up with somebody."

The man bent down and took his tin coffee cup off the rock. "That so?" he said, sipping. "Better have a shot of this here Arbuckle's Coffee, young feller. It's awful good fer growin' hair on yer chest if yuh ain't got none yet. Ha! Ha! Ha! Ma, get a cup outa the wagon for our friend."

"No, thank you just the same," Casey said. "Got to get travelin'."

"Wouldn't be a lawman yer tryin' to catch up to, would it?"

Casey's heart jumped. "A lawman?"

"Well, yeah, reckon we ran across one headin' south about ten miles down the line. He'd just caught up with a wanted killer and was takin' him back to Custer City."

Casey swallowed hard. "How long ago was that?"

The man looked at his wife. "That was yesterday, long about evening as I recollect, wasn't it, Olga?"

"Yes. Last evening."

"Was the prisoner—?"

"He wasn't no prisoner," the man said. "He was deader'n a doornail, stretched across the saddle and tied down to a big black horse."

"Jesus Christ, forgive me," whispered Casey. "God, forgive me."

The man cupped his hand behind his ear. "What's that?"

"Oh...Nothin'. Nothin'. What did the deputy look like?"

The man stood silent a moment, studying Casey. "Well, young feller, I don't rightly know if I ought to tell yuh. I don't know who yuh are, and maybe that lawman wouldn't want me blabbin' all about him."

Casey stared hard at the man. "I got to catch him, Sir. It's real important."

"What's yer name, young feller?"

"Casey Parkin. I got some information for that Deputy that shows he's killed the wrong man. I reckon he'd like to know about it."

"Humph!" Alex Hemming said. "I should think he would. Well, lets see, he's a slim feller, pretty tall, I'd say about in his early forties, dark hair, big mustache. You remember his name, Mom?"

She thought a moment. "It was Deputy Seth something. Drabble, or Dabble."

"Dalby!" said her husband. "Seth Dalby. He was ridin' a sorrel mare and leadin' the big black with the dead feller on." The man looked at Thief. "Nice lookin' dog there, feller."

Casey swung into the saddle. "Thank you, Mr. Hemming, for the information. Good-bye."

The piebald whirled and galloped back across the stretch of prairie with Thief close behind and the sun just dipping in the west. When they intersected their previous trail, Casey turned the horse south and the dog picked up the scent again.

He rode late into the moonlit night. The fires of Hell burned in his soul and tormented him almost to the brink of insanity. Sleep was out of the question; there would be none for him. His worst fears about his friend, Billy Aster, had been confirmed.

He no longer cared what happened to himself. One desire, and only one, lived in his brain, and all his thoughts and efforts were focused on that desire. He would catch up with Deputy Seth Dalby and kill him. Nothing less would do.

Chapter Eighteen

Seth Dalby rode into Custer City after four days' hard riding. He felt the town's eyes on him as the horses carried him and his prize down the pine-tree-lined street to the Sheriff's Office. He had waited long for this feeling, and he found it difficult to keep looking like a tough, serious man of the badge, when he wanted so bad to bust right out in a grin.

He dismounted at the hitching rail in front of the office. He climbed down and stood a moment on stiff legs, looking up and down the street. Wouldn't want anyone to see him misstep or falter. Even a little thing like that could cost him a vote come election day. He slipped the reins around the rail and sauntered into the office. Sheriff Brand looked up from his desk as Seth entered.

"Howdy, Sheriff," Seth said with a nod. "Good t'see yuh again."

The sheriff glared at him, frowned, and twitched his bushy grey mustache. "Where in the name o' hell you been these past weeks, Dalby?"

Seth pushed out his right cheek with his tongue and raised his eyebrows. "Well, reckon I been out chasin' a killer. Damn near got killed doin' it, but I got 'im!"

"Got who?"

"The kid that murdered his daddy. The Parkin kid."

"Yeah?" The Sheriff's frown deepened. "Where is he?"

"Right outside, tied on his horse. He ambushed me, and I had to kill 'im."

Sheriff Brand jumped up, and his chair crashed the wall behind him. "Yuh killed the Parkin kid?"

"Yup!"

Brand took long strides to the door and flung it open. "Good God and green apples!" he shouted, staring out. "Yuh killed him and brung him into Custer draped over his horse fer all t'see?"

"Uh...well...well, shit, Sheriff, I didn't have nothin' to cover 'im with."

Brand swung around and faced Dalby. "Why in the name of God didn't yuh take time to go to Judge Farnsworth and get a warrant before y'went after him?"

Seth felt hurt. This wasn't how the Sheriff was supposed to act at all. He was acting like there was something wrong with a deputy carrying out his duties and tracking down a killer. He ought to be happy about it.

"Gettin' a warrant woulda took too long," he said. "I wouldn't have caught him most likely." He could see the Sheriff was fuming mad and getting madder.

"Well, that would've been just fine, you imbecile," Brand rasped. "'Cause there ain't no want on the kid, and there never was no want."

Seth felt his intestines shrink up. "No want? How the hell could that be? He cut down his daddy in cold blood in the barn."

"That wasn't his daddy!" Brand roared. "That was his step daddy and he was an outlaw and a murderer himself. The County Attorney looked into him and found out he was wanted fer killin' his last wife in Saint Louie."

Seth stood with his mouth open. How in hell had they found that out? he wondered.

"The County Attorney and the Judge got together and went over the facts," Brand said. "They decided the Parkin kid should have a medal fer killin' the bastard. The Judge refused to issue a warrant."

Seth tried to find his voice, but for a moment it wasn't there. Brand's face was crimson.

"An' here you go out and bring the boy back draped over his saddle fer the whole county t'see. Yuh goddam ignorant imbecile."

Seth took a deep breath. Shivers were crawling in his spine and the room seemed to waver. "But...but...I had to kill 'im, Sheriff. He was tryin' to kill me. Look here, my shoulder here where he put a bullet through from his six shooter. An' another one here, on my left side here, where his bullet clipped me. It was a justified killin', Sheriff. Couldn't avoid it."

Sammy Bents, the office boy, came in the front door. He was a quiet kid in his teens, wearing a slouchy brown hat. He walked around Seth and opened the access door to the jail cells and went in. Seth glanced through the door. A prisoner stood inside the cell looking out, and in that moment his eyes met Seth's. He nodded recognition and raised his eyebrows. Seth felt another shock to his colon. It was Barty Hardwise, the man who had helped Seth and Hermund Grim steal the Parkin horses. Barty knew many things about Seth besides it being Seth who gunned down James Parkin by his front gate that day. Seth wondered if Barty would tell the Sheriff anything.

The kid came back out, closed the door, and took a chair near the gun rack.

"Sammy," the Sheriff said. "Don't go nowhere; I got a chore fer yuh. Jist set tight a minute."

"All right."

Sheriff Brand strode up and faced Seth. "Let's see that gunshot wound on yer shoulder."

Seth slipped off his vest and peeled back his shirt. Brand studied the injury.

"When did this shootout betwixt you and the Parkin boy take place, Dalby?"

"Uh...three, four days ago, I reckon. Why?"

Brand pointed to Seth's ribs. "Lets look at the other one."

"Don't worry about it none, Sheriff," Seth said. "I'll have the Doc look at it."

"Open yer shirt, Dalby, goddammit!" The Sheriff stuck his thumb in his chest. "I'm the one lookin' at it right now!"

Seth fumbled the buttons loose. The Sheriff pulled open the shirt and peeled it back. He studied the wound a moment. He rubbed his thumb and forefinger on the shirt fabric around the bullet hole, as if feeling the texture.

"What's this black gritty stuff all around the bullet hole, Dalby? Whole lot more on the inside than the outside."

Seth looked down at it. "Shit, I don't know what it is. Jist plain old dirt, I guess."

"It sure looks like black powder," Brand mused. "Like somebody stuck the muzzle up against yer shirt and fired. Only this is on the inside."

Seth felt the shakes creeping over him. "Ain't got no idea howsomever, Sheriff," he said. "Jist dirt, I reckon."

"And this here's a gunshot?" the Sheriff asked. He poked the side wound with his finger. "Four days ago?"

"Yup."

Brand stepped back a couple of steps and stood looking at Seth. He shook his head. Seth felt some anger mix with the anxiety. Damn Sheriff had no call to treat him like this. He snatched his vest and put it back on.

"What weapon did yuh shoot the Parkin kid with?"

"M'Colt Peacemaker. All I had time to do was draw and shoot. He jumped out from a rock dead ahead of me and started blazin' away. Didn't leave me no choice."

"How fer away was he?"

"Not much more'n across this here room."

Brand turned to the kid. "Sammy, did yuh see that black horse out there with the dead man in the saddle?"

"Yes, Sir."

"Well, you go take that horse and that man down to Doc. Wagner's office. Tell him the man is Casey Parkin, son of James Parkin. Tell him to start his autopsy soon as he can. I'll be down and fill him in when I'm finished here."

"Yes, Sir. What shall I do with the horse?"

"The Livery. Tell 'em to take good care of him."

The kid hurried out. Seth glanced through the window and saw that several townfolks had gathered around to look at the body.

"I'll take yer star, Seth," the Sheriff said. "Come back tomorra an' pick up yer wages." He held out his hand.

"What the hell fer? Yuh ain't got no call to fire me, Brand. I was just doin' my duty like any deputy would. I was actin' on a duly declared complaint from an upstandin' member of this here county that the kid killed his daddy — er, step daddy — and I went out and looked over the barn where the murder happened."

"I'm firin' yuh because I ain't toleratin' no liar."

"Liar?"

"Yuh say the kid shot you four days ago. Both of them wounds are weeks old. The shoulder one is almost done healed up. They couldn't have happened four days ago. And they sure don't look like no bullet wounds to me. They both look like a horse bite or some such. The star, Dalby, the star!"

"Now, just a minute, Brand," Seth said, pointing at the Sheriff. "You need a deputy. I can be a lot of help around here. Who yuh got to pin that star on, if not me?"

Brand shook his head. "Fella like you is hard to figure," he declared. "There's lots better than you." He thrust his finger toward the window. "Even that dead kid on the horse out there is better than you. I could pin yer star on him and not be no worse off."

Seth glared at the Sheriff. He ripped the badge off his vest and flung it onto the desk. "I'm a-goin', Brand," he rasped. "But yuh ain't seen the last of me, by God! I'm gonna run fer Sheriff, and I'll beat you come election time."

"You do that. But fer now, git out a my sight!"

Seth stormed outside, swung into the saddle and rode down the street to Alfie's Gold Mine Saloon. He tried to compose himself on the way down. He wanted to assure those he met that he was sheriff material. He tied the sorrel to the hitching rail and entered. No one was there except Alfie himself. Seth sauntered up to the bar.

"Howdy, Alfie," he called. "How's business?"

The barkeep grinned. "Well, reckon it's been gooder, Deputy. How's the sheriffin' business?"

"Couldn't be gooder. I'm thinkin' of puttin' my good name on the slate fer sheriff of this county come November. Can I count on yer vote?"

Alfie wiped a spot on the bar in front of Seth and set out a glass. "Might be. Don't rightly know yet, Seth. Ain't had time to give it no thought. You want whiskey?"

"Yeah. The usual stuff." He plunked down a coin. "Just leave the bottle."

Seth stood at the bar and emptied his glass. The hot liquid slapped at his innards, and he refilled and emptied the glass time and again, then moved to a table and sat. He went over in his mind several times the events of the day, and each time and each drink he got a little madder. All the fuss and trouble he went to to bring in a murderer and what thanks did he get? He got fired, that's what. How in hell was he supposed to know the kid had been forgave for killin' his daddy? Anybody else in Seth's boots would have done the same thing as Seth did.

He thought about Barty Hardwise, sitting in the jail. What did they have on Barty? Had Barty told the Sheriff anything about the horse stealing and killing of James Parkin? It was a most uncomfortable position to be in, and maybe he would be better off if he just rode back up to Claudia Morton's place and lived out his life in luxury. He tipped up his glass. The whiskey wasn't giving him quite the slap it did at the first drink.

He had his heart set on being sheriff, but he allowed that sometimes a fellow just couldn't have everything he wanted. He could do a lot worse than living with Claudia. He rolled a smoke and set fire to it.

He would sure like to get even with Brand for the way he treated him. That remark about pinning his star on the dead kid cut him to the core. It bit deep into his dignity, implying that he wasn't any more useful than a dead kid. Damn that Sheriff!

He puffed and watched the smoke drift to the dirty ceiling. He had finished most of his bottle, and all it had done was intensify his anger. He was just considering how he would like to put a bullet in that damn Sheriff when that very person walked into the front door of Alfie's Gold Mine Saloon. Seth turned and stared as the old man strode to his table and stopped, looking down at him.

"Seth Dalby," the Sheriff said. "Got somethin' to discuss with yuh. Are you sober?"

"'Course I am, goddam you!"

"We kin jist talk quiet like, Dalby. Ain't no need fer the whole town to know."

Dalby narrowed his eyes to slits and stared hatred at the older man. "If yuh got somethin' t'say, Brand, then say it. I ain't yer goddam deputy no more, y'know."

The Sheriff glanced over at Alfie, then looked down at Seth.

"It's about the gun you shot the kid with. You said it was yer Peacemaker?"

"That's what I said." Seth drew deeply on his cigarette.

"And yuh was on level ground with the kid?"

Seth shot Brand a quizzical look. "Yeah, that's right. What's that got to do with it."

"Doc Wagner says the boy was shot with a six or seven hundred grain bullet, like from a Sharps rifle."

"I don't know nothin' about that. I used m'Peacemaker. He was shootin' at me."

"Doc says the kid was shot from up above. High above. The bullet went into his chest and lodged in his lower spine."

Seth took a deep draw on his smoke and stood up. He dropped the butt and ground it under his sole. "Well," he said, "what is it yer tryin' t'say, Sheriff?"

"I'm sayin' that you lied about the whole thing, Dalby. I'm sayin' you ambushed that kid and shot him without givin' him no chance to surrender. I'm sayin' that's murder. I'm sayin' yer under arrest, Dalby, fer murder."

The words struck Seth's brain like a hammer. His anger rose to a high, red pitch as he stood facing this hateful old man that called himself Sheriff.

"Yer under arrest fer murder," Brand said. "An' it just happens that kid you shot down in cold blood wasn't even—"

Seth Dalby's Colt Peacemaker cleared leather in a flash. Sheriff Brand reached for his, but much too late. Seth's gun roared and the bullet caught Brand in the chest, sending him reeling back into the wall. He slid down onto the floor, his eyes surprised, his mouth gasping.

Seth looked back. Alfie was reaching under the bar, and Seth knew he kept a shotgun there. He whirled and raced out the door just as the shotgun blast ripped out the wall behind him. He swung up onto the sorrel and spurred to a gallop through town to the west. He heard the shotgun roar again, but it didn't touch him. His heart was racing and his eyes teared as he galloped into the pine covered hills. He didn't know how soon they might get a posse together, but he was going to get as far away as he could in the next hour, if he had to run the sorrel to death.

Chapter Nineteen

Casey, with the piebald horse and the dog that looked part wolf, topped the last ridge and gazed down into the valley at the lamplighted windows of Custer City. The moon was almost full and buildings not in shadow stood out brightly. He cursed the fact that he hadn't been able to catch up to the crazy deputy and kill him. Now he didn't know what to do. He dismounted and sat with his back to a tree for some time, listening to the crickets and trying to make sense out of everything. He'd be in deep trouble if he rode into Custer. The word was probably out about how he had killed Hermund Grim, and everybody would be watching for him, and if they saw him they would go get the Sheriff. He wanted desperately to find out whether his mother was still alive, so he arose and climbed back into the saddle.

It was late evening when he topped the rise and rode down the long hill. MacDoughall's windmill stood like a sentinel in the moonlight, its reflection distorted and eerie on the surface of the dike water, like a bad omen. Would he find Ma alive, or had she been taken away by Egor Baklanov in his shiny-black hearse?

He pulled up at the corral and sat gazing at the glow in the front window of MacDoughall's house. For a moment he thought about turning back. Maybe it would be better to ride away without ever knowing.

But he moved forward. He knew he could not bear it long without finding out. He tied Pie to the porch rail and rapped lightly. The door opened a crack and Birk MacDoughall peered out, squinting to see in the darkness.

"Hello, Mr. MacDoughall. It's me, Casey."

"Casey!"

"Yes, Sir. Is my Mom still here?"

"My God!" MacDoughall said. He flung open the door. "It's Casey." He turned and shouted, "Annabel! It's Casey!"

He heard his mother shriek and then she was at the door, hugging him. "Oh, thank God," she cried. "Thank God for bringing my boy home! Casey! Oh, Casey! It really is you, isn't it?" She was sobbing and holding him tightly.

"Yes, Mom," he said, trying not to weep. "I decided to come home. I had to find out how you were."

He pushed back and looked at her. Tears cascaded down her cheeks, but she was smiling and she looked wonderful.

"I'm so thankful you are all right," she cried. "It's been a nightmare here since...but come in, Son. Are you hungry?"

"A little. Can my dog come in too?"

"Of course," Birk MacDoughall said. The dog trotted through the door and sat down near his master.

"This is Thief," he told them. "We joined up along the trail."

"Uh-huh," his mother said, wiping her eyes. "I'm so glad you're back. Where have you been?"

"Running, Mom. I killed your husband. I'm sorry."

MacDoughall gripped Casey's arm and pulled him to the table. "Sit down, Case, sit down. Ain't nobody lookin' for you."

"They're not?" He pulled out a chair and settled in. "Lord, Birk, I figured I was as good as dead."

"Grim had it coming," Birk said. "Sheriff found out he killed his last wife."

"He did? And the Sheriff ain't huntin' for me?"

Birk stood looking down at him, half smiling, his hands out in gesture. "Only to tell you you're not wanted and to come home."

"I can't believe it!"

Birk moved a chair over from the wall and sat opposite him.

"It's true. Matter of fact, Sheriff Brand considers you a hero of sorts. Ain't no tellin' how many lives you saved by killin' that Grim feller. The County Attorney said he couldn't prove it wasn't self defense. Seems there was a pitchfork near the body, and Grim had told your mom he was gonna kill you. The Judge refused to issue a warrant for you."

Casey stared in amazement. "All this time I been hidin' out for nothing?"

"Yes." Birk was silent a moment. He looked at Ma, then back at Casey. "We didn't have no idea where you'd gone or where to start lookin' for you, Case. It's been awful hard on your poor mother. Deputy Sheriff Dalby brought in a kid he had killed and said it was you."

"I know," Casey said. "That was my friend, Billy Aster. I knew the deputy had killed him. We found signs—"

"We?" his mother asked.

"Yes, Hope and I. Hope is Billy's sister. We went looking for Billy when he didn't show up home after being out looking for livestock."

"You poor boy!" his mother said. "You poor, poor boy." She whirled and hurried to the cupboard. "You must be starved half to death. Let me fix you some supper." She pulled dishes from the cupboard and set them on the table.

"It was awfully tough for your mom," Birk said, "when she had to go down to the mortuary and look at that boy and assure them it wasn't you, even though Doc Wagner already told them it wasn't. The deputy thought it was you he had shot."

"He did shoot me once," Casey said. While his mother hurried about getting him a late meal, Casey told them about his flight up north, of meeting Thief and then getting shot and waking up at the Asters' place. He showed them his head wound. He recounted the story of Billy having taken Ebon and gone hunting livestock and not coming back.

"When we found the blood and tracks I knew darn well that deputy had shot Billy," he said. "I am awful bitter that he did that. I followed him down here intending to kill him, but he reached Custer before I could catch him."

"Oh, Casey," his mother said. "Please don't do anything more. Just stay home with us now. We need you to help with the farm. Haven't you been through enough already?"

"I owe it to Billy Aster," Casey said. "It was on account of me he got killed."

"No," said MacDoughall, shaking his head. "No, Casey, it wasn't your fault. Things like that happen."

Casey's mother set a plate of boiled beef, potatoes and peas before him. She buttered a baking powder biscuit.

"Eat, Casey. You need the nourishment. You look skinny."

"I'm glad you're better, Mom," he said. "I was worried about you."

She sat down next to Birk. She rested her chin in her hands and watched Casey eat. "I'm going to be all right," she said. "I had some internal bleeding, but it's healing good."

"Thank the good Lord for that. Where is Mrs. MacDoughall?"

"She's upstairs. She's very ill."

"Oh. I'm sorry. Shall I go up and see her?"

Birk shook his head. "No, please don't. She's not going to live long, Casey. She doesn't want anyone to see her in her condition. Your mother's been helping me care for her in her last few days."

"All right. I understand."

"It's ironic. Your mother came here needin' help and wound up helpin' us. I've been goin' over to your place and feeding the stock and taking care of things best I can. But the place needs more attention. I wish you'd stay and take care of it."

"Yes," Casey's mother said. "I do so wish you could stay. When you get married, I want you to have the farm."

"Thanks, Mom. That means a lot to me. I met a girl — Billy Aster's sister, Hope. Maybe now that I'm not a criminal...but first I want to know where that deputy is that killed Billy."

"Nobody knows," MacDoughall said. "Whole lot been goin' on here since Deputy Dalby got back with the dead boy yesterday. The Sheriff tried to arrest him for murder and Dalby shot the Sheriff and skedaddled out of town."

"Killed the Sheriff?"

"No. Didn't kill him, thank the Lord, but put him in the sick bed with a nasty shoulder wound. He's gonna be okay, but right now we ain't got a sheriff nor even a deputy."

Casey sat glaring into his plate. It was difficult to grasp all that was happening. It was so good to be back with his mother and to feel the weight of the murder lifted from his shoulders. The fact of Billy's horrible death tore at his innards, though, and he knew he could never let it rest. It was a debt, and those kinds of debts had to be paid. He knew he would keep his vow to kill the deputy. But he didn't yet know what the man looked like, never having seen him except perchance briefly at Dad's funeral, and he couldn't go out after him without knowing who he was looking for.

"The Sheriff tried to deputize me," Birk MacDoughall was saying. "He's plumb fallen to pieces about not havin' nobody to keep the law in the county. Don't seem to be a body around who can take the job, leastways nobody with the right stuff. I told him I couldn't handle it, what with my wife on her death bed and the farm to look after, and your mom's place needin' watchin' to boot."

"Is the Sheriff able to talk?" Casey asked.

"Oh, sure. He's all right. Just a matter of lettin' the wound heal some so's he can get up an' around again."

"I want to talk with him," Casey said. "Soon as possible. Do you know where he is?"

MacDoughall waved his arm. "Know where that ramblin' log house is, kind of up on the hillside, just south of the main road? Well, that's the Sheriff's place. He's there recuperatin'. We'll ride over there in the morning if you'd like."

Casey's mom put her hand on his shoulder. "Bet you're tired, aren't you, Son?"

"Yes."

"Finish your supper. I'll fix you a bed. You can go see the Sheriff after breakfast in the morning."

"All right." That sounded best to Casey. His muscles and bones ached from the long trip.

The bed felt superb after the nights on the hard, damp ground. Thief curled up on a braided-stocking rug beside his master.

The next morning Birk MacDoughall and Casey rode into Custer City to the Sheriff's log home and knocked at the door. Mrs. Brand, sixty, grey, and plump, ushered them into a back bedroom. The Sheriff lay propped on pillows, his face pale and haggard. He waved weakly as they entered. Mrs. Brand put chairs by the bed and left the room. The men sat down.

"You're lookin' good, Sheriff," MacDoughall said. "Specially considerin' what you've been through. This here is Casey Parkin, the boy Dalby was after when he killed the wrong lad."

"Figured that's who it was," the Sheriff said, smiling weakly. He held out his hand and Casey leaned forward and shook it.

"Casey's got a story to tell. It'll take some time. Hope you're up to it."

"Hell yes, I'm up! Let's hear it, young man."

Casey thought a moment, then began with the stealing of their horses and the murder of his father. He told about Hermund Grim coming along and winning over his mom, then turning wild. He related how Grim beat his mom unmercifully, and about how he had killed Grim. He then took the Sheriff through his flight, meeting the Asters, and the murder of Billy. When he was through, the Sheriff lay quietly a few moments, thinking.

"So the dead boy is Billy Aster. Glad to know who he is. Didn't know if we'd ever find out. I learned right quick he wasn't you, though. The Doc made yer acquaintance when he treated yer poor ma, an' soon as he laid eyes on that cadaver, he came runnin' and told me that sure wasn't Casey Parkin."

Casey buried his face in his hands and his mind saw Billy Aster lying dead across Ebon's saddle. The pain of the ages tore at his heart. "I'm going after Seth Dalby," he declared. "Please tell me what he looks like."

"I don't think I'd advise that, Son," the Sheriff said. "Dalby's a seasoned old salt. He's killed several people. I don't know how many. You might be interested to know he's the one that killed yer pa and helped steal yer horses."

Casey stared at the Sheriff. "He...he's the one that killed Dad?"

"That's right. I learned that just before Dalby shot me. A prisoner in the jail, feller named Barty Hardwise, told me him and Dalby was in the same outlaw gang, and when they went after yer horses, yer dad came runnin' out of the house and Dalby cut him down."

Casey clenched his teeth hard. "Goddammit! That goddam maniac, ridin' all over the Black Hills behind the badge of the law, pretendin' to be so holy, and all the time nothin' but a filthy murderin' swine! I'm goin' after the son-of-a-bitch, Sheriff. What does his face look like? I wanna burn it into my brain, so I don't forget it."

"Well, I know how yuh feel, Casey Parkin. But if you go out there and cut him down in cold blood, you'll be no better than him."

"I'll give him the same chance he gave Billy and me."

The Sheriff thought for a moment while Casey sat fuming.

"I was just thinkin', young man," he said, pointing a gnarled finger at Casey, "if yer so all fired rarin' to go after him, what say we make it legal? Let me swear yuh in as a deputy and yuh can tell him to surrender, and if he don't yuh can shoot him plumb dead if yuh want to."

"Me? A Deputy Sheriff?"

"Sure." Brand turned toward the door and hollered. "Ma! Send that office boy in here!"

A moment later Sammy Bents came in and stood beside the bed with his hands behind his back.

"Sammy," the Sheriff said. "Run up to the office and in that middle drawer of my desk, way back, is a deputy star and a pair of handcuffs and some of them fancy identification cards. Bring 'em to me."

"Yes, Sir." The boy turned to go.

"Oh, yeah, Sammy! In the cabinet in that little drawer of pictures and stuff there's a picture of Deputy Dalby. Know the one I mean?"

"Yes, Sir." The boy was off and running.

Casey squirmed. "I ain't sure I want to be a lawman right now, Sheriff. You see, I was plannin' on fillin' Dalby full of holes, an' if I'm a lawman, I gotta give him a chance to surrender first."

"All right. Give the bastard a chance to surrender. If he does, put the shackles on him, bring him in, and we'll see to it he's hung. If he don't, shoot him. But don't be a damn fool like I was, and let him get the drop on yuh. How yuh gonna find him? There's a lot of country up the way he left."

Casey didn't answer right away, but ran his fingers through

Thief's fur. He wondered just how good the dog would be at finding Dalby.

"Maybe I won't be able to find him. But I'm sure as hell gonna try. I got me a good trackin' dog, and if he can find the right trail I'll find him. Did he ride off on that same horse he rode in with?"

"Yep. Same horse. A sorrel."

"Then maybe my dog can pick up the trail, 'cause he followed that same horse all the way down here. Which way did he ride, do you know?"

"North, generally. But go down to the Gold Mine Saloon and talk to Alfie. He fired a couple shots at Dalby and watched him hightail it. He'll know which way."

Sammy, the office boy, returned, and Brand penned a Deputy Sheriff identification card for Casey. "Ma!" he hollered. "The bible!"

Mrs. Brand brought the bible, and the Sheriff put it on the stand next to his bed. "Put yer left hand on that bible and raise yer right. That's right. Now, do yuh swear to uphold the laws of the County of Custer, Dakota Territory, and of the United States of America, and to keep the peace and protect the folks and their property from evil men and women?"

"Yes, Sir, I do," said Casey.

"All right, bend down here."

He leaned over and the Sheriff pinned on the star. He looked down at it and read the words upside down:

DEPUTY SHERIFF, CUSTER COUNTY

"All right," the Sheriff said. "Yer a Deputy now. Yuh represent the law in Dakota Territory. Keep yerself alert and be careful. Don't take no damn fool chances. Here's the shackles. Hang 'em from yer belt. Here's the key. Don't lose the damn thing."

"What about my black horse?"

"Up at the livery. Sammy'll go with yuh and tell 'em I said turn him over. That yer saddle and Sharps, too?"

"Yep."

"All right. You'll have to view yer friend's body before yuh go 'cause yer the only one that knows him."

"Yes, I will."

"Here's a picture of Dalby. Looks pretty much like him, but he's got more whiskers now."

Casey studied the photo. The man in it had a day or two's growth of black whiskers and wore a black shirt and battered gray cowboy's hat. A big Colt revolver swung from his right hip, and he was showing the camera his pride and joy, a long-barreled buffalo rifle. Of course, Casey thought, he would want his killing tools in the picture with him.

"Let me know where yuh are if yuh can," the Sheriff was saying. "I don't know if you'll be near a telegraph station, but do what yuh can."

"Thank you, Sir, for the trust you put in me."

"Thank yuh for takin' the job. Yuh come from good stock, boy. I knew yer Uncle Bart, yer daddy's brother. We was in the war together, him an' me. Made outa damn good stuff." He shook his finger. "Watch out for Dalby. He's a cagey bastard."

"Thank you, I will."

"One other thing yuh might wanna know that Hardwise told me about. Might ease yer conscience a mite over havin' shot Hermund Grim. Old Hermund was one of the outlaws along with Dalby that took yer horses. He was jist as much to blame for yer Dad's death as Dalby."

The little bell over the door jingled when Casey entered Baklanov's Mortuary that afternoon. Egor showed him to the back and pulled the lid off a pine box.

"Ain't gonna bury him in *that*, are you?" Casey asked.

Baklanov shrugged. "My preference would be, of course, to send this young man on his final journey in a vehicle of more regal decor," the mortician said. "However, when buried at county expense, a pine box is the best the allowance will permit."

Billy's body lay beneath a sheet that covered it to the chin. The face showed chalky white in the dimly lit parlor. Casey could barely see the freckles that had been so vivid in life. He turned to Baklanov.

"The County better bury him in something better than that," he said. "That was a County Deputy that murdered him."

"Do you recognize the lad?" Baklanov asked.

"It's Billy Aster. I'll sign your identification form."

"Thank you, my boy."

Casey rode over to Judge Farnsworth's and got a warrant for the arrest of Seth Dalby for two counts of murder and one of attempted murder. He sat down at the dining table at Birk MacDoughall's and completed the bitter task of writing to the girl he loved and telling her of the death. He packed up his black horse with bedroll and trail grub. He handed the letter to Birk and mounted up.

"Would you mail that for me?"

"Sure will. You be careful, you hear?"

"Where's Mom?"

"In the house, crying. She can't bear to see you leave."

"Tell her good-bye for me, Birk." He extended his hand down. "And thanks for takin' care of her for me."

Birk gripped the boy's hand in both of his. "One thing before you go, Case. My darlin' wife is dying. Maybe it ain't right to say this while she's still alive, but with you goin' away an' all..."

"What is it, Birk?"

"I love your mother, and plan to ask her to marry me afterward. Would you approve of that?"

"Yes, Sir. I'd be proud to have you as my step father."

"Thank you, Casey. God be with you."

Ebon turned and trotted toward Custer City. Thief frolicked alongside, and Casey said a prayer of thanks. Then he said another and asked the Almighty to help him find Seth Dalby.

Chapter Twenty

Seth Dalby cursed the rotten luck that forced him to hightail it out of Custer City unprepared. One good thing was he had a place he could go where the law would have a mighty slim chance of finding him. Another good thing was there wasn't no law to come after him, leastways out of Custer there wasn't. With the Sheriff dead and no deputy, he didn't have to worry much. It would take them a long time to get any kind of a posse together. He galloped full chisel until he came to rugged hilly country, then slowed. It was good he did, for his horse showed signs of collapsing.

His first night on the trail was mighty uncomfortable. He had no bedroll — his belongings had gone with the Parkin kid's horse — and once the sun went down, a gut-chilling cold settled over the Black Hills. The next day he came across a group of gold prospectors and bartered them out of a couple of blankets and some trail grub.

The third day, about the time he got to thinking he was home free, he caught sight of a rider behind him. The fellow was a long way back, but it troubled Seth somewhat when, just for a second, he saw something reflect the sun. It had to be one of two things — a gun barrel or a badge. The man disappeared then, and Seth couldn't pick him up again. Oh, well, if the bastard got closer, he would hide and put a Sharps bullet in him.

Later that morning he brought down a deer with his big rifle. He roasted and ate a chunk and left the rest there. In the afternoon he spurred the sorrel up a long slope and stopped at the top for a look at the land behind. He saw the rider again, this time much closer, and his colon felt like it was puckering up. In fact he was so close now that Seth could see he was a young fellow, no more than a kid, wearing a black hat and riding a big black horse. A dog trotted just ahead. Seth drew in a sharp breath.

The kid was wearing a badge!

He stood motionless, hardly breathing, his eyes glued to the figure. It moved along at a steady pace across the wide prairie toward him.

"No, no! Cain't be!" he said aloud. "Ain't no such thing as ghosts!"

But there he was, the kid Seth had gunned down, coming closer. The Sheriff said something about pinning Seth's star on the dead kid and letting him be the deputy. He figured the Sheriff was just shooting off his old mouth, but hell, there the kid was, alive as life, riding toward him and wearing a star. Seth had already shot him twice, and the second time packed him clear into Custer across his horse. There was only one way a fellow could get out of that kind of mess, and that was to become a ghost.

He whirled and scrambled headlong toward his horse. The beast shied away, and he had to chase him around in circles to get his foot in the stirrup. He tried to throw his leg over, but the spooked animal sidestepped and Seth slipped back and flopped on the ground. When finally he did get mounted, on the third try, he dug in his spurs and galloped hell bent across the ridge and down the far slope.

Ambushing a lawman is one thing, but when it came to ghosts, that was a whole 'nother matter! The only way to treat ghosts was to vanish. And that's what Seth did, as fast as his mount would take him. He continued at full gallop for the next several miles, and would have gone several more if the horse hadn't slowed down to a walk. Then it stopped altogether, its nostrils flared and chest heaving.

"Come on, you damn Cayuse!" screamed Seth. He dug in his spurs and slapped the rump with his lariat. The horse staggered a few more steps, but its forelegs buckled and it fell forward. Seth landed hard out in front. He struggled to his feet and walked back.

The horse was dead.

"Damn the luck!" he moaned "What the hell am I gonna do

now?" He shuffled a few steps away and looked at the hills behind him, then glared down at the horse, half expecting it to rise up and be all right again and carry him quickly away from that specter.

He shut his eyes tight and tried to think. He would have to keep his head and figure things out. How do you fight ghosts? You can't shoot them, and that was the only thing Seth was really good at. You can't reason with them, especially if you're the one that caused them to be a ghost in the first place. The best way to handle them, he concluded, was just get the hell out of there.

He grabbed his Sharps and ammunition belt and took off running north as hard as he could go. He reached heavy timber and plunged through the thickets and underbrush and got his face and arms scratched. He fled in panic until he could no longer get his breath, then he hid in a briar patch near a stream and panted like a hound dog. He expected the ghost rider to overtake him at any moment, and he began to resign himself to a terrible death by however ghosts kill people.

He got his breath back and peeked out of the thicket. He saw no one. He crept to the water's edge, lay on his stomach and drank. He stepped in and waded knee-deep upstream. Maybe ghosts couldn't track you in water. He kept going until the creek deepened to where he couldn't make headway anymore, and he scurried up the opposite bank and on to the northward.

He figured Claudia's place ought to be another day's ride due north, but he'd never make it on foot. He stuck to the timber as much as he could, avoiding the open prairies where the ghost rider might see him. He kept up a fast clip in spite of the sloshing water in his boots.

In the late afternoon he entered a timbered valley where he saw smoke rising above the trees. Maybe a campfire, he figured. He struggled along on sore, tired feet. His legs ached, and somehow stickers had got inside his boots, but he decided not to take them out just yet. He smelled food cooking and he knew somebody had a campfire going. He sneaked along the river bank up to a big fallen tree and peered over. A few feet from him knelt a man in his fifties tending to a skillet over the fire. A hobbled roan grazed nearby, saddled. Only one horse, thought Seth. The man must be alone. That would make it easy. He'd just shoot him and take his horse. Of course, he'd eat whatever was in that skillet.

He reached for his Peacemaker, but stopped. Might be if he killed the fellow, it would just be another ghost to chase him. Besides that, maybe the ghost that was after him would hear the shot, if ghosts could hear, that is. Better not. He would try something else. He climbed over the log and walked forward. The man turned, stood up, and smiled through a long, grey beard. He was a frail little feller.

"Howdy, friend," he said.

"Howdy. Smelled yer campfire and had to stop and see who it was."

The man held out his hand. "Name's Griswold, Jack Griswold."

Seth shook his hand. "Mine's Seth Dalby. They call yuh Jack?"

"Sometimes. My friends call me Grizzly, though. Feel up to a steak and spuds? Got plenty here."

The aroma of cooking food sent Seth's stomach into convulsions. The old man filled a tin plate and handed it to him.

"Could be a mite flat," he said. "I ran outa salt."

Seth nibbled at the edge of the steaming steak on the plate. "What ya doin' out here?" he asked.

"Well, doin' a mite o' prospectin'. Been tryin' my luck pannin' along this creek, but ain't found much at all. Seems like there's more gold up around Deadwood. I might head back up that way. Where you bound fer, friend?"

Seth made up a little tale about himself to satisfy the old man's question. He had been on his way to Pine Valley and his horse went lame and he had to leave him.

"Might yuh be interested in sellin' me yer horse?" Seth asked.

Grizzly grinned. "Reckon not. Then I'd have to walk all the way to Deadwood, and that's a fer piece." He handed Seth a tin cup of steaming coffee.

"What yer sayin' is true," Seth said. He balanced his plate on a rock and took the coffee. "Tell me something else, Grizzly. Do you believe there's such critters as ghosts?"

Grizzly laughed. "Yep. Shore do. What makes ya ask?"

"I reckon I saw one. It was a feller I know is dead, yet I saw him."

"Understand what yer sayin', friend," Grizzly said. He threw dirt in the skillet and wiped it with his bandanna. "I seen ghosts a time or two myself. Folks that died and come back kinda faint lookin' so you kin jist about see right through 'em. Some makes a lot of noise with a chain or somethin', an' others is quiet as a cat."

Seth stood with his mouth hanging open, drinking in every word. "Can they...uh...Can they hurt a feller?"

"Never heard of none doin' nobody harm, but I seen fellers go plumb loco in their heads from gettin' pestered by a ghost. Sometimes they comes back and haunts a feller, partic'lar if he's the one killed em. Jist haunts 'em and haunts 'em 'til they go plumb loony and sometimes kill themselves." He looked over at Seth. "That ghost you saw some feller you killed?"

Damn this nosey old man! Seth thought. "No, ain't nobody I killed. Jist somebody I knowed." He slurped at his coffee.

Grizzly walked to his hobbled horse and slipped the skillet into the saddle bag. "Then I wouldn't lose no sleep over it, Friend," he said, strolling back. "Long as you ain't the one did the killin'."

When Seth was through eating, he stood up and drew his Colt .45 Peacemaker and aimed it at Grizzly. "Get yer hands up, old man. I need yer horse."

Grizzly turned and his jaw dropped. "Well, well, so it comes to this! Man welcomes you to his camp and feeds you and this is the thanks—"

"Shut up, goddammit!" Seth plucked the six shooter from Grizzly's holster and tossed it on the ground. "Put yer hands around that pine tree." He slipped the lariat off the horse and tied the old man's hands tightly around the trunk. "Yuh stay right here, and maybe somebody'll find yuh."

"Did you shoot that feller that's a-ghostin' after you?"

"Yep, and if yuh don't shut yer tater trap I'll shoot you too, by God."

Grizzly turned his head around almost backwards and looked at Seth. "If you do that, you'll be mighty sorry. My ghost'll haunt you 'til you go daffodils."

Seth gathered up the food and tin plates and wedged them in the saddle pouches. He replaced a small caliber rifle in the saddle scabbard with his own Sharps. The big rifle was a little bulky for the scabbard, so he tied it in with a leather thong so it wouldn't work out. He fished the bridle off the horn and slipped it on the pony. He removed the hobbles, swung into the saddle, and sent the horse splashing across the stream. He was off to the north at a trot.

Chapter Twenty-one

Hope Aster dismounted and led her little pinto down the narrow pathway into the deep canyon. She had never been this far north, at least not in this part of the Black Hills. She had heard things about it, though, that it was truly rough country with deep gorges and steep, slippery hillsides — the kind of terrain where one's horse could lose its footing and fall, and maybe one could lie injured and never be found and could die there. It was that thought that had kept her pressing the search for her brother. She doubted he would come this far north looking for the livestock, so this was an act of desperation. She had searched everywhere else since he disappeared. Some areas she had gone over three or four times. The far north part was all that was left.

She refused to believe the tale told by the signs she and Casey had found. The blood, the tracks, the appearance of Casey's mule. These silent voices were tearing up her insides, and she would no longer listen to them. Billy was somewhere about, perhaps lying injured in one of these canyons, clinging to life as Casey had done when they found him.

She had ridden to the Pine Valley Post Office twice during the week and a half Casey had been gone but there was no letter from him. She tried to push aside the thought that maybe some horrible thing had happened to him, too. Perhaps he had caught up with the deputy and got himself shot. She gripped the rein tightly and fought back tears as she had so many times the past few days. She stepped carefully down the perilous trail, measuring each yard for stability for her and her horse. Thus she arrived at the bottom of the canyon where a small stream trickled down. She removed her boots and bathed her feet in the cool water. She munched on her rations and thought about the range of mental torment she had endured the past few weeks, from euphoria to deep dread and depression. Her world had become so bright and wonderful when Casey had come to them and made his great recovery, and the gradual development of affection for him that had grown within her. If only she could have told him of her feelings.

Then the terrible realization that he was wanted by the law, and that her brother was missing — maybe murdered — and the man she secretly loved was riding away after that dreadful deputy person, perhaps never to return.

She climbed back into the saddle and rode up the stream, searching every foot of ground. If a man were injured but could still move about, he would probably seek a stream to rest by, she thought. Every few minutes she called out his name, and her voice echoed up the deep canyon and through the high pines. She continued on, sometimes actually coaxing her pinto into the shallow water when the bank became so tangled with overgrowth as to be impassable.

In the late afternoon she came to a place where the canyon opened up into a giant panorama surrounded by mountains. She was struck instantly with the feeling of peace and solitude. The birds sang sweet songs. Deer paused and contemplated her. The valley floor was green, and the trees were tall and straight and prolific. Through the woods came a sparkling of sunlight, and when she rode on she found a lake of shimmering blue water.

Perhaps she would find him here. If one had to die, she reasoned, this would be a good place, because it could not be far from here to heaven. She nudged the pinto down the shoreline another half mile through the trees. She found herself in a clearing, and before her stood a log cabin, and next to the cabin was a garden, and hoeing weeds in the garden was a woman.

"My goodness! Hello!" Hope called.

The lady turned, surprise on her face. "My goodness is right! Hello yourself. You plumb shooked me up, young lady." She hurried over and stood beside Hope. "What brings you up this way?"

"Looking for my brother. He's lost."

"Up here?" The lady shaded her eyes as she looked up. "How come him to be way up here, anyway?"

"Maybe he isn't. I've looked about everywhere else. I'm so desperate to find him."

"Are you all by yourself, Honey?"

"Yes."

"Well get yourself down off that pony and come in the house, for goodness sake. We'll get us something to eat. Are you hungry?"

Hope slipped from the saddle. "Not very. I'm so worried about my brother that I don't have much appetite lately."

"My name's Claudia," the lady said, snatching the rein from Hope. "Bring yourself along with me to the barn and we'll get Old Paint here some hay and maybe an oat or two. What's your name, girl?"

"Hope Aster. We live just above Forsythe Canyon." She followed Claudia to the barn. "My brother's been missing for over a week now. We think he might have been killed, but... well, we just don't know."

Claudia swung open the door and led Patches inside. She put her in a stall, slipped off her bridal, and closed her in. "There you go, old girl," she said. "Plenty of hay in that bin there. Help yourself." She turned to Hope. "You think he might've been killed? How so?"

They moved outside and Claudia closed and latched the door. "We think he might have been shot," Hope said. "We saw some signs that looked like it. You live here all alone, Mrs....?"

"My name's Mrs. Morton, but you call me Claudia. Don't get many visitors around here, and it gets mighty lonesome. My husband died of pneumonia awhile back, so I'm alone." She stepped up on the porch and opened the door. They entered a room that was kitchen and sitting room combined with stove and cupboards along two walls and a table in the center.

"Oh, I'm so sorry," Hope said. "It must be terrible being all alone."

"Set yourself down there, girl," Claudia said, pointing to the table. "I'll get us some grub together. If you want to freshen up, there's the wash basin and bucket of water."

In a few minutes Claudia Morton had supper on the table. Hope marveled at her ability to make venison steak, green beans and potatoes so tantalizing when she had no one to cook for but herself. It was a delicious change from trail food.

"My brother is a year younger than I," Hope said, cutting into her steak. "He has sandy hair and some freckles on his cheeks and bushy eyebrows. He was wearing a blue shirt and Levi pants and a black cowboy hat. Has anyone like that come by here?"

Claudia shook her head. "Nope. Nobody like that. The only visitor I've had in the past two years was a little older. He was a deputy sheriff from Custer on the trail of a murderer."

Hope's heart fluttered and shivers traveled up her spine. She sat staring at Claudia Morton.

"What's the matter, girl?" Claudia said. "You look like you saw a ghost or something."

"A deputy?"

"Yep. He hung around a spell, 'til he got a lead on the outlaw over at Pine Valley. Then he cut out of here in a hurry. Why you lookin' so pale, girl?"

"I...I think that deputy might have shot my brother."

Claudia's eyes widened. "Yeah? Well, I'll be..." She jumped up suddenly and went to the window. She stood a full minute, staring out. She turned back. There was concern in her eyes. "Your brother is young. Would you say he was sort of, eh...sort of...innocent-lookin'?"

"Well, yes, I suppose he is. Why do you...?"

"The deputy said he was after a kid, an innocent lookin' one. 'Fact, he called him 'The Kid.' He said he was a vicious murderer that killed his daddy and was as dangerous as Billy the Kid or John Wesley Hardin or some of them. He said he'd caught up with the kid once and the kid ambushed him and shot him in the shoulder. He shot back and thought he'd wounded him."

They sat in silence a moment, staring at one another. Finally Hope spoke. Her voice was hoarse and strained. "Do you think that deputy could have shot my brother?"

"Could be. He said the outlaw rode a...does your brother ride a big black horse?"

"He was last we saw him."

"Do you think he mistook your brother—?"

"Yes. He was after another boy..." Hope hadn't meant to divulge too much, but it had slipped out.

"Who was he after?" Claudia said. "Who was the other boy?"

"Just somebody I know of," she said.

Claudia got the coffee pot from the stove and poured. "That deputy was around here quite awhile," she said. "We went to Pine Valley and he learned from the bartender that some family had found a kid wounded and took him home and cared for him."

Hope was silent. She dug into the steak again.

"I'm beginnin' to see what happened," Claudia said. "And the more I think about it, the more I realize I was plumb wrong about that Deputy. It was your family that took care of that kid, wasn't it, Hope?"

She looked up. Claudia's eyes were gentle, true. "Yes," she mumbled. "We took care of him. But he isn't a vicious, heartless murderer. And he didn't kill his daddy. He killed his step-father in self defense. His step-father was very mean and beat him and his mother. Casey thought he would kill them, so he shot him before he could."

Claudia went to the cupboard and brought out pudding. She set a cup before Hope. "The deputy said the kid ambushed him," she said.

"That's a lie," Hope cried. "Casey never even saw that deputy, much less shot at him. It was the other way around. The deputy ambushed Casey from the bluff top. He never had a chance to surrender, even. We found Casey with a wound in his scalp."

Claudia sat and listened while Hope told her about nursing Casey back to health, about how much he looked like Billy, and about Billy borrowing Casey's black horse that day to hunt livestock.

"The way we see it," Hope said, "is that the Deputy mistook Billy for Casey and shot him. Ambushed him. There was no need to. Billy would never have resisted a lawman. Neither would Casey."

Claudia shook her head. "It's unbelievable," she said. "Just unbelievable."

"What?"

"The deputy said the kid ambushed him and wounded him. He showed me a shoulder wound, but I thought at the time it sure looked like a bite. Now I know it was — that mule bit him!"

"Really? We found the mule near where all the blood and tracks were. I'll bet when he shot Billy, he took the black horse and left the mule."

Claudia stood up and went to the window again. After awhile she turned back. "I sure hope I don't offend your tender ears, girl, but I have to say this. Deputy Seth Dalby is a rotten, no-good son-of-a-bitch and I'm just sorry I treated him so well. I wish I'd have fed him to the bears!"

"I'm terribly worried about Casey too," Hope said. "He vowed to kill that deputy. But he's only nineteen and not as wise or...or crafty like the Deputy. And he's not the kind that can shoot a man in the back, like from ambush. I'm just afraid I may lose both my brother and my...my friend."

"I got an extra cot here, Hope," Claudia said. "You stay right here tonight, and tomorrow we'll ride clear around the lake and see if we can find your brother."

"All right, thank you. I'll go unsaddle Patches."

Chapter Twenty-two

Casey thought about a lot of things while he was following Thief through the wild Black Hills region. He thought about Hope Aster and how he longed to see her again. He had wanted so desperately to express his feelings for her back on the trail, but his predicament with the law had held him back. How could he expect her to look with favor upon a murderer and outlaw? Besides, it seemed she already had a steady boy friend who took her to dances regularly. Maybe if he could settle accounts with Seth Dalby, he would see just exactly what the relationship was between Hope and that hired hand.

He sensed the grief she and her parents must be experiencing over the loss of Billy. They were a close family. Of course they didn't actually know, as he did, that Billy had been killed, but the evidence he and Hope had found was sure frightening enough to bring on deep despair. He prayed he could catch up to Seth Dalby and put an end to him. That was the least he could do for the Aster family.

But could he do that? Was he man enough to whip a seasoned old salt who loved to kill? Or would a bullet from Dalby's buffalo gun suddenly end his young life among the tall pines of the Black Hills?

He was grateful to have his strong, persistent gelding back again, and his powerful Sharps rifle. He had made good time since Thief picked up the trail leaving Custer. The dog was a wonder. He went quietly on his way, barking only when he needed Casey's attention, and never letting himself get so far ahead that Casey wouldn't be able to see him. Birk MacDoughall had given him a good supply of jerky and hardtack and he hadn't had to stop and hunt game nor to cook, except for an occasional pot of coffee and to fry up a little salt pork. He rode each evening until he couldn't see Thief in the darkness, then made camp and was up and away as the dawn turned. Ebon walked at a good clip and sometimes loped along when the going was easy while crossing the wide prairies.

Casey was ever conscious of a possible ambush. He had learned the hard way of Seth Dalby's penchant to shoot from hiding. As he moved he kept his eyes combing the hills ahead and to the side. He was confident Thief would bark and warn him if he sensed anyone lying in wait. Still, it was an uneasy feeling, especially when he chanced to recall the nasty furrow the deputy's bullet had plowed across his scalp.

He had been following the trail three days when he came upon Dalby's dead horse. Thief had barked and Casey leapt to the ground and crouched, thinking it might be someone in ambush. He crept forward through the grass, and when he reached the top of the gentle rise, he saw the dead animal. It hadn't been dead long. It was still lathery from having been ridden hard. Its lips were back and nostrils flared, and its wide eyes held the terror of a hard, horrible end.

"The son-of-a-bitch rode him to death!" Casey said aloud.

Thief was already on the move, this time sniffing out the smells of a man instead of his horse. Casey mounted and loped along northward behind the dog and entered heavy timber a half mile away. They came to a shallow stream and Thief lost the scent. He scampered to and fro along the bank and came back toward Casey, nose to earth and whuffing loudly.

"What's the matter, boy?" Casey called. "Lose him? He probably crossed over."

They waded to the other bank. Casey looked for tracks coming out of the water and found none. Thief sniffed up and down the bank but gave no indication he had found the scent. Casey halted Ebon and sat thinking. Maybe the man waded upstream instead of just crossing. Or maybe downstream. He decided to try upstream since north seemed to be the man's chosen direction of travel. For that matter it seemed he was sticking pretty close to the same general area he had ridden down from a few days ago with Billy across the saddle. This might even be the same stream along which Billy was murdered.

He continued north along the creek bed and kept an eye on Thief, hoping to see him pick up the trail. After a half hour he whistled to the dog and turned south, checking the terrain a half hour's ride below where they had lost the trail. That netted nothing, so he turned north again, this time swinging wide and riding across the prairie parallel to the riverbank. He continued thus until dark, then made camp along the stream.

They pushed on north again early the next morning. Thief locked on to a trail at the prairie's edge and followed it along the creek. Casey wasn't sure it was Dalby, but judging by Thief's excitement, chances were good that it was. After a half hour they entered a timbered valley where the stream came from the east. He pushed up the canyon and had gone a quarter mile when he heard a man's voice.

"Help!"

The foliage along the creek was heavy, and he could not see far ahead. Thief bounded through the thickets and out of his sight. He wanted to hurry, but common sense told him the voice might belong to Seth Dalby waiting to put a bullet in him. He swung to the ground and tied Ebon to a bush. He crept forward on foot, peeking through brush and over fallen logs. He heard Thief's bark from a short way ahead — not an angry bark but rather an excited one. If it would have been Dalby, the man Thief had trailed all this way, the bark would have been angry. It was something else.

He came to a large fallen tree and peered over. Thief stood with tail a-wag, sniffing a bearded man sitting on the ground with his hands tied around a tree. His campfire had long since gone out. Casey stepped out in the open. "Howdy!" he said.

The man looked up. His eyes were bleary, his face drawn and exhausted. "Oh, Great Saints above," he said. "A man with a badge!"

"Thief!" called Casey.

"I ain't no thief!" the old man declared. "It was a thief that tied me up here and took my horse and left me to die."

Casey moved over and knelt beside him. "I was talkin' to my dog. His name's Thief."

"Dammit, feller, I thought he was a wolf come to eat me.

Almost pooped in my long-johns. You a real sheriff?"

"Bet your hide, friend. My name's Casey Parkin."

"Mine's Jack Griswold. Friends call me Grizzly."

"I'm after the feller who took your horse," Casey said. "Man about six-foot, black hair, dirty black mustache, wearin' a dilapidated old gray hat. That the one that took it?"

Grizzly nodded vehemently. "Sure as hell is. Said his name was Seth somethin'. He was nice 'nuff t'wait 'til I fed him, though. Then he pulled his gun and tied me up here."

Casey opened his pocket knife and cut loose the cords.

"It's a wonder he didn't kill you. He likes to kill folks."

"He said he had a mind to, but I told him I'd haunt him if he did." He paused and rubbed his wrists. "Seems he's afraid of ghosts. He thought you was a ghost."

"He did?"

He shook his limp hands to restore circulation. "Yep. Asked me if I believed in ghosts. He said he saw a man he knew was dead comin' up the line behind him. He was plumb scairt to death."

"So that's why he didn't try to bushwhack me!"

Grizzly laughed. "Sure, that's why. You cain't shoot a ghost, you know. Bullets just go through and don't hurt him none." He gave Casey a sly look. "You *ain't* a ghost, are you, Deputy?"

"No." Casey grinned. "Not that I know about anyway."

Grizzly leaned down and brushed dirt off his buckskins. "You got a horse?"

"Hold on. I'll get him."

Casey moved down and brought Ebon back to the camp. Grizzly was rummaging through his pack. "Got some hardtack here somewheres," he declared. "That scoundrel took everything else."

"You're welcome to mine," Casey said. "I got some grub, too, and coffee we can make."

The two men got the fire going and made coffee. Grizzly retrieved his six-gun where Dalby had dropped it in the dirt. As they ate, Casey told him briefly about the murder of Billy and his having been deputized to go after Seth Dalby.

"I've trailed him this far," Casey said. "Rather my dog has.

Now I'll have to put my dog onto *your* horse's scent. What are you gonna do now, Grizzly, without your horse?"

"I was givin' some thought t'goin' back up around Deadwood. The pannin' around here ain't workin' out so good. But I reckon now I ain't a-goin' that far, least not 'til I can chase me down another horse."

"Sure wish I could help you," Casey said. "My horse could carry us both, but I just ain't got the time to take you all the way to Deadwood. I got to get on the trail of this outlaw."

"I know how that is, son. But it happens I do got a mount of sorts. I got a mangy old jackass tethered over yonder in that grassy prairie. He's my pack animal and ain't a very good saddle horse, but I kin ride him if'n I have to."

Casey laughed. "Got a saddle for him?"

"Nope, but I rode him bareback lots of times. I'd jist like to go along with you, Deputy. Like to get my horse back."

Casey chewed his hardtack and washed it down with coffee. "I can't promise to protect you from Dalby," he said. "He's meaner'n hell and likes to shoot from ambush."

Griswold grinned. "Kinda funny, kid like you protectin' an old salt like me. Most likely it'd be the other way around, me protectin' you. I been up an' down over these wild hills an' all across the Dakota Territory, outsmartin' Injuns 'n' outlaws 'n' fightin' my way out of scrapes fer nigh on to twenty years now. How long you been doin' it, Deputy?"

Casey grinned sheepishly. "Yeah, I see what you're tellin' me, Grizzly. Go get your old donkey."

Griswold hurried off through the timber and returned in a few minutes leading a large gray animal, only slightly smaller than Ebon, with a white muzzle and huge ears. Casey looked him over.

"He is a big feller, ain't he? Do you think he can keep up with my horse?"

"You got a thing or two t'learn about jackasses, kid," Griswold said with a smile. "Old Reuben here will run circles around your horse, both on the prairies and up them slantindicular hillsides. Don't you worry none, we'll keep up!"

Griswold flipped his shovel and pans and other mining

equipment under a small conifer and piled branches over them. "Gonna have to leave this stuff," he said. "I'll come back fer it when I get my horse back. I'll jist tie on these blankets an' my rifle an' my fryin' pan 'n' we kin be on our way."

"I just don't understand this feller Dalby," Casey said. "Seems like he's goin' right back up to Forsythe Canyon."

"Might be he's got someplace to hide up in there."

"Might be."

Casey introduced Thief to the hoof tracks that came out of the creek at the other bank and they moved into the timber. The trail was strong. Thief was eager and kept a good distance ahead. Casey was surprised to find he had to keep nudging his gelding to keep up with the high-stepping donkey. Griswold's legs clamped around the jack's belly, and his body rocked rhythmically with the animal's quick strides. Every now and then he turned and grinned back at Casey.

They rode on in silence awhile, then Casey spurred Ebon to a trot and pulled up alongside. "Where in the devil did you get that donkey, Grizzly?" he asked. "I never saw such a spry one for bein' that old."

Griswold laughed. "Hell, I had this bugger since he was first borned, back before the war. I had a little wife then, too. We worked a farm in Ohio, her and me. We didn't have no babies, though, and I expect that's why I loved Reuben so much. You got to have somebody to love, y'know. O' course I loved Rebecca too, that was my wife, but she up and died in '61. And after that I didn't have nobody to love except Reuben. O'course I love my Dolly horse, too, the one that rascal stole from me, in spite of I ain't had her near as long as Reuben. But she's a darlin', she is, an' I gotta tell you, young Deppity, if you wanna take that feller alive, you best catch up to him before I do."

The donkey was pulling away from Ebon again, but Grizzly slowed him up some so they could keep talking.

"There was a war then, wasn't there, Griz, when you was livin' in Ohio?"

"Yup. It was a hell of a war. You likely don't recollect it, bein' too young then."

"Yes," Casey said. "I remember my dad and mom talkin'

about it. I was only four or five then, I guess. Did you fight in the war?"

Grizzly looked down at the ground in front of Reuben and rode silently a spell. Then he looked up at Casey. "I didn't cotton to that awful war," he said. "I reckon I was a bad 'un fer not servin', but I jist couldn't get worked up over the idee o' killin' folks that was Americans jist like me." He shook his head. "I never got that excited about freein' the slaves, or if that was the right thing to do, even. So when Rebecca died, me and Reuben took off together and roamed about the countrysides. We been a lot of places, seen a lot of good times an' bad. The Black Hills suits us the best. Been here several years looking fer gold. Ain't found enough to get rich on, but enough to keep eatin' and buy a new pair of boots now and again. Lookee, Casey, here's yer dog comin' back."

Thief trotted toward them and when he reached a point just ahead of Ebon, he spun around and took up the scent again.

"He's just checking up on us," Casey said. "He gets a little far ahead and gets worried about me and comes back."

"Damn good dog," Grizzly declared. "He sure knows how to foller a trail!"

"Yep. I ain't had him as long as you've had Reuben, but I'll bet I love him as much!"

Grizzly laughed and shook his head. "Damn betcha! It don't take a fella long to fall in love with a fine animal. An' they're a hell of a lot truer than most womenfolk."

The dog led them up a tight canyon so overgrown with brush they could hardly squeeze through. The briars grabbed at their clothes and low branches snapped their faces. Casey found himself wishing he would have brought chaps to protect his legs from the brier. He hadn't even thought about chaps, although they were, indeed, a horseman's best friend in country like this.

They made their way out of the brush and up the side of a steep incline. Grizzly clung tightly as Reuben the Donkey stepped his way up the precarious hillside like a mountain goat. Casey, to make the climb easier for Ebon, dismounted and led him up. At the top they found a grassy plateau and Grizzly dismounted.

"Let's rest 'em a spell," he said. "Lookee back yonder. You kin see old Harney's Peak from here."

Off toward the south Casey saw the lofty landmark rising blue-gray in the mist above the tree tops. "Yeah, ain't she pretty? Dad and I were gonna go climb 'er one of these days. We never got to, though." He leaned down, picked off a long stem of buffalo grass and chewed on the end.

"Outlaws killed yer daddy, you said," Griz remarked.

"Yeah. This feller we're chasin' killed my dad."

"Then I reckon yer sure 'nuff itchin' to catch up to him. We both got good reason to find him. How's yer Ma takin' it?"

"Well, she's all right now, I reckon. She's offered to give me the farm, 'cause she's likely figurin' to marry Birk MacDoughall. He's our closest neighbor."

Griz slipped his thumb and forefinger into his shirt pocket and pulled out a shapeless white lump. He held it out in his palm, and Reuben the Donkey took it gingerly in his teeth, smacked his lips, chewed a bit, and swallowed. Griz withdrew another lump and fed it to Casey's black.

"What is that, Griz?"

"Sugar. Ever now 'n' then old Reuben likes somethin' a little sweet. He works harder when he knows it's comin'." He looked slyly at Casey, out of the corner of his eye. "You sure enough ain't married, are you, Casey? Smart young feller like you wouldn't be that foolish."

Casey laughed. "No, but I'm givin' it some mighty serious consideration."

"That little lady you said was the murdered boy's sister, what's her name...Hope?"

"Yep. If I can catch that damn deputy and get him hung, or shoot him, either way, I'll ask for her hand."

Thief trotted back to them and sat down next to Casey and received a pat on the head. "Reckon we better get on," Casey said. "I think we're probably gainin' on him. We been makin' pretty good time except for the briars."

They mounted up and continued on at a brisk walk. Casey was glad Grizzly was with him. The idea of traveling with a man who had fought Indians and outlaws was comforting, especially in light of Seth Dalby's dangerous nature. Besides that, Grizzly was a personable fellow and a delightful companion.

They followed Thief to Forsythe Canyon and right on past. The scent led them to high ground and exceptionally rough terrain, and eventually to a breathtaking lake that Casey had never dreamed was there. Seth Dalby's trail turned and meandered along the shoreline.

Chapter Twenty-three

It took Hope and Claudia Morton half the next day to ride around the lake. They stayed several yards apart where the terrain permitted so they could search a wider strip. Again and again Hope's eyes scoured the ground between the thickly flourishing evergreen trees and the bare places along the shore. Each time her heart became heavier with the terrible weight of despair. When they reached a point two-thirds the way around the lake, tears came and she wept aloud.

"What's the matter, Honey?" Claudia asked. She moved her white horse close to Hope's.

"I'm...I'm so terribly depressed," the girl sobbed. "It all seems so hopeless. There are so many places he could be, and the Black Hills is a huge place and so wild and...and so secretive. We'll never find him." She buried her face in her hands and the tears rolled down.

"There, there, don't cry, my dear," Claudia said. "Don't give up. We'll keep lookin' 'til we find him."

"I just know he's dead. I only wish there would be a letter from Casey. Even if it brought bad news about Billy, at least I'd know Casey was alive to have written the letter. I thought surely I would hear from him last week." She wiped her eyes on her handkerchief.

"Why don't we try the Post Office at Pine Valley tomorrow?" Claudia said." Maybe there'll be a letter from Casey. We can ride over in the buggy. Would you like that?"

"Yes. Yes, I would. Thank you."

Claudia smiled. "That's a good girl. Don't cry now."

By the time they approached the cabin, Hope felt much better with the prospect of a letter from Casey. But a moment later her elation vanished. The cabin door opened and from it stepped a bedraggled man with an unkempt growth of whiskers. Claudia gasped.

"Oh, my God! It's him!"

"Who?"

"Deputy Dalby!"

Hope clutched her throat. "Oh, Lord!" she cried, "What's he doing here?"

The man stood on the step and glowered out at them. His hands, arms and face were scratched and raw and dirty. His trousers were ripped and one sleeve was almost gone from his shirt. His face was red and sore looking. A trail-worn roan saddle pony stood at the southwest corner of the cabin.

"Claudia!" he growled. "Where the hell you been?"

Claudia and Hope moved to the cabin without breaking stride. "The question is," Claudia said, "where have you been and what have you done?"

Seth held out his hands. "I been runnin' for my life, that's what I been doin'!" he yelled. "You ain't gonna believe what's after me."

"One of my bears?"

"Lot worst'n thet. A ghost!"

"Oh, come on now, Seth. A ghost!"

"Yeah, yeah, that's what it is. A ghost. He's comin' after me. I gotta hide someplace, Claudia. Hide me someplace!"

She laughed, and Hope wondered how one could laugh in the presence of a horrible man like Dalby.

"Where could I hide you that a ghost couldn't find you?" She moved past him and up onto the porch step. "Ghosts go right through walls, you know."

"My God, I don't know. Gotta be someplace." Seth pointed back down the trail. "He's back there, after me. Be here purty soon. I just cain't run no more."

Claudia entered the house and Seth followed. Reluctantly, Hope entered behind him. He dropped into a chair at the table, poured whiskey into a glass, and drank it down without stopping.

"I see you found the booze," Claudia said. She hung her saddlebags on the wall.

"I needed some. I been through hell past few days." He

looked at Hope. "Who's this girl?"

"She's a neighbor, lives over the mountain. Her name's Hope."

"What's she doin' here?" He was staring at her, and she glared back.

"Visitin' me. Whose ghost is follerin' ya?"

Seth jumped up, went to the window and squinted through the glass. "Yuh recollect that murderer I was a-chasin'?"

"Seem to remember something about it."

Seth sat back down and took another drink. "Well, me and him got in a gun fight and I killed 'im. I took 'im back to Custer and that half-wit Sheriff was all upset about it 'cause it seems there weren't no warrant fer 'im. He took m'badge and I'm damned if he didn't pin it on that dead kid and somehow the kid came alive and started in chasin' me." He poured and drank again. "Now, ain't no man on this earth I'm afraid of, y'understand. But ghosts — them's a whole 'nother matter, by God. Ain't nothin' yuh kin do with ghosts."

Hope spoke for the first time. "Can't you hide along the trail and shoot the ghost?"

He looked at her with some surprise showing, although his face already looked so wrung out it hardly registered any change of expression. "'Course yuh cain't."

"That's too bad," Hope said. "That's how you killed the boy in the first place, isn't it?"

The whiskey was beginning to work and Seth's head bobbled a little. A faint trace of indignation showed in his eyes.

"The kid drew down on me. I wanted to take him in alive, but he drew his gun and I had to shoot 'im."

"Was it Casey Parkin you killed?"

"How did you know that, girl?"

Hope glanced at Claudia and saw a slight nod of the head that said, "Don't tell him any more."

"Because I heard about you and how you like to shoot people from ambush. It's no surprise the Sheriff fired you. What does this ghost look like that's after you?"

Seth tipped the glass again. "He's a goddam kid, about as tall as me, wears a black hat and rides a big black horse. It's Casey

Parkin's ghost, that's who it is. You know the kid?"

"As I said, I've heard of him." It took all the restraint Hope had to keep from registering her glee at hearing Seth describe the "ghost." By no stretch did she believe in ghosts, and the fact that a man of that description was following Seth meant that Casey was alive. Seth had brought Billy in dead, and the Sheriff had fired him and somehow Casey was after him, this time wearing a badge. Maybe he had been deputized, and maybe Seth was wanted by the law now. Maybe for murdering Billy.

Seth went to the window again, and then ducked quickly below the sill. "Baaah Gaaawd!" he rasped. "There he is, right outside there with another feller, comin' t'git me!" He turned toward Claudia, terror in his eyes.

"Quick, Claudia, hide me!"

Hope jumped to her feet and raced to the window. Her heart leapt as she saw Casey and an older man a couple hundred yards into the timber, riding toward the cabin, and Thief just reaching the clearing ahead of them.

Dalby turned back to the window.

"Oops! Oops!" he exclaimed. "Hold on a minute here! That there ain't the feller I killed. He ain't got the same face a-tall! He jist dresses and rides like 'im. That there ain't no ghost after all!" He straightened up, ran to the door, and snatched Claudia's Winchester '73 from over the entrance. "Shit! I shoulda knowed there ain't no such things as ghosts. I'm a-gonna kill the son-of-a-bitch!"

Hope turned and raced straight at Dalby. Her slender shoulder caught him in the kidney and sent him reeling. She raced out the door and turned and ran as fast as she could toward the riders.

"Casey!"

He pulled up, surprise on his face. "Hope! What—?"

"Look out, Casey! The Deputy!" She pointed back toward the cabin. "He's got a rifle!"

The shot from the Winchester whistled over her head and chipped bark off a pine tree to Casey's left. He and the man both swung to the ground, and the second bullet kicked up dirt beside Casey. He landed on his feet and crouched, Peacemaker in hand.

"Look out, Hope! Get down! Get down!"

She scampered forward with all the speed she could muster. She heard the clack! clack! of the Winchester's lever as Seth jacked in a new cartridge. The other man with Casey lay prone on the ground, and he was digging for his six shooter.

Casey pulled her down. "Lie real low, Hope," he shouted. "He's shootin' wild, but he might hit us."

Then she saw Casey take aim, and his Colt roared back. She turned and saw Seth run for his horse, fifty feet away. She had thought him too drunk to run like that.

"Halt!" Casey screamed. "Halt or I'll kill you, Dalby!"

The man reached his horse and swung up into the saddle. Casey's revolver roared again. Dalby ducked a little and dug in his spurs, and the roan was off down the shoreline at a gallop. The other man's revolver spoke but his bullet missed, and he leaped to his feet and climbed onto his donkey's bare back. Casey swung up on Ebon and both men dug out in pursuit of Seth Dalby.

"Casey! Wait! Don't go, please!"

She knew there would be no stopping him. He was the deputy now, and he would uphold his sworn duty. Oh, God above, if only he would stay with her and be safe. She realized, seeing him exposed to such danger, that she loved him and needed him more than life, and if he rode to his death, she thought, she might as well be dead too.

The donkey, in a full gallop, was faster than Ebon, and he pulled away. Thief was out front, tearing down the shoreline in a blur, with Grizzly on Reuben close behind. Grizzly still wielded his revolver, and he was straining to get a glimpse of Dalby. The ex-deputy had already entered the timber and was out of sight.

In a moment both Thief and Grizzly were out of Casey's view in the trees. He nudged the big horse into the woods at a gallop, then slowed. He caught a glimpse of Grizzly several lengths ahead then, still racing at top speed. He wanted to holler and tell Grizzly to watch for an ambush, but they were moving too fast and he would never hear him. There were many places where Dalby could be waiting in hiding. He still carried the lever action Winchester, and that was an accurate and deadly weapon for all but great distances, and it was a repeater. No need to load each time — simply lever in a new shell from the magazine.

Casey heard the shot before his eyes found Dalby. Grizzly jerked to the side, grabbed his chest, and spun off the donkey's back. He pitched onto the sod and rolled several times. As Casey galloped past he saw Grizzly writhing on his back with blood on his shirt. Then he saw Dalby standing a hundred feet ahead jacking a new shell into the Winchester. As the ex-deputy raised the rifle, Casey jerked the reins and Ebon lurched left. He heard the bullet zing! by his right ear.

The sudden move to the left found Ebon charging under a pine branch that snared Casey. It slammed into his stomach and swept him back over the pony's rump. The Colt flew from his grasp, and he landed flat on his back on the lake shore, four feet from the edge of the bank.

The tree tops were spinning above him. He struggled to breathe, but his lungs would not respond. He opened his mouth wide and gasped, over and over. He felt tears rolling down his temples. Then Seth Dalby stood over him, prodding his stomach with the Winchester, his face twisted into a grin that mirrored insanity.

"Well, well! So this is the deputy they sent after Seth Dalby, is it? They shoulda sent that dumb mule. He'd a come closer to gettin' me than a little boy what ain't dry behind his ears yet. You about ready t'die, Boy?"

Casey struggled for air and finally drew in a precious breath. Oh, Lord, how could he have let this happen? Now he was going to die.

Dalby prodded him again, and his grin widened. "Reckon I shot the wrong kid t'other day. It was supposed t'be you, wasn't it? You the one killed yer daddy?"

"No," Casey rasped, still struggling for air. "You're the one that killed my daddy."

"Yer a damn wise kid, ain't yuh?" growled Dalby with another prod. "Well, yer right. I killed yer daddy. What about Sheriff Brand? Is he dead?"

Casey shook his head. "No. Brand's all right."

"Too bad," growled Dalby. "But now it's yer turn. Any last church sayin's yuh wanna make afore I put a hole in yer belly?"

A low, throaty snarl came from behind Dalby. Casey rolled his head to the side and saw Thief a short way up the slope hunkered down, baring his fangs, ready to attack. Dalby whirled and brought up the rifle.

"Look out, Thief!" Casey hollered.

The shot was off-hand and in spite of the close range it missed the dog.

"Go, Thief! Run!"

Thief whirled and scampered up the slope out of sight. Dalby ran several steps after him, firing again, wildly.

Casey rolled to his left off the bank and fell four feet straight down into the lake. The icy water shocked him, and again he was fighting for his breath. He thrashed about, choking and sputtering. He tried to see where Dalby was but the bank was too high. He had no doubt the man would soon be looking over the edge and shooting at him again. He was about fifteen feet out, he guessed, and Dalby wouldn't miss from that distance. He glanced frantically up and down the shoreline. Willows and briars formed a thicket a few yards to his left, and he struck out swimming toward it. Dalby wouldn't be able to see him if he could get beyond that foliage.

He heard the Winchester bark again, and a bullet splat the water in front of him.

"Damn yer hide!" Dalby screamed after him. "I'll get yuh, yuh bastard!"

Casey swam as fast as his water-filled boots would permit. The clack! clack! of the Winchester's lever came to him, and he expected an impact on his back at any moment. Then he was beyond the thicket out of sight of Dalby, and he moved in as close to the shore as he could.

Dalby would find his way around the foliage in a moment and come after him. The bank was bare of greenery for the next thirty feet where another stand of willows grew. Half way to the willows the bank cut back in sharply and formed a small recess that was hidden from above by long shore grasses hanging down over the bank. He struck out swimming as fast as he could, and just as he reached the cavity, he looked up and saw Dalby peering down at him.

He ducked under the hanging grass and into the recess. There was barely enough room for his body. He felt a ledge of sorts under his feet and stood on it, struggling to get his breath back. Then he saw the rifle barrel poke down through the grass. He was sure Dalby couldn't see him, but it looked like he might fire blindly. He squeezed himself to one side as far as he could. The report was deafening in the small edifice as the bullet smacked into the muddy wall.

He knew one of the shots would get him if Dalby kept firing. He filled his lungs and ducked under the water with eyes open. The shoreline fell away below him into the green depths. He dove downward for several feet and swam along the bank until he couldn't hold his breath anymore. Moving in as close to the shore as he could, he broke the surface. He blinked the water from his eyes and looked back. Dalby was still there, leaning outward and peering down at the recess.

Casey took a deep breath and dove again. He swam another twenty feet and surfaced. He found himself behind the willows from Dalby now, and the bank had melted away to a steep slope.

He heard a shot and looked back. He couldn't see the man but he guessed he was still firing through the grass. Hardly daring to breathe, he gripped a tree root and pulled himself up onto the slope. He crawled quietly upward until he reached the end of the willow stand. There, tied to a tree thirty feet from him, stood Dalby's stolen horse. And in the scabbard under the stirrup fender rode Dalby's big rifle!

He took a deep breath. He had two choices. He could tiptoe away along the shore and try to find a place to hide. Or he could sneak across thirty feet of open space in full view of Dalby and try for the Sharps. That would mean he would have only one chance because the big buffalo gun had to be reloaded after each shot. He thought about Grizzly lying wounded and needing help. He decided to go for the Sharps and get this thing settled now and forever.

He scanned the ground carefully between him and the horse. He memorized each twig that might snap and each pebble that might crunch. He tiptoed out from the willows and moved ten feet, keeping his eye on the ground in front. He stopped and held motionless, turning his head to look. Dalby still crouched on hands and knees on the bank, trying to lean out and see under the grass overhang.

"Okay, damn you!" Dalby screamed. "I kin wait as long as you kin. I'll be right here when y'wanna come out!"

Casey crept forward ten more steps, then turned again. Dalby stuck the gun down and fired a round, then worked the lever. Casey moved another ten as water trickled from his pockets. He was almost there. When he turned again, Dalby was looking up the shore, and Casey knew if his head moved just a bit farther, he'd see him out of the corner of his eye. He crouched, frozen to the spot, not even breathing. Then, to his horror, Dalby turned and looked directly at him. His cruel face broke into a grin.

"Well, well, jist look who we got here. Looks like a drowned rat a some kind."

He raised the Winchester half way to his shoulder and stopped. "Wanna try fer the Sharps, Kid? Go ahead. See if yuh kin git it afore I put a bullet in yuh." He was making a game of it.

Frantically, Casey scrambled for the horse and grabbed the stock of the rifle, expecting the impact of Dalby's bullet. He yanked at the weapon, but it was tied in with a leather thong and came only partially out. He found a slip knot and jerked at it.

The rifle cleared leather.

He whirled toward the ex-deputy.

Dalby, still grinning, raised the Winchester ceremoniously and drew a bead. As Casey brought up the Sharps, he heard the click of Dalby's firing pin on an empty chamber.

Casey thumbed back the hammer and yanked the trigger.

The deafening roar of the big powder charge took him by surprise, and he staggered back. Seth Dalby was clawing for his six shooter when the .50 caliber bullet caught him dead center. The force slammed him backwards over the bank.

Casey dropped the rifle and staggered to the water's edge. His knees were weak and his breath came in short gasps. Thief galloped down from the timber and stood beside him, his tail whipping side to side.

Just under the surface floated the body of Seth Dalby. Blood poured from a massive hole in his chest. His arms spread out and bobbed slightly with the ripples left by the plunging body. The head drifted downward slowly, and the feet upward, and it looked like it might sink. Casey wondered what would happen if he lost Dalby's body. But first things first. What about Grizzly?

He hurried back down the shore and found Griswold struggling to rise. He knelt beside him.

"How bad y'hurt, Grizzly?"

The man grimaced and his eyes teared. "Hurts like purgatory. Knocked the stuffin' outa my shoulder."

"How bad are you? Is the bleedin' stopped?"

Griswold looked down. "Jist a shoulder shot," he said. "I kin wiggle all my fingers an' toes. I'm gonna be fit, I reckon. Where's Dalby?"

"He's in the lake, dead. I gotta go fish him out. Can you be alone awhile?"

"Hell yes, son. Takes more'n a bullet to do in ol' Griz. Go get him. Meantime, I'll try t'git up so's I kin help yuh."

Casey raced back to the shore. He could still see Dalby's body, a little deeper than before. He needed a rope to hitch on to it, but when he checked the roan, there was none. Then he saw Ebon through the trees, standing a hundred yards north. He sloshed as fast as he could in his waterlogged boots with Thief scampering alongside, and brought the horse back. He pulled his lariat loose from the saddle strings. He struggled out of his boots, slip-knotted the lariat in his belt, tied the loose end to a tree, and jumped into the water.

Dalby's body was about fifteen feet offshore, still drifting slowly downward. Casey gulped air and slipped under the surface. The water was so darkened by blood he could hardly see. The buckle on Dalby's gun belt glistened in the rays of sunlight streaking down from the surface, and he swam toward it. He wasn't gaining much. Now the water was murky green, and his ears began to hurt from the pressure. His lungs cried for oxygen. With great, frantic kicks he reached the body and grabbed onto the gun belt.

He shook his head violently several times, fighting off the strong need to breathe. He slipped the lariat end under Dalby's gun belt and knotted it.

He began his ascent to the surface. He threw his head back and looked straight up as he thrust himself upward. The surface looked far away, and for a moment he doubted he could hold his breath that much longer. It seemed he would never get there, and when finally he broke the surface, he took great gulps of air. He swam back and dragged himself up the tree roots onto the bank.

He lay a moment and rested. He was becoming unbearably tired. He moved around the willows to the rope and pulled on it. The body was heavier than he thought it would be and he could barely move it. It felt like it was bumping along, maybe on the bottom. He hoped it wouldn't catch on something. Then what would he do?

He heard hoof beats and turned to see Hope and a blonde woman ride up. They dismounted and tied their horses.

"Casey!" Hope cried. "You're soaked! What are you doing?"

"Fishin'! I've hooked a big one. Help me pull him in."

They stood beside Casey and looked at him, at his rope, and at the point where the rope stretched tautly into the water.

"Well," he said. "Are you gonna help me, or not?"

"Yes," Hope said. "This is Claudia Morton. She owns the cabin."

"What can I do?" Claudia asked.

Casey handed her the rope. "Pull," he said. "Help me pull this big fish out."

They all three strained on the rope, and slowly the prize slipped along the bottom.

"Hope!" Casey said. "Go look. Can you see him?"

She ran to the edge and looked down. "Yes. He's right at the bank."

Casey and Claudia took a stand closer to the water's edge. Dalby's dark form was visible just off the bank, five feet below the surface. His head was downward. The gun belt had slipped to his knees and he was being pulled up feet first.

"Oh, God!" Casey cried. "His belt's slipped. It's only hanging by the thong tied around his leg. Hope! Help Claudia. Hold him where he is if you can."

Hope joined Claudia on the rope and braced her feet. Casey slid down the bank into the water. He ducked under, swam alongside the body, and grabbed its left wrist. He treaded water and pulled, and slowly the body rose to the surface. He found a handhold around a large stone just under the surface at the bank and held on.

"Gimme some slack!" he yelled.

When the slack came, he half-hitched the lariat over the head. He tried to move the loop down around the chest but he felt the muddy body slipping from his grasp. He left the lariat where it was, around the neck.

"Okay. Hold him. Don't let him sink."

When the rope was taut again he swam up the shore as before and crawled out by the tree roots. He and the ladies stood at the edge and pulled. The body slithered up the wet, slippery bank, head upward this time. The loop tightened around the neck, and the tongue poked out between blue lips.

"Good God!" Claudia said, grimacing. "It's plumb like we're hangin' him!"

"Yeah," Casey said. "I wish my dad and Billy could see this! He murdered 'em both. He deserves to hang."

The body flopped out onto the ground like a big, rubbery catfish. Water dripped off, some from the bullet hole, and formed a puddle around it. A long stem of seaweed draped across the chest. Black mud from the lake bottom covered much of the body.

"Oh my Lord!" cried Hope.

"That is Seth, ain't it?" Claudia asked.

"Yes."

"Too bad! I've seen him look better."

"That's the best I've ever seen him," Casey said. He searched about and found his Peacemaker and his black hat. He slid the Sharps back in the scabbard and handed the Winchester Dalby had dropped to Claudia.

"Where is that man that was with you?" Hope asked.

"Dalby shot him. He's layin' back up there—"

"No he ain't," put in Claudia. "He's there by that horse."

Casey turned. Grizzly stood hugging his bedraggled roan horse that Dalby had stolen from him. Tears rolled down his cheeks.

"Thought I'd never see yuh again, Dolly, darlin'," he sniffed.

Claudia hurried to Griswold. "You poor man!" she said. "Just look at that shoulder. Let's get you to the house and get you patched up. Can you get up on your horse?"

"Don't rightly know," he answered weakly. "I'll do m'best. Can somebody get my donkey?"

"I'll get him for you, Sir," Hope said.

Claudia and Hope helped Griswold into the saddle, then the two ladies and Casey hoisted Dalby's slimy carcass into the saddle of Claudia's pony. "Hope you don't mind, Ma'am." Casey said. "I've got to get this body back to Custer somehow. I reckon the first step is to get him to your place."

"Don't mind a-tall. I'll ride on behind your friend. He looks like he might fall off if I don't."

She slipped up onto the roan's rump behind Griswold. "What do they call you?" she said in his ear.

"Grizzly," he answered.

She reached her arms around him and took the reins.

Chapter Twenty-four

Casey and Hope stretched Seth Dalby out on the floor in Claudia's barn and threw a saddle blanket over him.

"I'd like to get cleaned up a little," he said, "then I'll worry about how to get him back to Custer."

"You look very tired, Casey. You better rest."

His legs felt weak and he was beginning to shake. He wanted to plunge himself into the big stack of loose hay in the barn corner and sleep. Instead he plodded alongside her to the house. Claudia was there doctoring Grizzly.

"Come in," she said. "We'll tend to you too, Casey, soon as we can. Are you hurt a-tall?"

"No, don't think so. Just tuckered out and a might wet and a tolerable irritated. I've never had a day like this one that I can recollect."

Hope took his hand. "Thank God you're all right. Thank God for that."

"Some dry duds right there on that chair," Claudia said, pointing. "Belonged to my late husband. I think they'll fit. Overalls and a shirt and some long johns. He was right close to your size, maybe a mite bigger around the middle. You can bathe in the lake if your a mind to. There's a good spot right down yonder. I call it the 'bath.' It's got a gravel bottom."

Grizzly sat on a chair at the table and grinned weakly at Casey. "This is the life, Case, bein' treated by a lovely maiden. That ain't happened to me fer a spell."

"Thanks for takin' care of me, Griz," Casey said.

"What d'you mean? Yer the one killed the rat. You saved my hide, kid."

"No, it ain't so. You took the bullet I would've got if you hadn't gone ridin' in first."

Griz waved his arm at Casey. "Bawsh! You'd a had sense

'nuf t'dodge the dern bullet."

"Oh, sure I would've." Casey grinned and took the towel and duds Claudia offered and made his way to the lake. He peeled off his dirty, soaked clothes, bathed, and put on the dry ones. When he had finished and returned, Hope declared that he looked awfully good.

"You look doggone good yourself, Hope," he said. "I'm glad this terrible chase is over. Shall I tell your mom and dad about Billy when we get there?"

"Let's both tell them. I don't know if I could do it alone."

He glanced around the room. "Where's Grizzly?"

"He's takin' a nap," Claudia said. "He's weak and needs to get his strength back. Lost a lot of blood." She hustled about the stove and fixed a meal for them. Casey was famished. He started with a swig of the coffee and then went to work on the meat.

Claudia watched him eat. "I like a hungry man," she declared.

"Yeah, I sure am hungry. Swimmin' and fishin' gives a man an appetite." He broke open a hot biscuit and smeared on butter.

"Well, you just dig right in," she said, shaking her finger. "You earned it."

"Thanks. Do you have any canvas, Mrs. Morton?"

"My name's Claudia. And, yes, I have canvas. In the storage shed in back. Why?"

"I'd like to sew Seth Dalby up in it for the ride back to Custer. Ain't no reason people have to gawk at him. Besides, it'll help keep his perfume down."

After supper Casey and Hope went to the barn and rolled Dalby's body tightly in canvas. Casey stitched it shut.

"This is eerie," Hope said. "Tending to a dead man like this. Getting him ready to plop over a horse. Seems so undignified."

Casey thought a minute. "Well, this is pretty royal treatment for a slimy murderer like Seth Dalby. I ought to drag him back by his heels."

They strolled toward the cabin. About half way there, Casey

said, "Billy told me about your boyfriend, Hope."

They stopped and she looked up at him. "My boy friend?"

"Yes." He stared at the ground and kicked a pebble. "He was tellin' me the hired hand was takin' you to the dances. I was wonderin'..."

"Oh, yes. He was talking about Jim Boders. He took me to a couple of dances at the Seiden place. Not alone, of course. Daddy and Mother came too. But he's not my boy friend."

"He's not?"

"Gosh no. I don't have a fellow at all. Jim is nothing to me. Why are you grinning like that, Casey?"

"Because all this time I thought...I thought..."

"What, Casey? Thought what?"

"That maybe you were promised to that Jim feller."

She smiled. "Would it have mattered to you if I were?"

The smile left his face and he looked into her lovely eyes. "Yes. It matters a whole bunch, Hope. Because I'm in love with you, don't you know?"

"Oh, Casey..."

He took her hand. "I love you, Hope."

"Why didn't you tell me before?"

"Because I thought I was an outlaw. You deserve better than an outlaw."

She moved closer and their bodies touched. "Do you think Claudia and Grizzly can see us from the cabin?" she asked.

He glanced toward the house. "I expect so, if they're lookin' out that window. Why?"

"Would it bother you if they saw us kissing?"

"Not a bit, Sweetheart!"

He held her in his arms and kissed her for a long moment.

"I love you, Casey," she said. "I have from the very first."

That night Claudia fixed the rollaway bed in the main room for Grizzly, and Casey threw his bedroll on the floor. Hope shared the bedroom with Claudia.

The next morning Claudia fixed them bacon and eggs and all the trimmings. Grizzly dug in heartily. "I ain't had vittles like this in I jist don't know how long." he declared. "I plumb forgot what heaven was like."

Casey laughed. "I believe you look better this morning, Griz. Think you can travel?"

"Well, I reckon I can—"

Claudia shook her fork in Griz's face. "Now you know you ain't in no fit shape to ride, Mr. Griswold!" she exclaimed. "You just stick around here a few days and get your strength back. That horse and donkey of yours are all tuckered out too. They can rest up in the barn a couple days. Won't hurt nothin'."

"Well...I jist don't want t'be puttin' you out, Missus Morton. I feel fine, an' ridin' won't be no prob—"

"I ain't gonna hear no more of it!" she exclaimed. "I ain't gonna let you ride out there in the wilderness only half full of blood thataway. You'd get way out there somewheres and faint and fall off your horse and the wolves and bears and coyotes would come and pull your flesh off your bones an' eat you up and it would be all my fault fer lettin' you go."

"I think Claudia's right, Griz," Casey said. "You do look pretty pale and gaunt."

"Well, all right then, Missus Morton. An' I do thank you. I can bed down in the barn loft."

Claudia shot him a look of disgust. "An' just how in the name o' the Lord am I supposed to look after you there? You'll sleep right here on the rollaway, Mr. Griswold, where if you come down with the fever or need help I'll hear you holler. Don't that make better sense?"

"Yeah, I reckon. But some folks might be disposed t'frown on arrangements like that."

"Frown? Who's gonna know t'frown? You gonna frown, Casey? Are you, Hope?"

"No, not me," said Casey with a very subtle grin.

"I wouldn't," Hope said.

"All right, it's settled then," Claudia declared, cutting her flapjacks.

After Casey had saddled Hope's pinto for her, he cinched his own saddle on Ebon and tied the canvas bundle behind it. Grizzly came out and Casey shook his hand. "You come see us,

Griz," he said. "Hope and I'll likely be married soon and we'll live on the farm I told you about. You know where it is. You're always welcome."

Griz dropped the handshake and hugged Casey instead. His eyes were teary. "You're a true friend, Case. You saved my life twice and you rescued my Dolly horse, and I ain't never gonna ferget it. You can bet I'll come and visit." He glanced toward Ebon. "Say, Case, you kin take my big donkey t'haul that cadaver on if you'd care to."

"Thanks, but this'll do fine for the trip to the Asters. Then I'll load him on Bacon, my mule."

Claudia hugged both Casey and Hope and made them promise they'd come up and visit her from time to time. "You'll always have a place to vacation," she said, "as long as I'm alive. You can stay as long as you like and won't have to do a thing but lazy around and make love and maybe do a little deer huntin' and trout fishin'."

"No fishin'," Casey said with a grin. "Reckon I've had about enough of that. But thank you, Mrs. Morton. We'll sure be back to visit a wonderful lady like you. You can count on that."

With final waves they were off through the timber toward Forsythe Canyon, with Thief trotting proudly along next to them. The sun peeked over the eastern mountains, and the cool air brushed Casey's cheeks. The stillness was broken by the twitter of awakening birds.

"Hope!"

She turned her head, and the first rays of the sun brushed her face.

"When can we be married?"

She gazed down the ravine leading to the south. "I...I just don't know. Mama will surely give her blessings — already said she loves you like her own son. But Daddy...I just don't know. He's stubborn sometimes."

"Could you ride on to Custer with me now?"

She shook her head. "No, Casey. I'm sorry, but Daddy would never allow that. And I'd never go against his wishes."

"Oh." Casey dropped his face. "Too bad."

Their ponies turned into the ravine and started the steep descent.

"He *will* see it our way eventually, though," Hope said. "Right now there are so many things to iron out. With Billy gone I don't know what Daddy and Mama will do. I don't think Dad wants to work the farm alone. And if I leave too, well..."

"What will they do about Billy?"

"I'm sure they will arrange to bring him home for burial. Perhaps they will take a wagon down and bring him back themselves. If they do, I'll go too. Maybe they will visit you and your mother there. After Daddy has met her and Mr. MacDoughall, he might then give us his permission and blessings."

She was riding down the slope ahead of him, and she turned and looked back, smiling. "Don't worry, Honey," she said. "We will work it out, and we will be married. We must not rush things. We must do it right."

"Yes," he said. "It's a mighty big step, and it's important to do it right."

Her assurance uplifted him, and the mountain air suddenly seemed cooler and crisper, and the birds sang a little louder. For a moment he was carried back to the days he and his dad — always his best pal — had set out to fish or hunt game, or just enjoy the Black Hills. During the bitter days with Hermund Grim he had felt that without Dad his life was over and no more great joys could be found. But now, as he eased his pony through the mist, he knew the void was filled. This vibrant farm girl on the pinto would chase away the emptiness. So would Thief who trotted along ahead. He glanced down at the deputy badge on his chest. He was a man now. He didn't know whether one had to earn manhood, but if so, he had!

And he would be picking the guitar for his mom again.

Back at the lake cabin, Claudia Morton made Jack Griswold as comfortable as she could. She put the big armchair out under the sprawling branches of a pine tree and tucked the blanket around him against the early morning coolness.

"We'll keep you fed good," she told him, "and that wound

will heal up an' you'll be good as new in no time a-tall." She went in and brought out a small table and set a cup of hot coffee on it. She stood back and looked at him a moment.

"You know, Grizzly," she said with a smile, "I'll bet you'd be a tolerable fine lookin' man without that bird's nest on your face. Now, my late husband's razor and brush and strop is right there by the cook stove and..."

About the Author

Dick Clason spent his childhood in the Black Hills of South Dakota. Although he left to serve in the U. S. Navy during World War II and never reestablished residence there, his heart still beats within the shadow of Harney's Peak. He loved writing, and as a fifth-grader he penned an adventure serial for his class newspaper. He was an avid fan of cowboys and their horses, and he worked on his first western novel when he was twelve years old.

As a child he adored policemen, and as an adult he became one, serving first as a patrolman and later as officer in charge of the Criminalistics Laboratory at the Beverly Hills, California Police Department. He published his autobiography *My Life in the Eleventh Generation*. He publishes two family newsletters and has written three western novels.

He resides with his wife, Lillian, in North Hills, California.